'A soulful, breathtaking achievement
account of the horrors of brutal colo
First Nations women and an unbreakable connection to Country.
Tasma Walton has emerged as a masterful, mesmerising storyteller.'

LARISSA BEHRENDT

'*I am Nannertgarrook* is a story of both deep time and contemporary
resonance. Within these pages a heartbeat runs through Country as
it does our bodies. Through exquisite storytelling and with characters
of tremendous strength, Tasma Walton brings us a novel charged
with love and courage.'

TONY BIRCH

'A beautiful, heart-wrenching story of a proud woman whose world
is ripped apart and whose strength, resilience and love rises above
the brutality around her. A hidden Australian story that deserves
to come into the light.'

ISLA FISHER

'Beautiful and evocative storytelling. Joyfully uplifting and utterly
heartbreaking in equal measure.'

BEN ELTON

'Tasma Walton's extraordinary novel is a momentous feat – ancient
and urgent all at once. Nannertgarrook's heart-rending story echoes
across time, commemorating and continuing female lore and legacy
with a fierce, furious grace, and urging us to listen and learn. And it is
impossible not to. This is profoundly visceral and vivid truth-telling
that should be compulsory reading for every Australian.'

KATE MULVANY

'An extraordinary feat. Tasma takes you to a deep time, a world on the cusp of ending, that's both recognisable to us as a conquered land and unknown to most of us – the words and knowledge, and stories of who was there before. I wept through the final chapters at the tragedy of the end of a world, but will hold close the gift Tasma leaves – an understanding of the women who walked the lands I know, and the knowledge and love they held. The way I see the land of my childhood is forever changed.'

RACHEL GRIFFITHS

'Tasma's novel connects us all to the stories of our ancestors – their idyllic life on Country before the brutal realities of the not too distant past. This is truth-telling for a future with more humanity than Nannertgarrook could have ever imagined. Tasma's Old Ones would be very proud.'

NARELDA JACOBS

'Tasma continues our ancient tradition of storytelling with this important story of our stolen women, and their determination to hold family, culture and language so we can one day return and bring their stories home. *I Am Nannertgarrook* is a story of the Ancestors that is forever written on our Country and hearts.'

SENIOR ELDER AUNTY GAIL KUNWARRA DAWSON

I am Nannertgarrook

ALSO BY TASMA WALTON

Heartless

TASMA WALTON

I am Nannertgarrook

BUNDYI

First published in Australia in 2025 by Bundyi,
an imprint of Simon & Schuster (Australia) Pty Limited
Level 4, 32 York Street, Sydney NSW 2000

Bundyi books are published on unceded Gadigal land.
Always was, always will be.

New York Amsterdam/Antwerp London Toronto Sydney New Delhi
Visit our website at www.simonandschuster.com.au

BUNDYI and design are registered trademarks of The Gale Group, Inc.,
used under licence by Simon & Schuster LLC.

10 9 8 7 6 5 4 3 2 1

© Tasma Walton 2025

NATIONAL LIBRARY OF AUSTRALIA

A catalogue record for this
book is available from the
National Library of Australia

9781761426698 (paperback)
9781761426704 (ebook)

Cover design by Laura La Rosa
Cover image: Jensen Art Company/Adobe Stock
Typeset by Midland Typesetters in Adobe Caslon Pro 11.5/16pt.
Printed and bound in Australia by Griffin Press

MIX
Paper | Supporting
responsible forestry
FSC
www.fsc.org FSC® C018684

The paper this book is printed on is certified against the
Forest Stewardship Council® Standards. Griffin Press holds
chain of custody certification SCS-COC-001185. FSC®
promotes environmentally responsible, socially beneficial
and economically viable management of the world's forests.

For my Granny Nannertgarrook
Eliza 'No-one' Nowen/Gamble
I have heard you whisper, 'Bring me home'
So I call now to the Old Ones
And those of open hearts
Let these words ring out your truth
Stretching like an ancient songline
Through the spinning circles of time
To finally sing your murrup back to your Biik

Author's Note

From 1798 to the early 1800s, British men, along with others from many parts of the world, raced to our Southern Ocean to hunt seals. The industry was unregulated and the men ruthless in their enterprise. In under thirty years, more than 1.3 million seal skins (by conservative accounts) were traded, including females and pups, causing seal colonies across the entire southern coastline and neighbouring islands to collapse. In the Bass Strait alone, three species of seal – the long-nosed fur seal, Australian sea lion, and southern elephant seal – were eradicated, and the Australian fur seal was on the verge of extinction.

Whaling was next, and by the time the slaughter was waning, the southern right whale, sperm whale and humpback whale were all teetering on extinction. The largest animal on Earth, the blue whale, numbered around 225,000 pre-exploitation in the southern hemisphere. Today, there are fewer than 2000.

The sealing and whaling men who presided over this slaughter existed in a brutal world of lawlessness and savagery. They coasted along the edges of the rapidly growing British colonisation of an 'undiscovered' land, flouting the imposed law and government of Britain's 'New Holland'. They plundered as much as they could, with absolute impunity and scant regard for morality or sustainability. In a treacherous ocean and on foreign soil, their survival was tenuous, and often dependent on the knowledge and labour of largely kidnapped and enslaved young Aboriginal women and children.

Colonial sources estimate the number of young women and children abducted by sealers to be in the hundreds. Most likely, the number is much greater. The rampant kidnapping, beginning in Tasmania, soon spread to impact the saltwater people of Homelands across the entire southern coastline.

The story of *I Am Nannertgarrook* tells the events and consequences of one such abduction from Boonwurrung Country, documented in the early colonial records of Melbourne and Port Phillip. Around March of 1833, a group of young women, girls and a boy were forcibly taken by sealers from a beach at Point Nepean. Under the captaincy of George Meredith Jnr, they were shipped across the Bass Strait to King Island, Hunter Island and lastly, Gun Carriage Island. There they were sold in a slave market to sealers and separated, variously dispersed to islands around Tasmania. Three of the girls were eventually taken as far from their Country as possible, to the other side of the southern part of the continent: a desolate granite outcrop aptly named Bald Island, not far from Albany in Western Australia.

One of those girls was my ancestor.

References to the women and children enslaved by sealers are sparse in the colonial records, which usually only note the names given to them by their captors, rarely their traditional ones, and how many children they had. However, some extraordinary firsthand and key witness accounts have been documented in various journals and letters of the time, describing the treatment, conditions and experiences these women and children endured. A primary source is the extensive journals of George Augustus Robinson, a prominent, divisive figure in Tasmania who later became the Chief Protector of the Port Phillip Aboriginal Protectorate, as well as his Assistant Protector, William Thomas. The Victorian Public Record Office has also compiled a collection of historical documents in several volumes of their Foundation Series, which give important insight to the prevailing attitudes and events of the time.

However, most valuable are the stories gathered and gifted, passed down from generation after generation, by the descendants of these women. Cultural knowledge and stories, clues to identity and connection, fragments of a precious tapestry, guarded and preserved, and kept alive.

It is the weaving of the notes written in the white men's journals, successive historians' interpretations, and the yulendji passed down from mother to daughter, that informs my telling of Nannert-garrook's story. This is a fictional account of not only her journey, but the experience of the hundreds of women and children condemned to a similar fate. It is important to note that all of the events depicted in the novel occurred in real life. They are true stories. But as this novel is told with Nannertgarrook's voice and through her eyes, the chronology of those events has been adjusted to fit within the timeline of Nannertgarrook's odyssey from Boonwurrung Biik in 1833 to the southern islands of Western Australia.

It is with a heavy heart I acknowledge that the descendants of the extraordinary Boonwurrung women and children abducted from the calm shores of our beautiful Biik on a late summer day may never know with absolute certainty their ancestors' true traditional names. Many historians have assessed the records and linked the names given by the Boonwurrung countrymen to the Protectorates with the English names bestowed by the sealers. In this novel, I have embraced the names accepted by the descendant families, so that Nannertgarrook is Eliza ('No-one') Nowen/Gamble, Nandergarrook is Elizabeth Maynard, and Doogbyerumboroke is Margorie Munro.

Long have their stories been discarded and forgotten, their voices silenced and their bodies lost, in the ensuing decades after the 'discovery' of Australia and the consequent apocalyptic collapse of their world. *I Am Nannertgarrook* seeks to reclaim their voices and their lives, along with the hundreds of Aboriginal women and children like them, telling their truths and bringing a long-ignored chapter of Australian history back into the light.

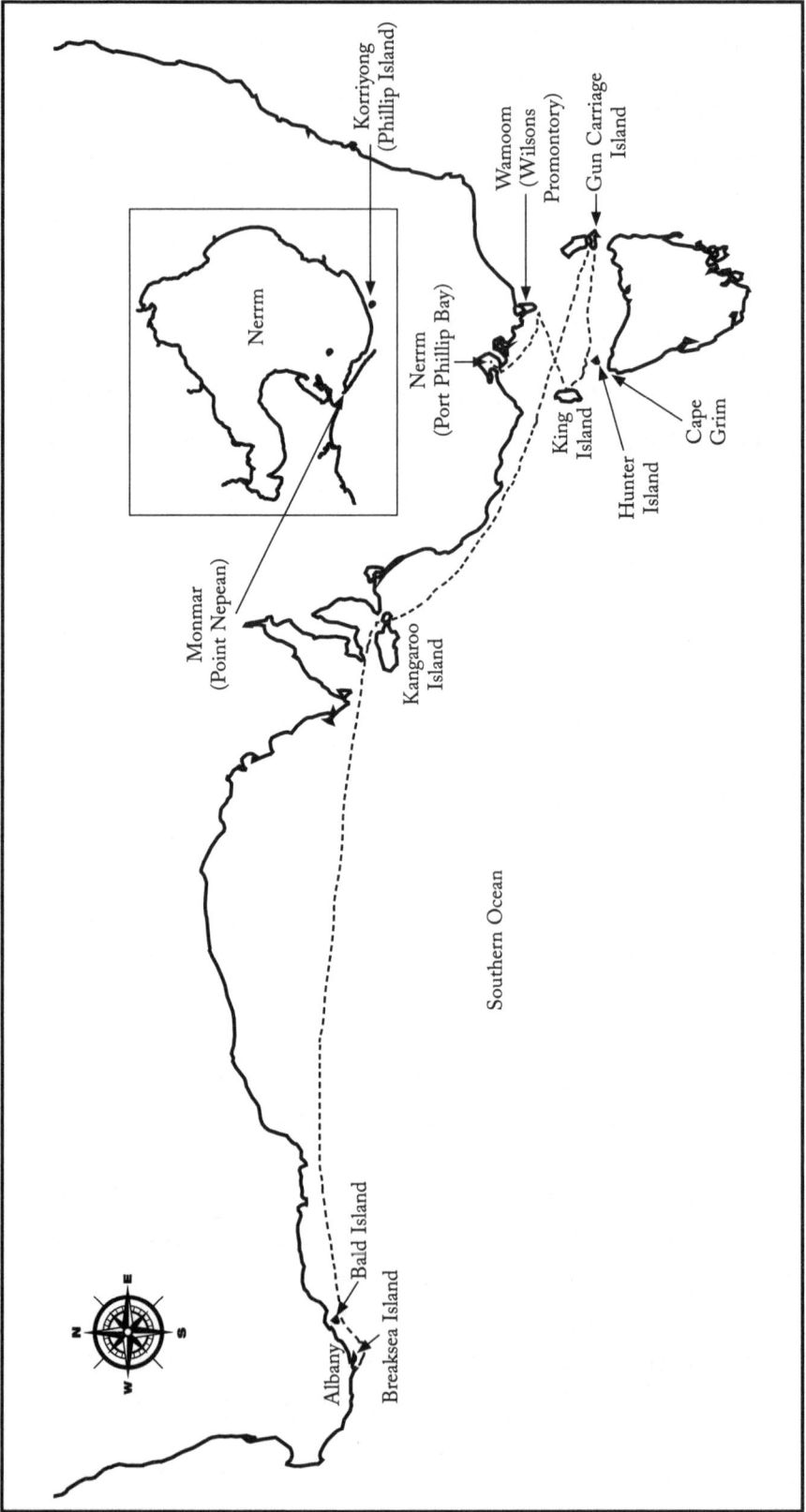

The route taken by Nannertgarrook's captor

Contents

Part Three
MUYIIPNALLOOK
Hell

Prologue

Do you hear that Wind?

*A roaring force hurtling towards your newfound
southern shores.*

*Screeching like a blood-soaked Koonwarra swan as
she storms across the wild ocean, ravaging sand dunes,
tearing at bended trees, in a furious search for her
threatened eggs.*

That Wind carries my Spirit.

*A murrup once soaked in ancient certainty, the
continuous connectedness of a deep time civilisation,
now severed from it all – children, Culture, Country,
Ceremony. My past decimated, my future thieved away.*

*Listen. That Mornmoot is Me. My agony, my despair,
trapped in the endless torment of the white man's savagery.
I am Nannertgarrook.*

*Belonging to Boonwurrung Biik. Born to Bunjil.
Married to Waa. Keeper of Burinyong-Balak.
Custodian of Babayin Betayil. Daughter to Dindoo.*

Mother. Myself.

Not no-one.

Can you hear me? Will you hear me? The sound of my Spirit, begging for my Whale to find me and take me to Karralk. To find peace in my place among the Ancestors in Sky Country.

I am Nannertgarrook.

And I am trapped. Condemned to fly tethered to this raging Wind. Thooamee! Listen! Do you hear me howl around your new houses of stone and glass?

Forever chained. Forever stolen. Forever screaming my fury at the invaders who destroyed it all.

Part One

BIIK
Country

BABAYIN BETAYIL
Mother Whale

Her arm stretches across my shoulder, hand resting open like a night flower blooming for the moon above. Velvety black, my girl's skin gleams in the luminous moonlight, bare chest gently rising and falling with a carefree grace. My little Boyerup, named so by the Elders at birth, when her first cries caused a flurry of butterflies to flee from their home among the banksia flowers. Delicate, this one, like the balambalam, and careful. Even when she dances, her favourite thing to do, she places her foot lightly on Biik.

Next to her, my youngest sleeps spreadeagled and face down on a possum skin fur. Although deep in slumber, Yearl Yearl still looks like he's about to take off running, quick and nimble, the complete opposite of the ponderous sea snail he's named after. Clasped in his tiny hand are three gangan, resting perilously close to his little button nose. I can't stop the smile from spreading across my face remembering his relentless pursuit of that cheeky Waa the raven trying to steal his pipis at lunch. No-one, not even the great bird of his moiety, takes food from Yearl Yearl.

My heart is full with these two, my bubup. They light every day, knitting each one to the next with love. Stories are sung for them, wisdom shared for them.

I trace my finger over the scars cut on my chest after the birth of each of my children. These scars that speak of knowledge and experience, a picture of my passage through motherhood. I still remember my own mother's expression, warm with pride, as she held me in ceremony, surrounding me in the calming resonance of ancient song, thanking Mother Whale for the blessings of these bubup. When the aunties, the murndigarrook, drew the blood and packed the sacred cut with soothing ochre, their eons-old wisdom seared a profound knowledge onto my skin.

Made from your flesh, forever marked on your flesh, these most joyous of creations, my babayin whispered. *And one day, as the cycles of our Time endlessly revolve, you will be them and they will be you. And so it goes.*

The low hooting echo of a distant owl travels across the still night, rousing me with a sudden restlessness. Ever so slowly, I lift Boyerup's arm from my shoulder and lay it carefully by her side. With a drowsy huff, she rolls over and curls back into herself, still lost in her dream world. In a few more years, she will be stepping into her own layers of knowledge, her own markings that speak of blossoming womanhood. But not just yet. Some part of me wishes to never let her go, not even on the day I travel to Karralk with my whale and back into the Dreaming. If I could, I would keep her hand held tightly in mine as we walk back and forth along our songlines for this whole life, and the next, and the next.

Picking my way carefully over the sleeping children, I head to the low-burning fire and add more sustenance to the flame. Spring might be just about to burst the land open with colour, but the night air of early Pareip still chills with the last echoes of winter. Around our camp, bodies wrapped in possum skin cloaks snore lightly. This time, our wilam is a women's place, tucked within the curving folds of a sheltering dune, stretching along the languid shores of the bay. While the men are travelling a different path on higher country, we come with our children for womindjeka, gathering in this place of women's song and dance with a singular, sacred purpose. To honour Mother Whale and her children at Yellodungo, her place of perpetual rest in the most stunning of Sea Country.

A low grumble nearby draws my gaze to where my mother, Dindoo, sleeps. Mouth falling open, her back rests against the warming curve of her werrun. Her dingo is an old, loyal one, with a warning growl that cautions any night walker to stay away from her babayin. They have been inseparable companions for many years and draw a mutual comfort lying together, especially after my father travelled into the Dreaming.

I study my mother's sleeping face. Wisdom has etched itself in the lines across her forehead, the corners of her eyes and the upturn of her lips. But in between those linear tracings of time, it warms me to see that her black skin is plump and soft with a pervasive peace.

The gentle glow of Meeniyan the Moon beckons me from our sand dune wilam to the glittering shore beyond. Are the whales gathering yet? As I get closer to the tideline, the night air is thick with the briny scent of an abundant Warrayin. I can hear the waves lapping at the smooth sands of the beach, their regular rhythm instilling a sense of rightness. Ears straining, I try to listen out for the telltale slapping of a whale's fluke on the surface of the sea. In Warrayin's mysterious depths, my family's totem travels. Guided by our Babayin Betayil, the great Mother Whale, the new mothers bring their calves into the safe embrace of Warnmarring. Arriving in the cooler seasons, these betayil families rest and wallow, feast and grow fat on the offerings of Mother Whale in her gentle bay, before they embark on their final epic journey, past the horizon and into the deep blue.

We women will gather over the coming days to honour them. Sacred to us is the Whale, the creator of the sister bays. Especially for my family, as she is our totem and custodial responsibility. With her care, we can live and our babies can thrive. With our care, she can live and her babies can thrive. A symbiotic relationship spanning millennia.

Ceremony will start tomorrow, an ebbing and flowing of song and story, dance and drumbeat, over a handful of Pareip's newly warming days and starry, brisk nights. For the first time, my mother will lead the yingali, moving further into her role as Knowledge Holder.

A shivering rush of excitement runs through my body. Since I was a young girl, Ngargee for Babayin Betayil has always been my favourite time. Just like my own little Boyerup now, I could hardly wait to wade into the water along the sandbar with my mother, aunties, cousins and children, getting as close to the majestic beings as I possibly could. To maybe, one day, be close enough to touch. And to maybe, one day, earn my rites of knowledge, the ancient yulendji, so that I can stand tall in the line of thousands of Old Women before me and lead our family's yingali for Mother Whale.

One day.

Holding my hand up to the gleaming darkness, I feel the rising of a brisk coast breeze. I whisper my wish to the Old Ones travelling on the gentle wind.

Liwik, if I am ready, let me be close enough to a betayil to touch, so I might learn just a fragment of the wisdom she carries.

Like a sudden, sharp inhale against my ear, a whispering flurry of mornmoot rushes past. My Ancestors have heard me. Waa the raven caws over the sand dunes near the camp and I head back to my sleeping babes, heart warm with anticipation.

As I lie down, I hear the calming crackle of the low-burning fire, the rise and fall of my bubups' breath, and the promising rumble of Warrayin in the distance. All is peaceful. All is perfect.

Gigantic shapes emerge from the shadowy depths of Warrayin. Great gusts of briny breath shoot out from blowholes, revealing the families of betayil gathering in Warnmarring.

I break into a blazing grin when a fluked tail waves to me from across the water, a glorious gesture of kinship. At my side, a clinging Boyerup gasps, nervous excitement shining in her eyes. She might be the careful one, but I know it won't be long before she succumbs to the urge of dancing for these incredible beings.

Shrieking behind us, Yearl Yearl darts all over the beach. Stomping across the breaking waves, scrounging through flotsam and jetsam, hurtling down the slope of a sand dune.

I shout a warning. *Enough, bubup! This is the Country of the Burri-barri, you must be very careful of their tiny eggs. Waa and Bunjil are watching!*

Chastened, Yearl Yearl shuffles in behind us, twiddling sticks impatiently with his busy fingers. A frown creases his forehead and he looks at me imploringly. *I'll always be careful around their eggs, babayin, always, always. But I didn't see any on that sand dune, I promise.*

Let's be still for a moment. I take both of my children's hands and walk back to Yearl Yearl's sand dune. *Thooamee,* I whisper, pointing to my ears. *Listen for the sounds of their song.*

Almost immediately, Boyerup's eyes widen and she points to a dense patch of old man saltbush just beyond the first crest of sand. I nod approvingly and look to Yearl Yearl. Screwing his nose up with intense concentration, he looks like he is trying to channel all of his power into listening. I can't help but laugh. Stroking his creased forehead, I reassure him to just be patient.

Then, a tiny black head peeks nervously through the leaves of the saltbush, the red circle around her eye blaring a warning. Carrying a piece of dried seaweed in her red and black beak, the hooded plover darts across the sand and into the neighbouring vegetation. Yearl Yearl's mouth falls open and a flush reddens his face.

I'm so sorry, babayin.

Konye, watch a little longer.

After a few minutes, more tiny heads pop out from the comforting foliage of the old man saltbush. Fluffy fledglings summon the courage to step out into the open. Judging the beach to be safe from predators, the adult hooded plover chirps the order for her family to return to the tide mark for feasting.

This one lays her eggs in a scraped-out hollow in the sand, I whisper to my children. *It takes many weeks for her babies to break free from their shells. And she has to be on the lookout the whole time to protect them from many dangers. Especially the clumsy feet of little boys!*

Yearl Yearl chews his lip and twists the twigs in his fingers nervously as we watch the fledglings huddle close to their mother on the shoreline. Although the bubup have heard it before, I continue the story of the burribarri.

And then it takes many more weeks before they can fly and survive on their own. Yes, old man saltbush gives them shelter. Or they can crouch and hide under rocks or driftwood, but their special wilam is the sand dune. This is their Country too. I look pointedly at Yearl Yearl. *And we must walk softly when we visit it. Just like Uncle Derrimut does near his wilam on the shoreline of Nerrm.*

Yes, babayin, the chastened boy whispers.

Will you remember for the next time?

I will.

And what do you say to Country?

I'm so sorry, Biik. I'm so sorry, burribarri. I promise to take better care of you.

A thumping splash breaks the sobriety of the moment. Our heads spin around to see the foaming whitewash aftermath of a breaching whale.

Let's go!

I squeeze my children's hands and pull them to their feet. Swinging our arms playfully, we pick our way carefully over the hooded plover's home, back to the edge of Warrayin. As soon as our bare feet touch the wetness of Sea Country, a baby betayil launches itself clumsily into the air. We all gasp and call out.

Kye!

What a joy to see the smaller ones roll and thrash as they try to copy the grace and power of their mothers. They are learning too, just as our young ones must. So we both, whale and human mothers alike, sing out our stories to teach them. Never do I have a fuller heart than at this time, when the embodiment of my family totems gather to share their knowledge and presence with me. To teach me and my sisters and our bubup the way of the great Mother Whale, giver of life, teacher of nourishment and replenishment. Babayin Betayil, she who made the sister bays and returned life to the Boonwurrung in their time of conflict and chaos. She who rests in Warnmarring to keep Sea Country alive and vibrant. The great Mother who enables that most sacred of journeys, Karralk, when we depart our time on the land and travel with our whale to the rays of the setting sun on the ocean horizon.

Catching up to our group along the curving stretch of shore, I let go of my children and they rejoin the other young ones in play. Yearl Yearl barrels ahead to throw himself enthusiastically into a digging race for pipis with his cousins. Singing sweetly to herself, Boyerup skips over to a gathering of girls who selectively scour the old tidelines for treasure. Soon their smaller bilang will be clinking with a variety of carefully curated shells for necklaces and bracelets.

Kye, Nannertgarrook!

My younger cousin calls out to me, waving. Painted in yellow ochre, the markings of the whale fluke fan out just above Meendut-garrook's eyebrow ridge. Down her arms and torso painted in various shades of yellow, orange and pink, the symbols of her personal and family totems make a beautiful, patterned contrast against her black skin. She has already fastened her liik around her forehead, a deli-cately woven band made of the softest possum tail, adorned with the finest feathers of ngayook, the white cockatoo.

Bright, gleaming eyes, this one, always lit with the glint of mischief. Younger cousin sister, just a baby when I was eight and heading out with the aunties for my first long dive in the deeper waters of Nerrm. On the sheltered shoreline of our fathers' Yalukit-Wilam clan estate, Meendutgarrook cried like a fledgling kwiyup-kwiyup, kicking her tiny feet impatiently in the saltwater. She wanted to swim too, out in the deep, a true Bubup Warrayin, Child of the Sea. Over the years we would play in the bay, diving and leaping like barrunan the dolphin or pretending to be secret, shape-shifting Koormamgarrook. And I would teach her in the shallows to hold her breath underwater, to be strong and assured in Warrayin's embrace like the Liwik in our family line. For Boonwurrung Sea Country is Women's Country, and if you were a girl who could swim like a fish in the water, the murndigarrook would make sure to find you a husband whose clan estate bordered the sea. That way, you could become a Knowledge Holder for women's saltwater Lore and Ceremony, a Bagarrook Warrayin. That way, we could hold fast the unbroken, ancient songline of Mother Whale and the glorious Sea Country she gifted our Old Ones.

Linking arms with my kin, I ask her to paint the markings of Babayin Betayil across my forehead too. As she focuses on her task, mixing the ochre with just the right amount of oil from barrimil the emu, I confess to her that, last night, I sent out a wish for our Liwik to help me get close enough to touch the betayil today.

Meendutgarrook clutches my arm with glee.

I did the same thing, she whispers conspiratorially. *Although my wish was to get close enough to stare into one of the bubup betayil's eyes.*

I burst out laughing, and my cousin playfully punches me in the arm.

Don't laugh! How else are we really supposed to know who's travelling with them this time around?

We're not meant to know, I admonish her with mock condescension. *We don't hold that knowledge yet. That's for the Elders to know and us to find out . . . so they always tell us.*

Cheeky grins spread across both our faces. We know the rules, but sometimes it would be lovely to find a way around them.

Meendutgarrook finishes the markings on my face and balances the wooden bowl of yellow ochre on a large driftwood log. She reaches for another tarnook, which holds a creamy paste of white ochre.

Neither of us says his name, but we smear our shoulders in ngar-rambil to show our love and respect for our father and uncle who has passed. Using my kin's palette of yellows, oranges and pinks, I paint the patterns that tell my story over the rest of my body. The tracks of koonwarra the swan, waving lines that speak of the sea, the shapes and stories of our Biik.

As we wash our hands in the lapping waves that lick at our feet, a boy's shriek suddenly echoes across the water. In a mad flurry of flailing arms and legs, all of the boys who had been paddling in the shallow depths of Warrayin dash for the safety of the sand, faces etched with foreboding. Meendutgarrook and I search the calm sea for the tell-tale fin of a lurking predator, but instead we see the whiskered, mischievous face of an inquisitive seal. Popping just above the water line, the koormam languidly lets the current carry her while she enjoys the spectacle on the beach.

On the high tideline, the girls had dropped their bilang of shells and were now cheekily trying to pull the boys back into the water. They would've been more successful if only they could control their raucous laughter, spurred on by the boys' terror.

No, no, no! The boys squeal. *Koormamgarrook! Koormamgarrook!*

Every baby in the Boonwurrung Nation has grown up with the wild and wonderful stories of the Koormamgarrook, the shape-shifting Women of the Seal and Kelp. For where there are koormam, these female water spirits will swim, hiding themselves among the blubbered creatures, sometimes even becoming them. Mermaids, shapeshifters, seal women, Koormamgarrook search for a morsel of human male to satisfy their lusty hunger. It is known that women can swim in the depths of Boonwurrung Sea Country because Koormamgarrook see us as their kin, ensuring our safety in the dangerous ocean currents and the entangling giant sea kelp forests. Providing for our sea harvest, keeping it plentiful and sustained, they might guide us to where they have left their iridescent scales against the rocks for the abalone to call home.

But best beware the man who dares venture into the deeper waters of Warrayin. He must cling tight to the edges of his gurrung if he chooses to fish beyond the breaking waves. For if he falls in and the Koormamgarrook are about, they will steal him down to their rocky lairs on the ocean floor. And even though the deadly descent means he will surely drown, they will revel in keeping his lifeless body in their underwater cavern for eternity.

No wonder the boys are squealing in panic.

Enough, munmundiik!

Trying to suppress our laughter, we furrow our brows in a stern frown and call the girls off their shivering prey.

The Koormamgarrook are not a joke! Just because you are girls, don't think you're safe. Those water spirits are not too fond of disrespect in any form.

As the girls scatter back to their shell bags and foraging, the now subdued boys dig sullenly in the moist sand for more pipis, grumbling among themselves about having to be around the girls, sharing a yearning wish that they were old enough to join their fathers on the hunt.

Looking back out to Warrayin, I see the seal's curious face still watching the proceedings of these strange two-legged creatures with an amused, yet wary, gaze. I murmur an acknowledgement to her and her kind. I pray to the Old Ones that she be protected in her search for a safe harbour. And just in case there are any Koormamgar-rook surveying the scene from under the surface, I likewise pay my respects to them and their Old Ones.

Satisfied, the seal twitches her whiskers and takes a final dive back under the briny sea, flicking her tail with performative aplomb as she goes.

Stay safe and travel well, lone koormam of Warnmarring, I whisper.

Hands clean, I untie my possum fur headband from its safe-keeping spot on my emu feather skirt. I straighten the glistening black gangan of koonwarra the swan, my cherished guide and guardian, that adorns the centre of the liik. Wrapping the band in its ceremonial position around my forehead, Meendutgarrook ties the leathery straps of possum skin securely at the back of my head. We are ready for our Ngargee of Babayin Betayil.

Ancient song starts to fill the contours of the bay, my mother's chant, swirling, echoing, rebounding off the landforms surrounding it, calling to Country, to our Old Ones, to the Mother Whale resting in her hidden channel. As each new Elder joins the yingali, the song swells with passion and purpose. A small group of women bring in the sonorous bass notes of possum skin drums and in turn, these are accompanied by the sharp clang of clap sticks. I see my radiant cousin, Kardingarrook, sister to Meendutgarrook, start the ceremonial dance of the Mother Whale. Newly wed, her lithe body glows with the honeymoon flush of new romance and young love, as she shuffles and kicks her feet in the cool sand.

A mighty splash erupts from the still waters of Warnmarring. Launching from the depths of Sea Country, a large, glorious betayil soars through the air, her eyes turned towards us as she crashes back into the blue. Suddenly, we can see the multitude of bodies that have been resting under the layer where water meets air, rising to the surface, fins slapping and flukes flying. They have gathered just like us, this clan of kindred whales, so that we can do our ceremony together.

My babayin, Dindoo, begins the ritual of venturing out along the sandbar. Her tone is raspy and quivering, filled with emotion as she sings the praises of the Creator of our Country's sister bays. Almost immediately, the closest whale slaps her fin on the water in response. A shiver runs through my body. I have seen this before, year after year, since I was a small girl, this miraculous call and answer. And it never ceases to fill me with wonder and awe. Continuing across millennia, this timeless song and dance, this yingali, has been etched into the very being of us who walk on two legs along the shore and our kin who glide like shadows in the sea.

Our family step forward to fulfil our custodial duty. Aunties, sisters, cousins. I am joined by Meendutgarrook and Kardingarrook as our bare feet slide into the brisk, lapping waves of Warrayin. Tumbling from our lips are the songs of a mighty songline. Carried from one Country to the next, coastline to coastline, the story speaks of our shared connections, the binding wholeness of every layer of Country no matter where your place is on it. I have known these songs for as long as I can remember. My voice is unwavering as I join with my family to sing it now and keep the songline strong.

Carefully, respectfully, I wade out along the sandbar. An energetic calf rolls her clumsy body towards me. A curious one, the bubup slaps her fin as if calling me towards her. My heart thumping, I sing back to her, and slowly make my way through the crystal-clear water of the sandbar, closer to her. Surprisingly, my voice holds strong even as a fluttering stirs in my belly when I see her focus a cheeky eye on me. I think I hear Meendutgarrook gasp from behind me but everything fades around the focal point of this extraordinary being and her soulful gaze searing into mine.

Such depth in the spirit of this newborn betayil, I marvel to myself. I wish I could speak in whale song, or find a sweet, shared language that we could both understand. *Who are you, little one?* I want to ask her. Your eyes speak of old knowledge, as if you've been here before. Have you? Are you my great-grandmother coming to say hello?

A delicious thought fires up from the base of my spine, sending tingles rippling through every cell. Or are you a new spirit, a returning bubup, lying in wait until the right time to land in my body and grow in human form again?

As if she understands the character of my thoughts, the calf rolls even closer to me, fanning her fluked tail merely metres from me. I hover on the very edge of the sandbar, just one step away from where the floor of Warrayin plunges down into a deep channel, the sacred resting place of Babayin Betayil. If only I could get a bit closer, if only I could stretch a bit further, my wish to the Old Ones would come true. Finally, I would be able to touch this magnificent being and feel with my own flesh the magic that courses through them.

A sonorous call comes from the calf's mother, as she effortlessly glides towards us. I call back in the tongue of my people and immediately the mother whale sings again. My whole body shivers with a great surging of emotion. A chant bursts from my lips and I slap the water's surface. She raises her tail in acknowledgment and taps it twice upon the water, like beating a drum double time.

Over and over, we mirror each other until I feel our very heartbeats are aligned. We are the same. Our black skins bearing scars with pride, showing the sum of our life's knowledge. Our fins and hands clapping in kindred harmony. I feel as if I am transported into her very consciousness and suddenly, in a blaze of brilliant illumination, I see with absolute clarity all the wisdom she holds within. The profound importance in the simple act of caring for Country. The right ways as a mother to tether a child just tight enough. The constant circling of our pasts and futures so that the songlines prevail across epochs. The entirety of Time itself.

And then, with one last exhale of air from her blowhole, the mother whale sinks back into the loving embrace of Sea Country. Without hesitation, her calf dives down after her, and the pair slip from view. Elated, I wade back to shore, forever changed.

Not much needs to be said around the campfire tonight. A humming blanket of happiness wraps itself around everyone at the wilam. Our spirits are full from our wondrous Ngargee for Babayin Betayil. Our bellies are sated from the feast of abalone, snapper, scallops and pipis. Each bubup is tucked up snug in possum skin rugs, in blissful repose after a marvellous day.

Gently, I prise the two twigs of driftwood from Yearl Yearl's grasp, lest they become an accident in waiting during his restless nighttime adventures. Always very loyal to the treasures he finds on the beach, my boy held the kalk tightly for the entire day, the sticks spinning with perpetual motion. Only now, in slumber, are they finally still. Likewise, it is safer to slip Boyerup's freshly made shell bracelet off her slender wrist. Creases in her skin have already begun to form as the weight of her hand grows heavier in sleep. One last look at the two vulnerable souls destined to be under my care, and I pad back to the fireside.

With the light from the fire flickering in her shining face, Meendutgarrook clasps my hand in hers.

You looked into her eyes! She whispers in wonder. *What did you see? What did you see?*

With a cascade of thoughts crashing through my brain all at once, I shake my head in a state of wonderment. How to possibly describe the depth of the unfathomable?

I saw it all, my liwurruk. I saw it all. I feel an evangelical zeal sweep through my mind as I try to wrap it around the complexity of the experience. *And the only thing I can say about it is we are lucky to be the custodians of such magnificence. So lucky.*

I squeeze her arm with a happy reassurance, laughing as she flashes me a wide, toothy grin. Those gleaming mischievous eyes twinkle back at me, forever shining with the eagerness and impatience of that brave bubup on the beaches of our childhood home. So quick to laugh and even quicker to rush where others, like me, might take pause, preferring quiet contemplation over impulsiveness. And yet I recognise the determination etched in her face, for connection, for knowledge, to be a true Bagarrook Warrayin.

Next time, she promises aloud, more to herself than anyone else. *Next time, the Old Ones will hear my wish.*

Maybe they did hear your wish, I quip. *They just gave it to the wrong person.*

I grin as Meendutgarrook snorts with amused realisation. *You know what, I think you're right!*

So next time, I declare, with the same fervour as my cousin, *maybe the Old Ones will let me finally touch the betayil!*

Standing, I sweep the detritus of dinner into a pile and fill my arms with the remnants of charred shell and bone. Nearby, strewn throughout the undulating hills of a special, windswept dune, stands our family Keeping Place. There is something strangely beautiful about seeing layers upon layers of feasted-upon shell, building up and mixing within the sands of the dunes. It speaks of certainty and continuity. Of the countless cycles of Ngargee for Babayin Betayil.

Glimmering before me, I see the very place where my great grandmother laid her shells, as did her great grandmother, as did her great grandmother. The older shells are cracked and brittle, weathered by the forces of salty wind, ocean mist and spinning Time. Nevertheless, they remain. A shimmering testament to the longevity of my Old Ones. As I run my fingers along the layers within reach, I thank those who created them for the gifts of their learnings and traditions. Knowledge that has kept us alive and thriving, kept our Country, our culture, our community and our children flourishing, year after year, decade after decade, century after century, millennia after millennia.

Returning to the warmth of the campfire, I see that the older women have joined our circle, a cluster of quiet murndigarrook whose faces are shadowed with concern. As I settle in beside her, my mother points to the barely perceptible shape of an island in the darkened distance, Korriyong.

Once part of the beautiful family estate of our neighbouring Boonwurrung clan, the Yallock Balak, this Country is now a lonely island devoid of its custodians. Following her pointed finger, I know why Dindoo is filled with a simmering resentment. Faint, but obvious in the dark cloak of night, a light flickers on the edge of the island. Men, white as the ochre of death, relentless slaughterers of the koormam. Sealers.

In years past, when I was a younger girl, I would lie on these very shores after our Ngargee for Babayin Betayil. Drifting off to sleep, I would hear the distant grunting and hollering, the splashing and slapping, of a restless community of koormam. Travelling across the Bay, the sounds of the seals would fill my sleepy mind with images of their mischievous, whiskered faces shape-shifting into the guardian water spirits of Sea Country, the Koormamgarrook. Dreams would take hold of fantastic adventures under the sea, diving in the forests of giant kelp, mermaids and whale calves by my side, glittering abalone shells lighting the ocean depths with their wurrdin iridescence.

But those sounds have stopped now. Each and every one of those seals that called Korriyong their home was bludgeoned to death by the white man. It happened so quickly, within the space of a handful of seasons. Silence rests heavily in their place now. Silence and sealers, still lingering on the empty island, claiming it as their own. No Boonwurrung can go there now, the place of their Ancestors since Time began, for if they do, they will suffer under the same club that decimated their koormam kin.

In hushed whispers, as the firelight flickers across listening faces, my aunty tells the story of a young mother and her eight-year-old girl snatched by a group of sealing men last summer. After searching for the better part of a day and night, her family finally found them both in a rocky cave. Disfigured, bloodied and broken, their lifeless bodies told the story of unspeakable violation.

Not men but monsters, my aunty murmurs. *Here on our shores. Buldjinganu, bad devils, who refuse to leave.*

Heads nod in agreement around the campfire. Over many seasons now, stories like this have filtered through the clan estates, becoming more and more frequent. From all over Country and the lands of our neighbouring Countries too. Women and children going about their saltwater business, diving for abalone, fishing, gathering shells and kelp, holding their sacred ceremonies, are no longer safe on the sands their Ancestors have walked since Time Immemorial. Desolate stories of being stolen away, brutalised and left to perish in lonely caves. Heartbroken whispers of young women and little girls vanishing, ripped from their Biik by sealers on wooden vessels, floating over Warrayin and past the horizon, never to be seen again. Never to see their family and Homelands again.

My mother begins the song. A cry to our Old Ones, to Mother Whale, Bunjil the wedge-tailed eagle and Waa the raven, to keep the spirits of these lost women and children tethered somehow to their Biik. Dindoo's voice breaks as the mournful lament fills the air. One by one, the older women raise their voices to help carry the song up to Sky Country. I imagine that somewhere across the ocean, our kin might hear the wailing call travelling on a persistent breeze. Maybe these stolen, vanished bagarrook and bubup might draw the strength and courage they need from our song. And maybe the sounds might weave a songline through the mornmoot's ether that could somehow draw them back to where they belong.

WILAM
Home

After several days and nights of women's ceremony, we gather up a stockpile of fresh eucalyptus and make our way to the highest ridge along the sand dunes of Yellodungo. Taking care not to disturb the fragile nests of the burribarri, we prepare the sand for a signal fire. Enough days have passed to see if the men and older boys have returned to our favourite wilam after the undertaking of their own special business. And, as the murndigarrook surmise in hopeful tones, their hunting exploits on the plateaus of our high country will make for a grand reunion feast.

Our firekeeper coaxes the flame with fire sticks from the grasstree and it's not long before her expertise has created an impressive blaze. Sweet smoke curls upwards in ribbons as the green leaves of the eucalypt transform in the kuunh. Deftly, Aunty waves the smoke in a practised pattern of questioning, then scans the horizon for an answer.

A few minutes pass, and a welcome funnel of smoke shoots into the sky close by. A cheer erupts from the aunties, the men have indeed returned to Kullurk, merely an hour's walk away. A flutter of anticipation ripples around the wilam, and my own heart skips a few beats at the thought of seeing my husband again. Absence works in mysterious ways. As eager as I am to embark on our women's business, with so much love in caring for Country and our totems in our women's way, the time apart from my nanggorrong makes me excited to be his wife again.

As the giggling and lively chatter reveal, many in our camp feel the same way. I see a spark ignite in my sister cousins as they pay special attention to the fall of their hair and the placement of their adornments. Kardingarrook can barely contain herself, zipping around the wilam, helping anyone who needs it, in the hope that it'll get our family moving quicker. Any glumness at having to leave her new husband over the last few days, and particularly nights, has dissipated like the morning dew in the heat of a rising sun. Even my aunties and mother smile with fondness at the thought of reunion, even though their role as Elders and knowledge keepers brings a different set of obligations when the community comes together.

Bilang full of bounty from the sea, we make haste back to Kullurk. All of my Country is beautiful, but there are some places that sing with particular sweetness. Walking lightly across the well-worn track of our women's path inland, I think about the great estate of Boonwurrung Biik and all of those places that make my spirit soar. The tumultuous coast that bears its weathered self to the open ocean, the glorious sweep of sand and cliff edging the bigger of the sister bays, the valleys of giant manna gum offering solid towers of shelter to so many creatures.

And Kullurk. The home we always return to. In this place, the song of Country is gentle, speaking of serenity and plenty, peace and ease. We make our wilams from stone because it's a favoured home for families, a place of permanence and respite whatever the season, teeming with bountiful gifts from Country and the Creation Beings. Alongside the resting place of Babayin Betayil, below the benevolent view of Bunjil the wedge-tailed eagle and under the protective wing of Waa the raven, Kullurk is a place of perfection.

Just as Nyawiinth the Sun ascends to the apex of Sky Country, we finally arrive. In a gush of frenzied joy, Yearl Yearl sprints to his favourite manna gum tree which towers above our family wilam. Secreted in the thickened boughs of this graceful wurrun are my mammam's prized treasures, and to this collection he now adds three glossy gangan from Waa. Boyerup and I duck inside the cosy confines of our stone-walled home, built strong with the sense of a perpetual returning to this most special of places. Inside, we lay out lines of delicate shells gathered from the shores of Babayin Betayil's resting place, ready and waiting for the time to string into lovely adornment.

Outside, a cheerful *Kye* draws us into the midday light, and my stomach flutters as I see my husband sauntering across the camp towards me, his shoulders draped with the body of a once robust kangaroo. A broad grin animates his beautiful face, and his dark eyes gleam with a mischievous light. My Bobbinary.

After lowering his bounty near the open fire, my nanggorrong leaps towards me and sweeps me up in his muscular arms. I shriek with laughter until his lips are on mine, tasting like sweet nectar from the warrak blossom. His kiss stirs a yearning in my belly and I can see by the glint in his eyes that he feels the same. But the moment is broken by two jumping bubup, impatient for their turn in their father's sunlight. Opening his arms wide, we all crowd into his protective embrace. Home.

Preparations begin immediately for the night's feasting, an exuberant reunion after business away. With fresh meat from the land, tasty delicacies from the sea, and tarnook full of fruits from the trees, it promises to be a monameit occasion, an evening of full bellies around warm fires telling stories of the time apart.

Even as we all launch happily into the industry of readying ourselves for celebration, a rumble of concerned murmuring begins to roll around the wilam. A tense whisper that has travelled on the ether to us. A warning message from our neighbouring allies. There is trouble in the north.

With Boyerup and Yearl Yearl in a race to see who can collect the most firewood before dinner, I take the moment of privacy to ask my husband what is happening. Grimly, Bobbinary grasps both of my hands and pulls me out of earshot from other family.

Word has come from the other Kulin Nations that a celebrated wirrirap from the mountain people was shown a terrifying vision. The liyan holding up the sky has started to rot.

A sharp intake of air fills my lungs and I feel a surge of panic ricochet through my body.

We don't really know what it means, but the clevermen agree it's a warning, Bobbinary continues, *so an urgent call has gone around all of our clan estates for the strongest axes to be delivered North as soon as possible.*

To make a new liyan? I enquire, my voice high-pitched and strained.

Perhaps. It is not decided if the vision was about fortifying the props that hold up the sky or . . . he pauses, speaking low so as not to be overheard, *or to fortify against something else*

My mind is racing with a thousand thoughts, questions and fears. What could the wirrirap's vision really mean? Is it even possible to make a new liyan? How long will that take? What possible threats are coming from the mountains to the north? Will they reach us here?

A precious memory quietens the cacophony of anxiety in my mind. I remember sitting on my father's knee, looking up to Sky Country. It was early morning and the golden rays of the newly risen sun were beginning to ascend the sky. Drawing an arc overhead, my father tracked the passage Nyawiinth would travel that day and described all manner of miracles his journey would gift our Country. Light for us to see, heat to keep us warm and dry, sustenance to help the plants grow, and a way to measure the passage of Time.

But this journey of Nyawiinth had not always been possible, my father had explained, as I bounced restlessly on his knee, pulling on his beard. Lacing my small, fidgeting fingers through his long, toughened ones, he patiently described the texture of the sky. Like a many-layered blanket that long ago lay heavy across the barely formed earth. It was so dense that most creatures struggled to thrive underneath its weight. There was hardly any light or heat, no tall trees, and an endless monotony to the shape of Time.

One day, the old spirits of that long ago Time, the Murrumbunguttia, gathered at the highest point of their Country. Much discussion was had about the nature of their existence. They wanted to mark the changing of day into night. They needed a sun and a moon that could journey over the land but how was that possible when the blanket of the sky lay so heavy upon it. Then Barrawarn the magpie, thinking about the sticks she used to build her nest, had an idea. If they found a kalk strong enough and secured it to the very top of the mountain, maybe the cloak of Sky Country could be lifted.

And so it was done, and so it has remained across millennia. Sky Country exalted in a raised blanket of starlight, and the land and sea taking shape below, flourishing under the custodianship of grateful kulin and bagarrook. All sustaining in a careful, harmonious balance. Until now.

Clutching at my husband's powerful hands, seeking their comforting reassurance, I try to assess his level of concern.

Can we get the axes they want?

Yes, my birrimbayin, we have exactly the materials they need.

A strange glint of mischief twinkles in his eye, and despite the awful reality of the catastrophe that might befall us, I find myself laughing at his casual bravado.

Why do I feel like you're planning something dangerous?

Not dangerous if one is careful, he replies flippantly.

Hmmm, so where exactly are these extraordinary materials that will keep the danger away or the entire Sky Country from collapsing?

All will be revealed, but not tonight. Tonight is for yingali.

Even as I bask in the certainty of my man's courage and valour, an insidious wisp of fear curls up from the base of my spine. I can't name it or pinpoint its origin, but I feel it take hold. A sense of the shifting of an axis. A feeling of strangeness, of being off-kilter, has simmered under the surface of Boonwurrung Biik for many seasons now. Since Time Immemorial, we have known our rhythms, our structures, the symbiosis of Country and Kulin working together.

But change of a kind never experienced before is forcing its way into our world. The very foundations that hold up our universe are starting to rot. People in the mountains feel it coming from the north, we catch glimpses of it gliding across our seas in the south.

The rising of the Buldjinganu. As a young girl I remember overhearing my grandmother whisper this to her sister, words that chilled me to the bone. Late at night with the campfire low, I should have been asleep. But I was fascinated by the thing my grandmother held in her wizened fingers. Silky and white, threaded from material I had never seen before. Not leather, not fur, not reed, not feather. A covering for a man's chest.

The ngamudji are here, my granny had whispered. *And if they don't leave, I fear it's the end of our world.*

An icy grip seizes my heart.

But what will happen if the wirrirap's vision was about the ancient liyan? What if it really is rotting to nothing? I murmur.

My husband clutches my hands in his and shoots me a disarming, wry smile. *Then Sky Country will fall upon us and everything will change. But that's not going to happen today. And I'm praying to the Old Ones that it doesn't happen tonight.* His dark eyes blaze a seductive promise, wrapping me in delicious heat. *Because you and I have other things planned.*

Laughter and song echo around the towering trees. All the families in our clan estate are reunited again at Kullurk. Every belly in the clan is full and satisfied, and the remnants of our great feast are gathered to feed to the werrun, patiently waiting on the edges of the camp.

A sharp clap rings out through the crisp night air. The aunties and uncles are playing their daal kalk and the yingali has begun.

Dust flies around the camp as feet thud upon the sand, casting a hazy glow over the men dancing in full splendour.

Beating happily on her possum skin drum, my cousin Meendutgarrook gazes lovingly at her promised one, Barrunan. Ever since the men had arrived back at the wilams, she would steal secret glances whenever he was close by, desire flickering in her munmundiik's eyes. And impatience too, for while she had been long promised to Barrunan, Meendutgarrook had to wait until the murndigarrook decided she was ready to wed.

I wish they would hurry up, she would often groan in frustration, particularly when she saw her sister revel in newly wedded bliss.

I look for Kardingarrook, but she is nowhere to be seen. And neither is her man. A knowing smile plays on my lips as the Elders sing the stories of the Old Ones and our revelry buzzes up to the stars. Staring upwards at those twinkling points of light sewn through the black booroonth of Sky Country, I send a wish to the Seven Sisters, asking that they hold up the blanket for as long as they can.

My bubups' eyelids grow heavy and their spent bodies start to slacken. It is time for them to drift off to sleep, so I wrap them in their wallert wallert rugs and kiss them lightly on their foreheads. Around the campfires, the family groups slowly disperse and the Elders take their whispering conversations to a separate kuunh. At last, Bobbinary comes for me and links his arm with mine. We find ourselves a place of quiet seclusion. On the cool sand, under a show of shimmering stars, Meeniyan the Moon high and bright, my nanggorrong lays me down.

The hypnotic lapping of the lulling ocean nearby mirrors the rhythm of our bodies merging and we move together in blissful harmony. When a djurt shoots across the sky above me in a blaze of light and awe, I know that all is perfect. Right here, right now, for this moment. All is perfect.

*

Low tide peels back the water from the rockpools, exposing to daylight the abundant treasures of Warrayin. Following the line of the ocean floor on the curving shore around Kullurk, I see that the eternal pendulum governing the undulating tides now swings to the extreme.

For weeks now, the men have been biding their time, watching as the days roll onwards and Biik blossoms under the warming Pareip sun, swarming with bursting flowers offering themselves to a myriad of fluttering balambalam. Finally, the saltwater is shallower and glassy, its rhythms gentle as the open ocean pulls the currents back into her expanse. One more cycle of the moon and Warnmarring will be at her emptiest.

Heaviness pulls in my stomach. This is what the men have been waiting for. A chance to cross from the safety of our Burinyong Balak peninsula to the island of Korriyong, once home to the seal and the shape-shifting Koormamgarrook, now claimed by the insatiable white ghosts.

Long canoes built from sturdy river red gum are patched with clay, reeds and grass tree resin. Using the unyielding granite of greenstone axe, my man pierces through the outer layer of a willing river gum. A buzzing stirs in my belly as I secretly watch the tightening and flexing of Bobbinary's powerful arms. Fierce pride and deep longing wind their way around every fibre of my being at the sight of my nanggorrong, his body, his knowledge, his skill and his innate nobility.

He is mine, I think to myself, smiling in a flush of love. *And I am his.*

Carefully, Bobbinary makes a practised cut, long and wide, down the rough skin of the tree. Sized for three men, the shape of the gurrung emerges from the bark which is skilfully eased away. As the new canoe is shaped and toughened, the men speak in agitated whispers. Every detail is examined as they meticulously plan their precision raid on the sealers. It has been so many turns of a full

Meeniyan moon since any kulin have walked on the shores of Korriyong but the memory keens with the knowledge of the sealers' gunfire and ruthless slaughter.

We must only take what's necessary to assist the people in the north, what their wirrirap asked for. The white man's axe and stone, the thick-ened rope, whispers Bobbinary. *We get in and out while the tide is at its lowest tomorrow night.*

Knowing well the perils of such a trip, my husband's grim face makes it clear they will take this risk for one purpose only. But a restlessness pervades in some of the men, a stirring of darker emotion. Dread gathers heavy at the base of my spine and I try to push it away, grasping my women's digging stick tight in my hand and bracing the largest tarnook against my hip like a babe wrapped in a wallert wallert cloak.

As I leave our Kullurk wilam to join my countrywomen on the day's spring harvest of our growing fields, I hear Bobbinary say, *This is not the time for revenge. That will come. Someday, that will come.*

Fat fingers of murnong yam spread their bodies through the churned-up soil. With the pointed ends of our kanaan, the women of my clan strike the ground with utmost precision. Careful farming of Biik's abundant plains over many seasons means our murnong grow long and strong in their family clusters, often bigger than a man's hand.

With a wide, taunting grin, Meendutgarrook gently prises one of the larger yams away from its snug family and waves it enticingly in front of Kardingarrook. *Look here! Remind you of anything?*

Her sister flushes bright red and jabs Meendutgarrook's yam with her murnong kalk. *Nah! Too small, that one! Not nearly as big as I'm used to!*

Hoots of laughter sound around the field and even Dindoo and the older women break a smile at the girls' bawdiness. Happily, we gather the yield into our tarnook. These precious yams are lifeblood, a constant source of sustenance for the whole clan. As always, when we separate the yams from their family cluster, we make sure to put one back. This way, she can sprout new babies for the next harvest, and the cycle sustains itself over again.

Back at our burgeoning camping place, the joyous shrieks of children rocketing around the wilams echo through the towering wurrun groves. Our community is growing, with more men arriving to join the quest to save the failing liyan holding up Sky Country, and their families follow in solidarity. Reunited with their distant cousins from all over Boonwurrung Biik, the bubup are bubbling with newfound excitement and purpose, eager to show their friends the secret wonders of their patch of Country.

Make sure you tread gently in those dunes, Yearl Yearl, I warn. *Those tiny burribarri have fragile homes and the Old Ones are always watching.*

My boy nods with a solemn reassurance. *I most certainly will.*

Then, in a burst of glee, he sprints off after his band of brother cousins, singing out with exuberance to his Liwik as he goes.

Threading arms with her newly arrived clan sisters, Boyerup likewise takes great delight in leading them to the best patches of river reed and the most abundant tidelines rippling with shells. Quick and nimble, the girls' fingers weave threads of delicate reed string under the watchful gaze of their accomplished aunties. Once satisfied, they clasp hands and skip along the tracks to the sea for an afternoon filled with threading their favoured shells onto the freshly made twine.

Running my fingers over my own threaded creations, shells necklaced and gleaming across my breasts, I relish in the memory of making them. Each tiny, pierced shell a keepsake of cherished moments, marking time spent with sisters on the beautiful shores of Warnmarring.

Kye, Nannertgarrook! You dreaming again? Meendutgarrook calls from beside the rekindled fire. *We have some cooking to do. Old Man Sun not gonna wait for us!*

I look up to Nyawiinth on his ascent overhead and sigh. Sometimes it would be nice to be a girl again with only the shells and the sea demanding my attention. I settle beside my grinning younger cousin with a tarnook full of murnong, and count the long, fat fingers of nourishing tubers sitting ready to be slow-roasted in the warm stones of the hearth throughout the afternoon.

Just as I start in earnest the task of cleaning and preparing the first batch of yams, Meendutgarrook gives me a sharp nudge with her elbow.

Following the direction of her pointed gaze, I see a young woman arrive at our wilam with her family, a densely reeded basket strung around her neck. Solemn and drawn, the bagarrook's face is pinched with deep emotion. Yet, evident in the determined set of her jaw, a grim resolution appears to push her forward.

My mother catches our curious gazes and she motions for us to quickly finish our work. Quietly, Dindoo explains that the young mother's name is Bindergarrook from the Lowandjirri clan estate and she has travelled a great many days from her home at Wamoom, the very far end of our Boonwurrung Biik.

For a long time now, my babayin whispers gently, *she has carried her specially made binuk for sorry business. Always keeping close to her heart, the sacred remains of her only child.*

A rush of sadness sweeps over me as I steal another quick glance at the bereaved young babayin. Trepidation tugs at my heart when I imagine her carrying her bubup close over many months, riding the waves of grief as best she could, mourning the untimely loss of her baby. There is no assumption, no rules or guides, on how long a mother may take to move through her own cycles of grief. But there will always come a sorry time when she must embark on the last ritual in her journey of letting go.

Bindergarrook has chosen the murndigarrook of our clan estate to walk with her towards this final ceremony. Still speaking in a whisper, Dindoo gathers the clean murnong, positions them carefully in the roasting hearth, then slowly stands. *We will all travel together before Nyawiinth rises in the morning. The place of Ngargee Karralk is many hours away and we must get there with enough time to dive and gather the wurrdin.*

Sitting beside her sister Meendutgarrook, a crestfallen Kardingarrook barely stifles a disappointed sigh. I follow her yearning gaze to the wurrun trees where the men gather and see it has alighted on her newly anointed husband. My own heart is heavy knowing I am leaving Bobbinary again so soon, but one glance to the precious binuk at the young mother's breast and my duty to her little one's murrup, to the ceremonies of our Liwik, to the honouring of our ancient Lore, rears up strong and determined.

Let us embrace her now, Dindoo nods, compassion thick in her words.

My countrywomen and I gather around Bindergarrook, running our hands over her arms as a welcome into our fold. There is no need to labour over the young mother's precious cargo and the story of how the sorry business came to be. She was not the first to walk on this journey and she would not be the last. So many times, I have felt an awful shudder rock the core of my being when I contemplated the possibility of my young ones being ripped from me. More often than not the trigger making my knees weak would be the recklessness of Yearl Yearl as he flung himself up a possum tree or across a fast-flowing stream.

When the story reached our wilam, of the young girl and her mother kidnapped and brutalised by the sealers, I remember pressing my hands hard against my ears in a vain hope to unhear the details. Because all I could think of was my Boyerup. My beautiful butterfly with her generous heart and gentle touch. Any thought of her suffering made the cells in every part of my body lurch with a sickening churning. I would not, I could not, bear such agony.

Yet before me stands a mother carrying the sacred remains of her beloved baby against her breast. A bereaved babayin, whose suffering we all pity and fear. As we gather around her solemnly, the upwelling of our compassion rises into a plaintive wail. Immediately, her shoulders curl under the heaviest blanket of grief and Bindergarrook succumbs to the cries. Together, we rock in empathetic unity, letting the solemn release of sadness rise up like smoke into the endless ether of Sky Country.

That night, Meeniyan the moon hangs lower in the darkening sky. Her radiant crescent form is beginning to swell like the pregnant belly of a bagarrook whose bubup is starting to show. With her changing form, Meeniyan holds command over the ebb and flow of Warrayin. Soon, she will pull the waters of our Bay further out to sea, an epic low tide, the perfect scene for a daring raid on the ghosts who won't leave the now silent Korriyong.

Time also for us women to travel with Bindergarrook, taking the quickest passage to where our Old Ones have held Ngargee for the journey of our murrup to Karralk since Time Immemorial. A beautiful bay fronting the surging swell of a wild, southern Warrayin, flanked by soaring basalt cliffs and graceful folding dunes. I have journeyed throughout my entire life to that hallowed Biik on the Burinyong-Balak estate. Following the winding, fresh water of the Burrabong creek from the high ridges to the sandy shore, my mother would always explain its significance for Warrayin Bagarrook.

Konye, look see, wherever fresh water flows into saltwater on our monameit Biik, that is the place for mothers and their children. Her wise face would glow with the profundity of our Old Ones yulendji. *A place of many ceremonies, much learning, joy and sorrow, birth and rebirth.*

But that is the journey for tomorrow. Tonight, resting in my husband's cradling arms, I stare up at Meeniyan, moving like a shrouded beacon across the night sky. I send her a secret wish that she might slow her journey, just for this night, so I can spend a longer time in his comforting embrace by our wilam's kuunh.

When will you leave? I question softly.

Bobbinary turns his gaze away from the flames that lick at the cool night air. We have feasted on lemon-scented wirrap wrapped in paperbark, slow-baked murnong yam and fresh greens from the bush. My belly is full, my mind is clear, but my heart persists in an irregular beat as I foolishly hope my man will say he is sending the others while he stays behind.

Tomorrow night. We will have darkness to shield us and the waters low enough to make the journey to the island quick and easy.

You make it sound so simple.

My monameit wife, I promise I will make it there and back before you even know I'm gone.

I can't help but smile, knowing he is probably right. *But I leave in the morning*, I qualify. *Bindergarrook is ready, so we will walk the songline to the coast for her baby's next cycle.*

Ah, I see. A shadow of disappointment crosses Bobbinary's features but is quickly replaced by a warm and seductive smile. *Then we should make tonight count, shouldn't we?*

We most certainly should, dear husband.

A plaintive call from a restless mopoke wakes me from my dreaming. Nestled next to my nanggorrong, I feel his body rise and fall with slumberous breaths. Warm to touch, his dark skin melds into mine and in the shimmering moonlight we look to be one and the same.

Next to us, Boyerup rests curled on her side, a loosely balled fist stretching towards the strong sinews of her daddy's shoulder, reaching for the reassurance of his presence. As always, Yearl Yearl lies in a mess of tousled hair and flinging limbs. I stifle a laugh as I marvel at his uncanny ability to appear to be in perpetual motion while in the deepest of sleeps. *My family*, I think, as a haze of sleep clouds my midnight brain. *Mine, so lucky.* Blissfully I succumb once again to the lovely drift of dreaming.

Dawn breaks in streaks of pale light, pink and gold over the blue of the bay.

I'll look for your smoke, I say to Bobbinary, clutching at his hands for a reassuring promise. We kiss and he strokes my cheek. I feel a penetrating love burn along the line drawn by his fingertips, tracing the tension in my clenching jawline, which eases under his soothing touch.

And I'll look for yours, he whispers.

Just as I turn to join the assembling procession of women and children on our journey for Bindergarrook, my husband pulls me in a tight embrace.

Watch for them, on the horizon, their vessels on the open ocean, he says, low and urgent, dark eyes searing into mine. *Make sure you come home to me.*

YULENDJI
Knowledge

Following southward along the sweeping coastline of the gentle bay of Warnmarring, we walk the time-honoured trails of our Old Women to our estate's glorious wind-blasted cliffs and salt-spraying seas. Winding through forests of towering coastal banksia, blooms are erect and buzzing with bees. Golden powdered wattle bursts with the colours of Nyawiinth, a feast of nectar for flocks of many feathered kwiyup-kwiyup. Soon we will reach the meandering creek line which carries fresh water to Warrayin. It is the time of Pareip, when darting poorneet sprout their jumping frog legs and glassy young yurok journey from saltwater to fresh, finding refuge in the plentiful, sweet waters throughout Boonwurrung Biik.

Ahead, as Watcher for the whale and Keeper for the story of Werrun the dingo, my mother Dindoo sings out to Country, the Old Ones and her Ancestral Dingo, alert for the signs that say Biik and Liwik are listening and guiding. Our Elders, the murndigarrook, lead the way and set a steady pace, slow but purposeful for this solemn procession to the place of Ngargee Karralk. I can feel Yearl Yearl's rising impatience as he struggles to contain his urge to run free, chasing any unwitting animal soul that he spots moving. Gripping his dusty hand tighter, I try to teach him right ways.

You must be patient, my boy. Just walking now, with respect. This is not the time for playing and running.

Out of the corner of my eye I glimpse the edges of Boyerup's lips quiver with a barely smothered smirk. Yearl Yearl sees it too and he promptly thrusts a vicious tongue out at his sister, directing all his frenzied frustration her way.

Thooamee! Listen!

From a distance, a sonorous yelping has travelled to us on the lingering breeze. Our dingo companions pause in their walking, ears erect, senses alert. Dindoo stops too, a smile broadening across her knowing face. Werrun has joined us, her dingo totem, a sure sign that Mother Whale will be waiting in the Warrayin to greet us for ceremony.

The breeze grows momentarily stronger as the Old Ones use mornmoot to send the howl of the dingo to us. Werrun's mournful cry seeks out Bindergarrook and envelops her in a gentle cloak of humming melody.

The young mother weeps and the Elders know to keep moving forward so that she might find comfort in progression. My children's eyes are wide with wonder.

Whispering, Boyerup asks if that was her grandmother's ancestral totem.

Of course, manggip, I nod, finding myself filled with the same awe. *He has called to remind us of the sacredness of our journey. And do you remember Nana Dindoo's story?*

About the dingo being Mother Whale's baby? offers Yearl Yearl, a hint of pride that he remembered.

That's right! A whale travels mighty distances far out to sea to meet Old Man Sun as he rises from and falls into Warrayin. But betayil will always return to Biik to be close to her baby.

And a dingo can travel across a long distance without tiring too, adds Boyerup, eager to show she has been listening.

And you are also right! Look at you, my clever bubup. I squeeze both of their hands in admiration and encouragement. *Yes, you will see werrun sniffing the wind to catch the scent of his mother. And when she returns, he will run to the coast. Even though her migrating path loops over and over, betayil will make sure to stay close to the cliffs and the beaches so that they can travel together on their endless journey.*

For a moment I pause, a cold uneasiness threading its way up my spine. A dislocated thought crashes into my mind, rolling over and over, like an uprooted strand of giant kelp tossing and turning in a thrashing sea. *What if they lost each other? What if they lost each other?*

Shaking my head with a sudden jolt, I grip the hands of my children tight and pull them under the shade of a blossoming banksia. This warrak's flowers are heavy and ripe so we pick a bloom each to make a sweet drink at our destination. Pushing the intruding thought away, I finish the story of the whale and the dingo, sharing with my bubup a fragment of the sacred knowledge that has been passed to me from my mother.

You see, I murmur so that only their ears can hear. *Sometimes a mother may have to leave her child to take care of her own special business. And sometimes a child will have to leave their mother to make their own way in the world. But remember this.* I pull their small bodies into a close hug. *A mother will always return to her baby because she loves them so much. And a child will always look to see that their mother is close in case they need them. Whale and dingo, mother and child, are always connected, their bond can never broken. They will never lose each other.*

Boyerup turns to the young woman carrying her sacred binuk so close to her breast and whispers, *But what about when the baby dies?*

Well, that is why we are doing ceremony today. Because in our Ngargee, our songs and our dances, we are asking Babayin Betayil to take the spirit of the little one across to Karralk. The place where the sun touches the sea, the lowering of Nyawiinth on Warrayin's horizon. There, the bubup's murrup will climb up the golden rays of the setting sun to visit Sky Country and our Liwik. And once they have done what they need to do, the spirit will return on their whale to be close to their mother again.

Boyerup nods solemnly, and Yearl Yearl stares up to Sky Country, wondering what adventures await there.

Can I tell you the most amazing part?

The children lean close, bright eyes gleaming with a thirst for knowledge.

It is in this ever turning journey of spirits that the dingo on the land is both baby and mother, and the whale in the sea is both mother and baby. One and the same, with a bond that is never broken.

A wondrous realisation illuminates Boyerup's face. *And that's the same for us, isn't it?*

Tears prick the corner of my eyes as I take in my glorious manggip and her intuitive understanding. All swirling around in her wise, soulful eyes.

Yes it is, my bright spark, yes it is.

Impatiently, Yearl Yearl stamps both feet, bends his knees and waves his legs open and closed, mimicking a move performed by the men around the campfire.

Nah, he says dismissively. *I don't get it.*

With a burst of laughter and a shake of my head, I grab their hands and we race to catch up with our clan.

Stretching across the full length of the beachfront, another Keeping Place stands as testament to the thousands of women who have come before us. Built with layer upon layer of bounty from the sea, shells and charcoal weave through the sand, fortifying the undulating dunes that emerge between Mother Whale's cliffs. Tonight we will make our wilam here, next to the place of the Ngargee Karralk, ensuring our hearts, heavy with sorry business, will be lovingly ensconced in the calm embrace of the midden dunes, sheltered from mornmoot's ocean winds, nestled within our history's unwavering arms.

Warrayin is whisper quiet, as if patiently waiting for us to arrive. Still and clear, her crisp saltwater sings like a siren, beckoning the women to swim free and safe in her depths.

Our Elders smile with loving appreciation and sing out their praises. *Thank you, Babayin Betayil, thank you, Liwik, thank you, Koormamgarrook, thank you, Warrayin.*

My countrywomen join in. I prod Boyerup and Yearl Yearl, and our voices rise happily, for as we gaze upon this paradise laid out before us, how can we not thank our Mother Whale, our Ancestors, the Women of the Seal and Kelp, and our stunning Sea Country. My mother calls me over, and as she grinds pieces of ochre, orange and pink in her tarnook for the ceremony to come, she delegates the day's responsibilities.

The grannies will watch the children in the rockpools while your aunties and I make preparations with Bindergarrook for tonight's Ngargee Karralk. Choose your best swimmers and you girls can collect the abalone. We need plenty, some for tonight and some extra to take back to the mob tomorrow.

Armed with my bilang and special women's tool for prizing wurrdin shell from rock, I wade into the sea with the other bagarrook. Icy water stabs at our tensing muscles but we have learned to be like the seal and the Koormamgarrook, smearing our bodies with animal fat to insulate our susceptible skin. Diving for the fruits of the sea has its challenges. Not just the cold, nor the tangling tendrils of giant kelp and holding our breath for many minutes. But out beyond the rock ledges and reefs, we enter the home of Wiyagabul Darrak, the Old Man Shark. Open ocean is his domain, and while he shares it with Mother Whale and Barrunan the dolphin, he is not so fond of splitting the bounty with the Boonwurrung, especially when he can eat us instead.

You know, I saw one of Darrak's children last time we were here, just out past the reef, Meendutgarrook says with a hint of trepidation. Standing waist-deep in the placid Warrayin, the young girl's usually bright, laughing eyes flicker with concern as she scours the depths for a patrolling dorsal fin.

Gliding past Meendutgarrook with a well-practised ease in the water, her older sister is nonchalant.

I've seen plenty, Kardingarrook declares airily. *Best thing you can do is make like a rock and they glide straight past.*

Easy for you to say, I snort.

Yeah, adds Meendutgarrook, gazing at her big sister with a reluctant admiration. *Helps to be the one with the record for holding her breath the longest!*

This is true, smirks Kardingarrook cheekily. *I run rings around you mob.* And proving her point, she dives quickly, with the streamlined grace of a dolphin, out to the deeper water.

I go with what my gugungiyup told me on my first swim, I say reassuringly. *Remember to keep listening to Liwik, they will guide you. Look around you, watch for the signs. A jet of cold water, movement of the fish, a tap from a Koormamgarrook.*

You've been tapped by a Koormamgarrook!? Meendutgarrook squeals in disbelief. *Did you see her face? Did she try to talk to you? What do they really look like?*

Well, I lean in close and lower my voice. Some knowledge is not for the ears of a curious boy. *I thought I heard a whisper and then I felt this weird tapping on my shoulder. When I turned around, I saw her swimming away through the kelp forest. She looked like the kelp, long and black, slender, but with scales flecked with light, iridescent like the abalone shell. Somehow I knew I should head up to the surface, and that's when I saw the fin.*

Meendutgarrook's eyes are oyster wide. *Was it coming for you?*

Well, liwurruk, I wasn't staying in the water to find out, was I? I got up on that reef quicker than your soon-to-be-husband going up a possum tree.

My Barrunan climbs lightning quick, she grins with lustful pride. *Exactly.*

I swim alongside the peninsula of reef jutting out from the headland cliffs to a swaying forest of giant kelp, where I know the precious wurrdin shell clings in Warrayin's depths. As I pull myself down the slippery stem of an enormous stalk, I feel the cold water press ever closer against me. The deeper I dive, the greater the force of Warrayin's grip.

There is something strangely comforting about these depths. The peaceful silence, the squeezing pressure of the water like a full-body embrace. I am at one with the saltwater, a Bagarrook Warrayin, a woman of the sea. Searching out the rugged crusts of the abalone shell, I know where to look. Sea Country has taught me many of her secrets. Familiar and steadfast, I move easily through her comforting density. My second home.

A burst of bubbles shoots up in a jet stream to the surface. I quickly slide behind the waving strands of kelp, watching to see what is sharing these depths with me. To my shock, it is Bindergarrook, swimming forcefully towards the bottom of the seabed. Fluid and strong, she moves with the grace of a Koormamgarrook. She knows this Country too, a striking likeness to her own clan estate further along the coast at Wamoom. Without hesitation, she heads straight for a rocky ledge, pulling out the lobster cowering there. I watch with admiration as she glides along the sea floor finding more bounty tucked away. A kindred spirit.

At that moment, Bindergarrook sees me, veiled behind my seaweed curtain. A quick flash of surprise and then a grin stretches across her face. She points upwards and I nod. Together we ascend to the light above us, breaking the surface with an expulsion of air.

Thank you, Warrayin, Bindergarrook breathes.

Her tone is low and hoarse with emotion, and I sense the multitude of layers held in those three simple words. Sea Country not only shares her resources and knowledge, her cleansing waters can heal. I rub the young mother's arm and we pick our way along the rocky reef, back to the shore in unspoken understanding.

Ochres, in shades of orange, pink and yellow, adorn the sacred remains of a beloved bubup, now tenderly swaddled in the possum skin cloak given to the little one at birth. Beats of gentle drumming merge with the subdued taps of clapping sticks. Women's voices vary in wavering pitch, a ritual of melodic weeping and release through song. We tell the spirit of this little one that they have been loved, are loved still and will always be loved. We tell the murrup of this little one that their mother is ready to let them go so they can start the next lap of their looping journey. And that their special whale is waiting to carry them across the Warrayin to Karralk.

Now, as Nyawiinth the Sun begins his descent to the far edge of the ocean, the Elders gather around Bindergarrook. Gently, they encourage the young mother to pick up her precious bundle and, cradling the bubup tight to her breast, she follows her teachers to the place of letting go. This is sacred business, and only the knowledge keepers who hold the ritual of Karralk can tread this path. I watch greedily, like a famished eagle, hungry to learn all of the intricacies of my culture and the deepest layers of knowledge it holds.

Desire grips my heart, watching my mother pick her way across the reef pools to the rock of Babayin Betayil. A yearning to be able to walk the ancient paths of the Elders and Ancestors, to soak up their teachings, to come to that place of intimate understanding of all the ways that have seen my clan thrive over epochs. All this so that, one day, I might ascend to the same stature of Elder as my mother and grandmother, teaching the ones coming after me all the beauty, wisdom, and revelation of our Country and her culture.

The women disappear around the far edge of Mother Whale's giant boulder, shaped in her image, rising out of the waves. Forged by the thrashing of her enormous fluke as she attempted to rescue her beached baby whale Djou-Djou, the rock stands against the forces of Time, heralding the enormity of the love a mother bears for her child. And this evening, as the aureate rays of the setting sun bathe Country in a glorious, golden light, this rock stands unshaking beside the spirit of a beloved bubup, waiting for their whale to carry them onwards.

Beyond the headland, the streaming rays of gold and pink emanate upwards from a sinking Nyawiinth. My eyes stay fixed on the place where my Elders disappeared, leading Bindergarrook to the place of letting go. As Sky Country colours purple and deeper blue, I think I hear voices on a gathering wind, the wail of the murndigarrook carried across the waves on a sympathetic mornmoot. Waiting for their return, I wonder about the songs and dances of Ngargee Karralk. I yearn to know them, to earn the right to sing the ancient yulendji, to grow old and wise like my Elders before me and teach the young ones the sacred ways of thousands upon thousands of years.

Just as the last light fades under the darkened cloak of booroonth, the murndigarrook emerge from behind Babayin Betayil's rock. Supporting between them a tear-streaked Bindergarrook, no longer carrying her precious, sacred binuk against her breast.

Another layer of charred shells mixes with history at our Keeping Place after tonight's subdued feast of bounty from the sea. They mark the solemness of Bindergarrook's loss and the beginning of her next journey forward.

As I gaze past my children's sleeping bodies to the soft curves of these women's sand dunes laced with shells, I wonder how many strands signal the same loss from women thousands of seasons ago. Time is a circle, I remember my grandmother explaining. And we travel its loops to learn love. Love of Country, and every soul on it, from the smallest grain of quartz to the wild expanse of the sea. From the tiniest speck of biting mite to the wondrous, wizened spirit of our oldest bagarrook.

As I ponder on this, my eyes following the ragged cliffs glowing silver in the moonlight, I see a shape emerge from behind the distant rocks. Out at sea, its triangular form cuts across Warrayin like the sinister, cruising fin of Wiyagabul Darrak, the giant old man shark. And a shard of fear stabs into the base of my spine.

It's them, I think.

Casting a panicked eye over our women's wilam, I feel some relief seeing my sleeping family hidden in the sheltering folds of our sand dune.

A low growl hums from my mother's werrun as I creep to where she is sleeping.

Hush, I whisper to the dingo, who settles when she recognises my scent.

I press against my mother's arm until she wakes. Without speaking I point to the ominous shape gliding along the horizon. Like me, Dindoo glances an appraising eye over her sleeping clan. Assured of their hidden safety, my mother and I pick our way over blissfully unaware bodies to a grove of banksia at the end of the beach.

Our fires are low, I whisper. *I think we're safe.*

I'm not worried for us, Dindoo responds, her brow furrowed in calculated thought. *It's the men. I wonder if they've made it back across the Bay.*

A sudden sickness grips at my belly. Of course, the men. And their daring raid to gather the tools needed to satisfy the distant wirrirap and his dreaming, to repair a rotting liyan and prevent the collapse of the blanket of Sky Country. Quivering with panic, I search my mother's face for reassurance.

It wouldn't take them long, would it? With the tide low like we saw it today.

My mother doesn't answer straight away. Her gaze sweeps along the course of the shore, measuring the height of the tideline against the revealing of submerged rockpools. Looking up to the night sky, she follows the arc of Meeniyan the moon and I see her stiff frown loosen.

If all has gone well, they should be back at Kullurk by now, Dindoo nods.

Relief washes through me like the mercifully rising tide. Until my mother searches the darkness of booroonth with questioning eyes and adds:

If all has gone well.

Dawn's first light stirs me from my restless sleep. Sitting bolt upright, I immediately scour the top of the cliff opposite the rock of Mother Whale and see the smoke of a burgeoning fire curling upwards like a signalling beacon.

My mother did not return to the sleeping sand dune wilam last night. Instead, she waited, vigilantly, for the precise moment to send her message back to the clan at Kullurk. *Did the men come home?*

I watch her body language, riveted with anticipation. After a few long minutes of stillness, Dindoo leaps up as sprightly as a munmundiik, her long thin arms pumping the air with jubilation. A bubbling giggle of relief bursts from me.

My daughter snaps awake, looking at me with still sleepy eyes. *What happened, babayin? Is the sky okay?*

My sensitive manggip, so perceptive, so watchful, with a mind that churns with questions. Cut from the same cloth we are.

I wrap her in comforting arms, soothing her busy mind. *Yes, my bright spark, everything is okay.*

And did the bubup find their betayil?

I curl back the strands of hair falling across her forehead and nod. *Their murrup travels with their whale across the western Warrayin, even now.*

For how long?

That is not for us to know.

Round, brown eyes scour the ocean horizon, searching for a betayil splash or gust of blown spray.

But Sea Country is still this morning.

Come, my manggip. Time to sing our goodbyes and head home to Kullurk.

That night, dusty, dancing feet thrust into Biik's cool soil. Pictures and patterns painted in ochre contrast vividly against dark skin. Flashes of white shine from jubilant grins and laughing eyes. Leaves on trees tremble with the pounding of drums and the clapping of sticks. Many voices, young and old, fill the darkness with song and story. Tonight is a celebration of pure joy, community connection and our all-encompassing love for our Biik and culture. Tonight, we have filled our bodies with the finest delicacies from our women's harvesting of Warrayin, the sweetest fruits collected by the children from Waa's pantry and the richest cuts of game from the men's successful hunt.

Under the rippling black cloth of booronth, studded with brilliant flecks of light from djurt, Bunjil, his family and the cluster of the seven Munmundiik, we celebrate the continued miracle of the holding up of Sky Country. And with it, the reassurance that our way of life will prevail alongside our ever abundant Biik and the generosity of Warrayin. My husband Bobbinary dances with his brothers, his son in front mimicking their every move.

Later, as the women's voices begin, I too stand with my sisters and our daughters. Emu feathers tied with the string of kangaroo sinew wrap around my woman's body as I move to honour the essence of my totems. The long glide of Betayil the whale, with the sudden flick of her cliff-making fluke. The long-necked grace of Koonwarra the swan, coupled with her blind ferocity defending her young.

Beside me, Boyerup lifts her arms with a delicate lightness, perfectly capturing the fragility and artistry of her totem, the butterfly. As the light of our wilam fire flickers in her eyes, I am struck by her blossoming beauty. I see her marmin sitting in front of her, a proud smile playing on his lips as he watches his daughter and wife move through the dances of our Old Ones. Lying across my husband's lap with his arms flung open and his mouth agape, Yearl Yearl is happily lost in the land of sleep. My family. At peace.

As I press my feet onto the sandy earth of our women's dancing circle, I feel a subtle movement low in my belly. Almost imperceptible, nearly missed, if it wasn't for my sudden awareness of an exquisite change taking hold in my body. The feeling of fullness in my breasts as I raise my arms to form the fluke of Babayin Betayil. A quick calculation in my mind of Meeniyan's cycles and the dawning realisation that my own womanly cycle has shifted. Goosebumps prickle all over my body and I shiver with an exhilarating under-standing. A profound knowledge that, within me, another being has started to grow.

My heart expands with happiness, to a near bursting fullness. Deep breaths steady my trembling limbs and slow my racing mind so that I can stand, present and true, in this moment of magic and wonder. I feel its breathtaking perfection etch into every cell in my body. I let myself steep in its bliss, the fibres of my flesh supple, love radiating from every pore. Suddenly I sense that I am standing at a pinnacle, the very peak of another revolution in the turning cycle of Time.

Hold onto this moment. This is the knowledge you need. A gentle whisper of my grandmother's voice in my head. *This yulendji is yours.*

DJAMBANA
Gathering

The hollering of a boisterous gang of boys playing marngrook on the beach shatters an otherwise placid, late summer day. A ball fashioned from possum skin is kicked high by the pack's young star, Yanki Yanki, light and quick on his feet, able to drop the ball and kick while simultaneously dodging his opponents. My mammam Yearl Yearl is two years younger and two feet smaller than most of the other boys but, judging by the determined set of his jaw, this won't dissuade him from throwing himself vehemently into the game. A pass from Yanki Yanki gives him a chance to reach the dazzling heights he imagines in his restless dreams. A long kick with his short legs, a pat on the back from his older cousin accompanied by a cheer from the rest of the pack, and Yearl Yearl beams with the elation of a long-held wish come true.

Monmar is busy today. The peninsula's curving stretches of shore sing the songs of eons-old life and play. Families from all over Boonwurrung Biik gather on this favoured Country, womindjeka, as the warmth of a blazing Wiyagabul Nyawiinth begins, at last, to wane. For us, on our Burinyong-Balak clan estate, it is a mere two days walk from our stone wilams at Kullurk. For others, the journey has taken many more days, weeks, but they come without hesitation every year. Such is the magnetising beauty of our Biik at Monmar. Such is the strength of the bonds that bind our family estates to each other as one Boonwurrung nation. Such is the abiding desire to come together and share any knowledge gathered over the changing seasons, to reconnect in ceremony and celebration, culture and community, to simply see each other again and enjoy the receding summer by the gentle waters of our Nerrm bay.

Yurok harvest promises to be plentiful this year, as the long, slender bodies of smoked eels, dangling from the branches of warrak and moonah, testify. Large binuk brim with an array of molluscs and seashells, next to stout fingers of murnong and lily bulbs, all holding the promise of feasting when night falls. For those of us with babies growing quickly in our bodies, tarnook full of the iridescent shells of the wurrdin promise a special sustenance from Warrayin for our women's sacred work.

On the ridge rising along Monmar's spiny centre, the men gather their spears and boomerangs for the hunt of kangaroo and emu. Many weeks' worth of artistry have been etched on their timbers, waiting to be compared and celebrated when the countrymen in arms finally got to reunite. I see Bobbinary standing beside my younger brother Derrimut, inspecting the newly cut shields, testing their form and function. A rousing call from Baddoorup rallies the men and they set off on their hunt.

A childhood image pops into my mind. By the Koonwarra wetlands on the Homelands of my birth, the glorious estate of the Yalukit-Wilam clan, I remember Baddoorup, much older than me, practising his dance behind the cover of the water reeds. Fingers splayed and arms outstretched, legs parted with knees knocking together, he made a lovely sight for a blossoming girl. Even though he was my poison cousin, same moiety, family connections, it was the first time I saw a male as something more than a strange figure of mostly perpetual annoyance. Glancing over to my manggip, Boyerup, patiently entwining dried grass into string, I wonder if this flash of new insight has fired in her mind yet.

Another chorus of shrieking slices through the harmonious air. The boys rough and tumble through their game of marngrook, as though incapable of sitting still or embracing silence. Boyerup's eyes roll upwards and I chuckle to myself. *They are still annoying.*

In contrast, our weaving circle of mothers and daughters sit in a space of softly spoken story, trying our best to ignore the imposition of screeches and hoots nearby.

Nandergarrook, my sister-in-law, languidly chewing on a morr currant, holds the attention of the younger girls with the tale of the sacred moonah tree. Married at this time last year to my brother Derrimut, Nandergarrook has a belly that is swollen like mine, her first bubup growing strong on the juicy fruits she guards jealously in a tarnook by her side.

Even though they knew it was against the strictest rules of their culture, the two would-be lovers couldn't help themselves, Nandergarrook whispers conspiratorially.

Nimble fingers suspended mid-weave, the bubup Barebun, tender age of six, youngest daughter of Doogbyerumboroke, loses the rhythm of her string-making as she soaks up every detail of the captivating story of poison love.

Choosing the time when Meeniyan was fully clothed in her black veil, the boy and girl of wrong skin decided to leave the clan forever. It was the darkest of nights and they were confident they could sneak away unseen. But alas, that wasn't to be.

Nandergarrook pauses for full dramatic effect. Seeing she has her audience enraptured, she takes her time, plucking another morr currant from her tarnook and chewing on it pensively.

Unable to contain a building impatience, the oldest of Doog-byerumboroke's manggip, Borodanger, bursts forth with a groan. *Oh, hurry up!*

Instantly, her hand is slapped by her mother sitting beside her. *Kye! I never taught you to be so rude. You might think you're all grown up because you've just turned twelve, but you're not a munmundiik yet. You have much to learn!*

Doogbyerumboroke's stern expression makes her daughter shift uncomfortably on her cushion of sand.

Even though this formidable bagarrook is much younger than my mother, the ceremonial scars decorating her body speak of Doog-byerumboroke's growing wealth of knowledge. A strict one, she is a quick study on how to keep the young ones in line, but the twinkle in her eye reveals the certainty of her mother's love.

Sorry, babayin, Borodanger murmurs.

And anyway, pipes up Kardingarrook with a bemused smile, *you've heard this story a hundred times before so why are you getting so worked up?*

Catching Nandergarrook's smirk, still casually chewing on her currant and enjoying the scene playing out in front of her, I shake my head and try to stifle my laugh.

Finally, she finishes her fruit and continues on as if nothing has happened.

Just as they reach the calm waters of the bay, where the boy has prepared a canoe for them to escape, boom! Nandergarrook punctuates her sentence with a loud slap of her palms and everyone in the circle jumps.

Unnecessary, Doogbyerumboroke admonishes, clutching at her breast. *Some of us have a fluttering heart you know.*

Is that what happens when you push out four bubup back-to-back? I tease.

Just you wait, liwurruk, it will happen to you. Doogbyerumboroke warns, her eyes twinkling warmly.

Once again, unable to handle the tension of an unfinished story, Borodanger blurts out a desperate prompt, willing Nandergarrook to continue. *Boom! Bunjil appears. And then . . .?*

Indeed he does, nods Nandergarrook wisely, picking up the threads of the tale with the dramatic tones of a natural born storyteller. *Bunjil appears as the wedge-tailed eagle, enormous in the night sky, his beating wings creating a gust of wind that makes the runaway, poison lovers shiver in its wake. Panicking, the boy grabs the girl's hand and pulls her towards his gurrung. But this makes Bunjil angrier and he lets out a piercing shriek. Scared, the girl stands frozen at the very edge of the shore.*

Any weaving from small fingers has stopped now, all the younger girls staring wide-eyed at Nandergarrook, fully immersed in the story she has conjured in their imaginations. Barebun nestles against my manggip, Boyerup, finding comfort in her older cousin's steady presence. The bigger sisters, Borodanger and Naynar, only two years between them but a lifetime apart in their views of the world, both hang on Nandergarrook's every word.

Laying my own weaving to rest for a moment, I place my hands on the swell of my abdomen, feeling for the movement of my growing bubup. Looking around our women's circle, a glow of contentment warms my body as I imagine our families expanding over the years to come. My newborn arriving around the same time as Nandergarrook's, alongside the hope of a bubup from the newly-wed Kardingarrook. Perhaps even from Meendutgarrook, waiting on the murndigarrook's word to unite with her promised, Barrunan. Still further into the future I imagine, a great many full moons from now, the little girls before me emerging as bagarrook, their own bubup swaddled in possum skin and rocking in cradling tarnook beside them. Like the lines of glittering shells in a many-millennia Keeping Place, I see the continuum roll before me, a looping songline on the shores of our beautiful Biik, from that which always was, to that which always will be.

Jump on the canoe!' Nandergarrook's dramatic cry pulls me from my daydreaming. *'Quickly!' calls the boy, as the gurrung drifts out to sea with him in it. Waves made by Bunjil's beating wings start to lap at the girl's feet. Bigger and bigger they grow, until they rock and crash against the yanyean's canoe. He cries out to his poison love, 'Help!' But she remains rooted to the shore in fear. One mighty gust from Bunjil's wings and a giant wave crests over the gurrung, knocking the boy into the angry Warrayin. The munmundiik screams and takes a step into the sea, but it is too late, the boy has disappeared under the ocean. 'No!' the girl cries, reaching her arms out to where she last saw him, to her poison love with the wrong skin. And there she stayed, frozen in horror, until she transformed into —*

A possum skin ball crashes into the centre of our weaving circle and bounces into Doogbyerumboroke's lap. Yanked from the all-encompassing thrall of Nandergarrook's story, the two older sisters, Borodanger and Naynar, leap to their feet with piercing squeals. Seconds later, a pair of panting boys race over to retrieve the marn, apologetic grins already visible.

Sorry, babayin, winces Yanki Yanki to his mother, Doogbyerumboroke. Then the strutting yanyean adds, with more than a hint of self-congratulation, *That was probably one of the biggest kicks I've ever done, though.*

Behind him, Yearl Yearl nods in fervent agreement. *Definitely.* Then he flashes a glance to me and adds, more subdued, *Sorry, babayin.*

Bravado filling his chest, Yanki Yanki quickly glances at Boyerup as he continues, helpless to resist the boast. *Actually, I think it was definitely the biggest kick that anyone's done today.*

Definitely, Yearl Yearl agrees effusively.

Oblivious to Boyerup's growing annoyance, Yanki Yanki throws a jaunty grin her way and tries his best to sound humble and apologetic. *So yeah, sorry about that.*

Reaching past our collection of basket reeds and sinew, his lanky arms grab at the ball, eager to leap back into the fray, but Doogbyerumboroke holds it aloft.

Sorry, my boy, you will have to wait. She shows him where the seams have split, tufts of stuffing fur peeking out.

The boys' faces fall.

Oh no, cries Yearl Yearl. *I was just getting really good at kicking it!*

With a pointed sigh, Doogbyerumboroke lays down her tools and pushes her weaving aside. *Come on, mammam, let me see if I have some more wallert to fix it.*

You stay, Aunty. Kardingarrook whips to her feet. *I'm sure some of the murndigarrook will have extra skin we can use.*

Monameit, Doogbyerumboroke grins gratefully, then turns sternly back to the yanyean. *You boys, why don't you collect some wood for tonight's Ngargee. The marn will be ready when it's ready.*

One glance back to Boyerup, then Yanki Yanki nudges into Yearl Yearl's shoulder. *Race ya.*

Instantly, a cloud of sand sprays over our women's weaving circle as the boys tear towards the scrub, eliciting more squeals from the unimpressed girls.

Clutching a handful of now gritty currants, Nandergarrook also rises to her feet.

I think Derrimut might have some spare at our wilam, she offers.

Wait! Borodanger's face creases in exasperation. *Are we going to hear the rest of the story?*

Kardingarrook hoots and shakes her head, making a start towards the huddle of murndigarrook stoking the fires of their camp.

Oh sorry, little cousin, laughs Nandergarrook, picking the sand off her fruit. *You'll just have to wait until I get back. I'll try not to be too long.*

And with a cheeky grin, she saunters off, leaving the young girls crestfallen.

Well, that was a big letdown, mutters Borodanger to Nandergarrook's retreating back. *Next time I'm going to tell the story.*

But I like it when Nander tells the story, a softly spoken Naynar says wistfully. *And my favourite part is when she tells how the girl turns into the moonah tree.*

Begrudgingly, Borodanger agrees. *I know, she's the best at telling stories.*

Leaping to her feet, she dusts off the sand and holds out her hand to her middle sister. *Come on, Naynar, while we're waiting for her to get back, let's see if the snapper are swimming.*

And let's look for Koormamgarrook! Excited that her older sister is taking an interest, Naynar grabs her liwurruk's hand before she can change her mind and skips to the shoreline. Arm in arm at the water's edge, I watch as the girls meet up with Kardingarrook's sister through marriage, Tootkuningarrook, and the trio of blossoming munmundiik examine the water for signs of snapper and the Women of the Seal and Kelp.

Tying off the trailing ends of reed coiling around my growing basket, I move over to sit by the two smallest girls. Barebun's string has loosened and frayed, a reminder that it's only pieces of dried grass after all. Beside her, perfect braids of string lay neatly along the sand in front of my daughter. Even at the tender age of nine, Boyerup shows a delicate dexterity in her work.

This is exactly like your grandmother's string, bubup. Holding both ends of a piece, I tug forcefully. *And strong too.*

My manggip beams up at me and I want to hold those broad cheeks in both hands and give her a big kiss on the forehead. But before I can, she studies her lap and asks, shyly, *Babayin, how many more seasons before I can wear an emu feather skirt?*

Across the now disbanded weaving circle, Doogbyerumboroke smiles knowingly.

I can't say for sure, Boyerup. Everyone is different and we each grow in our own time. Clasping her hands between mine, I squeeze them gently. *But you'll be a big girl soon. And when the Old Ones let you know you're ready, we will make the most beautiful dilburnayin together for your special ceremony, I promise. Now, I think that's plenty of string so do you want to find some pipis with your cousins?*

With her younger cousin Barebun following wherever she goes, the two bubup link arms and head down to the tideline. The three older munmundiik call the children over to see the bulging collection of shells poking out of their stuffed bilang. Like a fledgling flock of burribarri, the girls move in unison as they pick through the flotsam and jetsam on the shore.

My girls have been talking about their emu feather skirts as well. Doogbyerumboroke watches her two older daughters help

Barebun and my bubup separate some clinging molluscs from a piece of kelp.

Is Borodanger close, do you think?

Very much so. We may well be doing our dance of the dolphin at the next full moon! Observing her eldest daughter, Doogbyerumboroke is pensive. *It's funny though,* she muses. *As much as she yearns to wear her dilburnayin, she still has the whims of a child. Still wants to play games with the younger ones. Although she is beginning to get obsessed with boys. Ones she shouldn't, mind you!*

Don't tell me she has the makings of a moonah tree! I joke.

Well, she teases, *don't we all have a little of the moonah tree in us?*

But you have Baddoorup!

And you have Bobbinary!

Kye! Too true! I laugh. *We have ourselves some good ones.*

Returning to the weaving of her binuk, Doogbyerumboroke selects some reed stained with red ochre to fashion the last coil around the top of her basket. My project beckons but a strange restlessness starts to hum in my stomach. As it builds, sending ripples of fluttering through my belly, I assume it is simply a pang of hunger, so I check Nandergarrook's tarnook for supplies.

Did that girl eat all those morr currants!

Yes, but I have returned with other offerings, Nandergarrook exclaims grandly from behind me. Flopping onto the sand, Kardingarrook and Meendutgarrook in tow, the three bagarrook replenish the bowl with a tasty selection of more currants, seeds and ripened kangaroo apples. *No luck with the wallert skin though.*

Popping a couple of seeds in my mouth, I once again reach for my unfinished basket. But once again, an eerie feeling of dread snakes its way through the joints in my arms. Suddenly, a gust of mornmoot makes me look to a grove of warrak fluttering on the ridge.

Then I see it.

A giant gurrung in the Warrayin, gliding quickly, silently, to the shore. Behind it, in the distance, the unmistakable triangular cloth of the white man's boat cuts across the sky, appearing on the bay as if from thin air, at once obscured and illuminated by the harsh mid-afternoon sun.

An invisible hand grips at my throat, squeezing shut any sound I try to make. All I can do is slowly rise to my feet and point. The swift gurrung is in the shallows already, powered by a single figure, skin of garish white, pulling relentlessly on giant poles, thrusting in and out of the calm ocean. The vessel is canoe-shaped, pointed at both ends, but so much wider and thicker than any gurrung I have ever seen, with the middle of the vessel packed with lumps of mysterious cloth.

But it is a woman standing stiff at the helm of the gurrung that draws my attention. Tall, her gazed fixed, black skin gleaming in stark contrast to the white of her strange dress. Like a warning vision in a wirrirap's dream, she stands erect, unmoving, her arms outstretched, laden with items, unknown, unimaginable.

Within moments the vessel has reached the shore and the woman jumps onto the sand with a beaming smile. Behind her, steadying the boat, the white man pushes his long poles against the sea floor, a growing smirk pulling at the sides of his lips.

This clutching sense of dread curls around every bone in my body now. I am shaking, a fine tremor that ricochets up and down my spine. For some inexplicable reason, my eyes keep returning to the objects strewn along the black woman's arms. Unnaturally bright colours, glittering stones, cloths made of material never before seen. And the garish grin, frozen there, as if painted on in the white ochre of grief. The ngarrambil of death.

The first of our kin to see the intruders' arrival is Tootkuningar-rook, closely followed by Borodanger and Naynar. They are hesitant, but curious, and I can see the white-dressed woman beckon them kindly. Attracted by the shine of the new, the young girls edge closer to the boat. The constriction around my throat tightens and tightens. Only a whisper can escape my lips.

No.

The munmundiik are inquisitive, watching, deliberating, wondering what it might all mean. Doogbyerumboroke's girls are the first to make the decision to shift closer again, step by inevitable step, nearer and nearer to the woman with the beguiling, outstretched arms.

Desperate, I push through the iron grip squeezing my throat, and say in a louder, trembling voice.

No.

Loud enough for the others weaving their baskets to stop and glance questioningly at me. Another no, even louder and I keep my hand, now shaking violently, pointed to the rowboat on the shore.

With striking clarity, as if I was standing right beside them, I see my bubup grip Barebun's hand with a tight intensity. Doogbyerumboroke's youngest manggip is intrigued and wants to follow her bigger sisters to this strange floating tarnook and the tall woman covered in treasure. Tugging on Boyerup's arm, Barebun takes one step forward and a lightning bolt slams through my body, jolting me into action. My scream ricochets around the sand dunes cradling the beach.

No!

And then I am running. Straight for all of those little girls. Behind me, the other women are running too, the happiness on the beach flipping to confusion and fear in an instant. All I am focused on is my Boyerup.

Run! I scream to her and she catches my eyes, feverish and piercing, and her instinct kicks in.

Grabbing her young cousin she turns and runs as fast as her little legs can carry her, dragging a wailing Barebun along behind her.

That bubup's wail is like a sudden signal for action.

In an instant, a fateful chaos erupts from the black stranger's boat. Not one white man, but five, leap forth from under the mysterious cloths in the vessel like burrowing spiders from their underground lair. Carrying thick bands of string to bind.

Hurling ourselves across the sand, like Koonwarra the swan in a desperate battle to save her children from the bunyip, we mothers reach our children at the same time as the men. In the flurry of bodies and rope, panic and confusion, I see Yearl Yearl running towards me.

Your father!

At my screaming command, he turns and runs as fast as he can, spindly legs darting across the sand like a frightened emu terrified by the chase. The other smaller boys call in confusion to their fathers as well, unsure what to do, pacing on the sand. All except brave, foolish Yanki Yanki, just a boy of eight but with the heart of a warrior, trying to prise his mother and sisters away from the ropes and arms of grown men.

I am knee-deep in water, legs smashing against the wooden vessel, rope slashing into my wrists. A man's fist connects with my temple and I feel my eyeballs jolt in my skull. Vision blurring the peripheries around me, all I can see now is Bobbinary, spear raised, hurtling down the ridge towards me.

Then suddenly, I am in the boat, along with my clan's sisters and daughters, Yanki Yanki too. Our men have their spears raised ready to strike into the heart of the ngamudji. But the white men seem to have played this game before, and they use our bodies as shielding mulga.

Rough hands yank my arms as the vessel lurches away from our gentle curve of Country. Swaying in a shuddering line, arms bound in burning rope, pulled taut by the cowering thieves behind us, we women and girls can only watch as our men hesitate to launch their spears at the departing gurrung. They race into Warrayin, swimming out past where their feet can touch.

But they cannot catch us. It is too late.

We are too far out to sea.

Watching it all, standing stiff and unyielding at the helm of the vessel, is the woman, a ghastly grimace still stretched across her lips. Again, a tremor shoots up my spine and radiates along my limbs. I cannot control the quaking through every cell, muscle, sinew of my body.

It only stops when I see my daughter. Her face is as clear and focused as if I was there on the beach, standing by her side. In those eyes, I see a mirror of my own. I see the fear, I see the bewilderment. I see the loss. And I see the love.

A sob catches in my throat. Flooding every single piece of my body, spirit and soul is a crashing wave of love.

Those eyes. My firstborn baby's eyes. Beautiful, deep and brown, seared onto my soul the moment she opened them. Pierced my heart then. Piercing through me now. Once again, a mirror of my own, full of desperation, ache, grief.

Full of love.

And a growing, incomprehensible loss.

Part Two

WARRAGUL
Savage

WARRANA WURRBA
Song of Sorrow

Faces thrust out towards us, etched in the weathered cliffs of our Homelands. The Seven Sisters of the Pleiades, our Munmundiik, standing as the sentinels guarding women's ceremony places along our surging ocean coastline. So often I have walked the length of these magnificent cliffs, following the ancient tracks of our songlines. I know these faces of the Old Ones, every detail, the power in their weather-beaten forms, portals to other times and places, other layers of hidden knowledge. But I know them from the solid embrace of our clan's shores. Not from the rocking insecurity of a white man's wooden vessel on the rolling waves of Warrayin.

Our men are positioned on the highest points of Monmar, spears raised, but paralysed with impotence. We are too far away, they cannot reach us now. And yet, not so far that I think I can see my husband join the others, two little ones trailing behind him. Only silhouettes in the hazy distance.

Staring with unblinking eyes, I try to fashion them clearer in my mind. I remember them gripping each other, a desperate comfort, as they watched me pull away on that foreign gurrung, out into the darker blue of the bay. Picturing them on the dunes, I imagine them huddled close to each other, trying to make sense of what they were seeing, the gurrung holding their babayin, their birrimbayin, hauled onto a much larger vessel waiting in the deep water, its triangular cloths of white engorged with a growing mornmoot. Pushing out between the narrow passageway of the bay, the sealers' giant vessel cuts through the open ocean with taunting ease and I imagine my family running to the ridgelines of our sacred Country as the tall ship glides along the edges of our Biik, so close but deliberately out of reach. Then, as Nyawiinth begins to descend on his western arc to Mumilam, my family stand pressed together, knowing they can do nothing more, only watch. To bear numbing witness.

I can picture them so clearly in my mind, even as their silhouettes on the now distant ridge darken into shadow. I hold the knowledge of every dip and curve in their bodies, every rise and fall of their spirit. I can see in painstaking detail, as if they were each standing alongside me on this cursed, quaking vessel, the confusion creasing Yearl Yearl's forehead, the rage searing in Bobbinary's eyes, the terror etching itself on Boyerup's trembling face. And the dreadful sorrow now threatening to engulf them all.

My heart seizes with a fearful grief and a sob bursts from my lips. I lurch towards the side of the boat, willing to throw myself into the arms of the rolling sea in the hope I will be carried home, back into the embrace of my fading family, but a rough hand yanks on the ropes that bind me and pulls me back down to the wooden deck. In desperate longing, I search for the junctures of the thickened thread that holds the gurrung to the side of the sealers' masted boat. If I could unweave its bindings, along with my own and that of my kin, we might find our freedom in the very vessel that captured us. But one push against the namudji's rope around my wrists and I know I am bound tight in a brutal reality, swaying sickeningly on a sealer's ship, witnessing all I know move further and further away. Seeing the shimmering image of my family fade into the looming shadows of my Homelands.

Passing by the lonely spectre of Korriyong, the once thriving island filled for millennia with ngargee, song and dance, home fires and feasting, I whisper, *Koormamgarrook*. Said like a prayer, an incantation, to the looming black boulders that signal the homes of the Women of the Seal and Kelp. I know that their home is a silent and barren island now, not even an echo of the thousands of years of life that have come before now. And yet, I still search in desperation for the flicker of movement beneath their Sea Country's gleaming surface.

My mind runs wild with more wishes. That they might hear my whisper on a compliant breeze and unite to rush their revenge at the slaughtering sealer's boat. A mighty horde of Koormamgarrook launching upwards from under the sea to push the thieves out of their vessel and carry them down to their underwater lairs, where the ngamudji will drown and stay forever. A bitter laugh burns my throat with the realisation that it is the likes of these very men that have made my fantasy impossible. As the raiders have massacred the Koormamgarrook's companion, the seal, the number of kelp women will have plummeted too. For they need the seal to shape shift, they are one and the same.

In mournful silence, the island of ghosts slides away. Further we sail along the coast of our Homelands towards the far reaches of Boonwurrung Biik, until the clan estate of the Lowandjirri, Bindergarrook's Country, reveals her sweeping splendour. A magnificent Keeping Place rears high along an undulating stretch of dune, laced with an untold number of shells glinting in the late afternoon light.

My mind gets stuck. A loop plays around and around in my head, of grandmothers, mothers and daughters, grandmothers, mothers and daughters, over and over stretching out in an eternal line through Time. The spirits of the women in my line, the murrup I descend from and whose essence has forged my flesh, built these Keeping Places shell by shell, day by day, season by season, epoch by epoch. And so it has continued since Time Immemorial.

But now, could it be that it might stop? If I can no longer journey to that Keeping Place in the season my Ancestors always did, harvesting the bounty of the sea at the time it has always been offered, cooking in our hearths, roasting in our fires, laying our remnants and building our history, does it stop? How could that be? After so long, since memory first began, how could it just stop because I am not there?

A sickening ache presses into my bones. On my shoulders, a heavy weight descends, permeating my flesh and dragging me to my knees. My lips part as if to scream, but no sound comes out. Instead, I feel as if my murrup, my very soul, is rising from my belly like a frenzied snake writhing to get free. As it travels up into my heaving chest, I try to clamp my teeth shut so it cannot escape, but I'm paralysed in a state of horror.

With growing urgency, it pushes into my throat, desperate to be free, to be returned to her Biik and her family, forever tethered to the murrup of the Old Ones who have come before. I cannot stop it.

As it flees through my mouth back to the bosom of my Country, a howl, deep and guttural, launches from me, followed by another then another. I am powerless to stop the wailing pouring from me, powerless to prevent the tremors along every limb, powerless to dry the tears flooding down my face.

Around me, the ragged voices of my kin join the cry. I see in their distorted features, twisting with indescribable pain, the same agony as my own. I know they feel it too, the rising of their spirits surrendering to the inexorable pull of Country, an ancient tethering that spans millennia, that cannot be broken. Our wailing reaches a crescendo and I wonder if our murndigarrook standing helpless on the shore can hear us.

Slap!

The bones in my cheek shudder with the force of the man's strike. A face presses into mine, brown teeth bared, eyes bulging with a dark rage. I don't need to recognise the white man's language to understand the meaning of his words, spitting at me through clenched teeth.

But I cannot, will not, stop. Once again, my voice mingles with the cry of my countrywomen as we mourn the flight of a part of our very souls back to the Country we are being pulled from.

The men rush at us. I am pushed with a vengeance to the deck, my back scraping against the splintered wood of the vessel's edges. The sickening crunch of the bodies of women and girls resonates around the boat and the vessel lurches with the force of it. Well-adapted to the rocking of a boat on the sea, the men's thick legs stay resolutely upright, even as my kin and I flail and fall in the chaos. Only two black women manage to stay standing. The one who held treasure to entice our girls into entrapment.

And Tootkuningarrook.

Steadying herself with an unbound hand gripping the side of the ship, Tootkuningarrook's eyes are wide and searching as she stares into the churning Warrayin, so far below. Loosened rope dangles from her wrist as she clutches at the teetering edges of the towering, masted vessel. I watch as a grim determination sets into the thrust of her jaw. In what seems like both lightning fast and the slowest of motions, she launches herself into the frothing sea.

Tootkuningarrook!

My voice is strangled, barely able to be heard above the frenzy on deck. Half running, half falling, I make my way to where she stood, a dim hope willing me to take the same plunge. But my arms are still tied behind my back. And my sisters would still be on this boat.

Tootkuningarrook!

This time my call carries further, its timbre laced with an echo of envy. One of the men shouts a command to stop the subjugation, pointing to the woman's figure cutting purposefully through the waves.

We all stop and watch Tootkuningarrook's graceful dance with Warrayin. Pride warms the cold enveloping my heart. Strong, this young bagarrook, brave. Even as the men shake their heads and laugh, the courage of my countrywoman is undeniable.

As I watch her push deeper into the territory of Wiyagabul Darrak, the Old Man Shark, I whisper to the Koormamgarrook and Mother Whale. *Be with her now.*

Further and further away from us she swims. Closer and closer to the dim outline of Wamoom. Light reflects off the looming granite boulders of the promontory in the distance, marking the far edge of our Boonwurrung Biik, the very end of Waa the raven's Country. If she makes it there, she is home.

Shadows stretch long as Old Man Sun sinks towards the meeting place of Sea and Sky Country. Soon his rays will bounce against the horizon and shoot back upwards in an arc of brilliance. The forming of Karralk, a bridge of light, for souls to walk their journey to Pindayi. With a shudder I wonder if Tootkuningarrook might make that journey tonight. She was a tiny speck of spinning arms when I lost sight of her in the surging currents. So small within the ocean's expanse, could she really make it to the refuge of the shore? And if not, would she still be able to travel the loop of the Old Ones, without ceremony, without song, without ochre on her bones?

I send a whisper to my Liwik. *Help her.*

Gusts of wind fatten the pieces of cloth strapped tight to towering props in the middle of the ship. Each time they fill with mornmoot, the vessel pushes forward with renewed vigour. Further and further away from our Biik, hazy and sinking in the distance.

Then suddenly, she is gone, slipping beneath the line of the horizon in a shocking, soundless instant. *We have lost sight of our Biik.*

A shudder sweeps through the huddle of my kin, bagarrook and bubup, overwhelmed and trembling in desolate disbelief. Confused. Uncomprehendingly lost.

How can we lose sight of our Biik? When every second of our life to this moment has been inextricably connected with Country, how can she now disappear? Yet, our gentle Biik is gone. And now, all that surrounds us is a hostile sea and the menacing will of the warragul men.

A forceful banging from one end of the vessel jolts our attention away from Warrayin. Thudding his fist on a timbered shelter rising from the deck, a sealer waits impatiently for a response. After a while, another white man emerges tentatively, casting his eye out to sea as if searching for any sign of impending danger. His smaller form is clothed in material of a different colour and softer texture than the rougher weave worn by his friends. White and red with bursts of round, shining rock, like shells made of golden quartz, which are sewn in a line from his neck down to his waist. Unsteady on his feet, he grips the boat and scours the distant horizon. Once satisfied, his furrowed forehead eases and he turns his attention to us, casting an appraising eye over our bound bodies.

Huddled at the curving end of the vessel, pressing together for warmth and solidarity, we meet his gaze with accusing stares.

A sly grin spreads across his face and he pats the nearest sealer warmly on the back. His gesture speaks of a job well done, and I understand that he believes himself to be in charge, and that he is happy with the work of the kidnappers. Pointing to the ropes around our wrists, he barks at his crew and they obey immediately. Shrinking from their touch, I try to keep my body clean of their wandering, calloused hands. As soon as my arms are freed from behind my back, I rush my fingers to my belly and interlock them across the breadth of where my baby grows. Nandergarrook does the same, a babayin's instinct of protection rising fiercely against the threat. Likewise, Doogbyerumboroke spreads her arms wide to shelter her three children in a tremulous embrace. Squeezing the hand of her sister Kardingarrook, my young cousin, Meendutgarrook, links her other arm through mine. Shaking uncontrollably, her munmundiik's body, barely fourteen, quivers with a fear never before felt. It reverberates through all of us, a sickness never imagined possible. A pulsing dread foreign in our bodies after lifetimes of peaceful days walking the songlines of our tranquil estates, nestled in the bosom of our beautiful Biik.

Standing nearby, silent and watching, steady legs planted rigid on the rolling deck, the strange figure of the black woman in the white dress is silhouetted by the setting sun. In studied stillness, her expression stays carefully unreadable as the man in softer cloth grabs the top of her arm and pulls her to him. After one last approving glance our way, he manoeuvres the bagarrook down into the depths of the vessel and the two of them disappear into the darkness below.

Doogbyerumboroke's two young daughters press against their mother. A devastating loss sucks all life from their usually smiling cheeks, now lined with streaks of dried tears, and they stare hollowly out to sea, glazed with shock and confusion. My heart burns with a fierce need to protect them as if they were my own.

I see one of the older men turn towards the two young girls. A hungry shadow darkens his face as he runs his eyes up and down their children's bodies.

Shifting my head, I try to surreptitiously scan the other ngamudji.

The same shadow plays across their faces. With a greedy sense of absolute ownership, the men stare at our bodies, our breasts, our thighs, the sacred space between.

Strict law governs the marital rights of everyone in our society. Morality runs deep in our culture. Songs and dances speak of the right ways to be and behave. Ancient stories tell tragic tales of the dire consequences of defying these rules. Wrong skin, poison lovers. Most importantly, the rituals of ceremony prepare the initiate for the next part of their journey. Only when the Elders determine a person is ready will they learn the knowledge they need.

Two nights before, not so long ago and yet a whole other existence, around the murndigarrook's campfire on Monmar, the old women agreed that it would only be a few more cycles of Meeniyan the Moon before a delegation of women would journey with Borodanger to our sacred place for secret women's business. Merely a handful of weeks past the age of twelve, the girl stood on the edge of her blossoming into the knowledge of the Munmundiik. Not long until she would have journeyed through her coming-of-age ritual, understood a deeper layer of women's yulendji, had her blood drawn and a scar raised to mark the momentous occasion. From that point on, she would have danced in her dilburnayin, the emu feather skirt of the munmundiik and bagarrook.

Her younger sister Naynar is not much older than my Boyerup. Many more seasons need to pass before their little bodies would be ready for that same coming-of-age ritual and all it signified. Children have their own business to attend to. Playing marngrook with their cousins, picking for treasures in the tidelines, chasing schools of silver wirrap in the safe shallows of the Bay. Their tender minds and bodies are not ready to be instructed in the knowledge of adults yet. Plenty of time for that when the Old Ones give the right signs.

So we had thought, only two nights ago.

Yet here we are. Rocking perilously on a wooden vessel in the middle of an unknown Sea Country. Surrounded by men who know nothing of our Law, who care nothing for our Law, as they run their restless eyes over us in wanton abandon.

Suddenly, in three long strides, one of the men reaches Borodanger and grabs her wrist.

As if already galvanised for this exact action, Doogbyerumboroke springs to her feet and pushes the offender away from her daughter.

No, she demands, shaking her head, voice humming with a righteous rage. *Konye! She is only a child.*

Knowing the ngamudji wouldn't understand her words, Doogbyerumboroke stands ferocious in front of her trembling daughter, promising a bitter contest if he takes one step closer.

I stand as well, in solidarity with my kinswoman, even though my knees feel weak and loose like water runs through them. Constriction pulls at my abdomen, taut now with both a growing bubup and an impending dread. Kardingarrook also rises, followed by Nandergarrook, the brave set of her jaw belied by quivering hands holding the curve of her pregnant belly. Then Meendutgarrook stands and my trembling legs nearly fold under me with fear, seeing my younger cousins place themselves in front of the building danger.

The sealer studies our show of defiance. I think I see a flicker of shame wash over his face when he looks from the mother to the child and back again. Whether his conscience prevailed or he weighed his options and thought better of making his predatory move, the man gives a derisive snort and casually sways back to his original post. Even though he turns away when he sits back down, I cannot shake the feeling that he is simply biding time. That they are all biding their time.

As the rays of Karralk darken, I know it is nearly time for Wiyagabul Nyawiinth to disappear into Warrayin's depths and seek out his place of night time rest. In those last vestiges of fading light, I see that greedy desire surge once again in the men.

This is what they are waiting for. Under the cover of booroonth, I realise without any doubt that they will come for us. Hiding their weakness under the darkness of a moonless sky, they will not need to heed the teaching of our proud women's eyes. They will not need to see the scorn of our shaking heads, the shameful truth of their lack of self-control, their failing of moral strength, their cowardice in thieving what is not theirs. They will be able to take what they want with impunity.

Cries are subdued with thudding blows. Screams are muffled with hands over mouths. In the thickness of the cloak of night, my senses stretch towards every sound and movement. The creaking of wooden floors, the stifling of my kin's voices, the pushing of bodies to the ground, the smothered cries of children, the thud of footsteps drawing closer to me. And then the suffocating weight of a man on top of me, the stench of his sour sweat. The sounds of his grunting freezing my blood. The pain of his violation tearing at my insides.

Boom!

A splitting crack like roaring thunder cuts through the darkness and the desperate cries of women and children struggling for their freedom. Sound distorts in my ears as they pound with a ringing reverberance.

Immediately, the man on top of me leaps up and I see, behind him, the figure of the captain holding a flickering flame aloft and a rifle pointed to the sky.

With a quiet ferocity he barks orders to the men, who slink away to the opposite side of the boat. In the dim light, I see Doogbyerum-boroke's face covered in blood, seeping from severe cuts across her head, the blood of the fierce Koonwarra swan protecting her young. Behind her, Yanki Yanki is likewise wounded, his lacerations telling the valiant tale of his efforts to help his sisters. The shadowy figures of the girls cower in a far corner, clutched to each other in solidarity.

Surveying the scene with barely concealed anger, the captain pushes forward with his light to inspect the damage to his cargo. As he moves around the circle of women and girls, I see my cousins Meendutgarrook and Kardingarrook sitting on the deck, their knees drawn to their chests in a protective embrace. Nandergarrook folds her arms across her stomach as if to shield the baby growing there from the violence wrought on her body.

When the light swings my way, I stand and turn to the men, my head held high, gaze burning with righteous accusation. I want them to know that their actions prove they are not worthy of us. That they are, all of them, thieves, thugs, Law-less desecrators of married women, repulsive violators of children.

My voice is firm as I say, *I am Nannertgarrook.* Sweeping my stare over every one of the pitiful, cowardly captors, I remind them of the truth they are bound to know in the fibre of their being.

You are no-one.

That night, eyelids closed, body aching, I take my mind to another time. Sitting in the cool sand of Burribarri Country, a ring of women encircling me, lit by the flickering embers of a warm kuunh. Quiet joy steeping through my body, still buzzing from the ceremony for our Mother Whale and the moment of closeness with my own babayin betayil, holding the gaze of each other, sharing her infinite knowledge as our souls connect. Bubup asleep, I listen with the murndigarrook to the noises of the night. But one empty echo overtakes all else, from the thickness of silence surrounding Korri-yong, the island across the bay of Warnmarring. The Elders murmur the story of the young woman and her eight-year-old manggip, dying violently in a lonely cave. Hushed whispers of other vanished women and children, thieved away over the seas by warragul ngamudji. I hear my mother begin the yingali, and one by one the women join her. The song is a cry to our Old Ones, to Babayin Betayil the Mother Whale, Bunjil the wedge-tailed eagle and Waa the raven, asking to keep the spirits of any lost women and children tethered to their Biik. The murndigarrook's voices waver and crack as the lament fills the air and travels up to Sky Country.

Sobs claw at my chest and tears sting my eyes as I crash back to where I lie now, on a splintered, rolling deck, seared by the memory of that night on the shores of my Biik. When I sung a calling song with my murndigarrook, hoping that my kin who were caught some-where across the expansive ocean, stolen women and girls adrift and alone, might hear our voices travelling on the breeze. That night, when I was still surrounded by the comforting circle of my kin and Country, praying to our Liwik to help a lost bagarrook draw strength and courage from our song. When I hoped our yingali might weave a songline through the ether that would draw her back to where she belongs. With her children, her beloved, her family, her Country.

Yet here I am, my heart splitting with a terrible realisation. That I am she. I am that lost woman adrift in the unknown, straining to hear a guiding song, my murrup reaching out to be tethered once more, but finding no songline to follow home. I am she who is vanished. How could I know, on that glorious, sacred, fateful night, I was really singing the song for myself.

MOORROOBULL
Ghosts

A wild mornmoot, howling in from the West, whips at the flapping sails of the sealer's boat. Cursing and spitting, the men rush between ropes, tying and untying, furling and unfurling, to keep the vessel moving ever onwards. Queasiness has seeped into every limb and I spend most of Old Man Sun's long passage hurling burning liquid out of my mouth into the sea. At least the wracking sickness keeps my mind from thinking. Thinking about the steady shores of my Biik, the comfort of a warm wilam, the soul searing eyes of my children, the protection of my Bobbinary's arms.

Silence surrounds my kin now, lost for days in a formless sea on a quaking ngamudji's ship. Even with no words spoken, I understand so much from our shared, wordless language. Huddling together, we try to mend the scars etched into our bodies and murrup from that first night. But the cuts are deep. I can barely look at young Naynar's bewildered face. Pressed against her mother, her small arms are laced tightly across her chest and belly. Her shoulders roll inwards protectively and a strange urge hits me for the first time to find something to help the bubup cover herself.

Not once has that thought entered my mind before now. Of course, as the cool turn of the seasons demanded, we would sew and strengthen our possum skin cloaks to protect from the rain and cold. But this thought of covering a little one's body for an entirely different reason is new and not welcome. Suddenly, I feel an anxious compulsion to cover all of our bodies, for the sole reason of protecting against violation from lascivious men. I understand now why the black woman wears her white dress.

Another wave of nausea crashes over me and I lean as far over the side of the boat as I can for relief. All of us are untied now, the men having calculated the risk of us leaping overboard in hostile waters as minimal. They are right. This is not the Warrayin I know. Not the comforting lapping waves of our sister bays, nor the rumbling whitewash of our rocky coastal shores. This is a thrashing, angry ocean, like Wiyagabul Darrak the Old Man Shark losing his battle, and some of his teeth, to Mother Whale.

For a moment I think I see a child of Darrak in the sea below us. A flash of a fin, sunlight illuminating a dark shape in the water. It breaks clear of the choppy waves so that I can see its curious eye.

Gasping, I look to my sisters. They see it too. Barrunan, our dolphin. A small family pod keeping secret just under the surface. Companion to our whales, communer and sentinel in our cere-monies, showing himself to us now in our time of desperate need. Secret smiles spread fleetingly between us. We may be so far from home, but Barrunan is swimming beside us and for the briefest moment of joy, we feel found. Reaching out for each other, we hold tight. This will not be taken from us, we say to each other through stolen glances. This, our kinship, our totems, and the sacred signs of our Liwik.

As the dolphins shimmer and fade back into the blue, land appears on the horizon. Launching into action, the men position themselves around the vessel, tugging on ropes and hoisting their vessel's masted cloaks in new directions to guide the boat towards a sheltered cove. My heart skips a beat as I foolishly hope it may be our own land we are returning to. But, as the shape of this country looms into full view, I see that its contours are not what I know.

Sheltered from the perpetual wind, a sweeping stretch of sand dotted with the rounded humps of partly submerged rocks promises a refuge from the endless rocking of the boat. Clumps of salt-laden scrub hunker down on the beach, turning their scrabbly backs against the bite of a chilly breeze. Even with Wiyagabul Nyawiinth still arching high in the sky, radiant with late summer warmth, the air of this unknown Biik is much colder than our own. A reminder that we have travelled far across the expansive Warrayin, ngamudji masts catching propulsive mornmoot from the West. That we are many days and nights from home and no matter how much we yearn to place bare feet on steady sand, the Country before us is another People's. And we may not be welcome here.

As I scan the shore for signs of community, I see one of the submerged boulders begin to move. My breath catches in my throat. Tell-tale tufts of whiskers and fur seem to sprout from the rock and I rub my eyes, sure that the shadows are playing tricks on me. Again, the enormous dark shape moves. This time I feel a squeezing on my hand and it's Doogbyerumboroke. She has seen it too.

Koormam? she whispers the question, raspy with emotion.

I nod in wonder as I gaze at the biggest and strangest seal I have ever seen, with a body the size of a whale calf and a bulbous, fleshy snout drooping over most of his face.

The subtlest splash gives the creature away and a deafening holler comes from the man closest to me. In an instant, the men have loosened the rope on their smaller rowboat and it tumbles into the sea. Gathering their weaponry of spears, rounded clubs and long pieces of sharpened steel, the men launch themselves into the gurrung.

Catching their scent on the wind, the seal is suddenly alert, whiskers twitching with concern. He starts to roll his enormous body but its lumbrous size makes him clumsy and slow.

Glistening in the afternoon light, I'm transfixed by the knives gripped in the sealers' hands. So many stories spoke about these men and their brutal tactics, slaughtering the seals on Korriyong without mercy until there were none left. I wonder if the same might have happened here, making this lonely warrior the last of his kind.

Tugging at their oars with a frantic zeal, the men speed closer and closer to the koormam.

Move, I urge him through gritted teeth.

Thrusting into deeper water, the seal is finally able to shed some of the weight of his gigantic form. Weaving around the boulders with a growing agility, he senses the freedom of the open bay is only metres away.

But so are the men. Standing precariously upright, one of them raises his barbed spear high. As he readies himself to plunge it into the seal's blubber, the animal darts cunningly in the opposite direction.

Doogbyerumboroke shoots me a look of jubilance and we are both trying to resist the urge to cheer. The other women and girls notice our excitement and we all gleefully watch this giant of the sea triumph against his would-be murderers. Dodging around the remaining boulders with ease, the seal pumps his powerful fluke and outpaces the frustrated men heaving their wretched gurrung. Sinking into the shadows of the water, the seal merges with Warrayin's depths and disappears. The thwarted ngamudji return to the larger boat, grimacing faces dark with failure.

Turning the vessel away from the now deserted shallows, we continue along the coast without stopping. With innate understanding, I follow the hushed contours of this foreign island, vast rocky platforms, towering boulders, bays of curving pale sand. Eerily quiet and painfully empty, this Country should echo with the yapping of hundreds of seals. Underneath them, the Koormamgarrook should be swimming, keeping Warrayin in balance, exchanging form with their kin as they dive together under the water. Instead, silence. This is a place where the dead are buried.

Crossing into open ocean once more, I yearn to stand my feet on solid ground. Sickness hangs heavy on my shoulders, refusing to release me while the vessel endlessly rocks. But the boat ploughs on, heading for yet another rocky outcrop on the horizon. A flock of gulls follow our path towards this new place, promising land ahead.

Finally, we reach a sheltered bay and the men drop the rowboat into the waters, pushing our huddle of hesitant bodies into it. Rising before us like her neighbouring sister, this Biik emerges with lichen-covered boulders, ragged cliffs and the respite of scrub backed swathes of sandy beaches. The calmer shallows feel familiar and I dare to drag my fingers across the surface, introducing myself to this new Sea Country.

Jumping shakily from the lurching gurrung, the water icy cold on my bare legs, I am grateful to feel my feet on the granular seabed.

Wading cautiously towards the stable comfort of land, Doog-byerumboroke calls first to the Liwik of this foreign Biik and the rest of us follow, raising our song to ask for safe passage. Like a band of jittering burribarri, we move in an anxious group, heading for the grassy slopes of the hilly shore.

Nandergarrook sees it first. Layer upon layer of shells, weaving through the sandy striations of the dune. A Keeping Place, enormous, ancient. Just like ours. A gasp of wonder fills my chest and I suddenly feel the presence of another Time weaving the echoes of its energy around us. This is a place where women have gathered with their children over thousands of years. But where are they now?

Wind and dune, hand in hand with Time, have layered sand over the shells, reclaiming the Keeping Place in the absence of a clan. Country needs her People, People need their Country. Else the testaments to this glorious symbiosis become hidden, forgotten, bereft.

Standing at Warrayin's edge, the sealers' black woman watches us, seeing our recognition of the story held in the land. A mournful shadow passes over her face, hinting at what it seems she has lost. She knows the story of this lonely Biik.

Oblivious to the enormity of history underfoot, two sealing men stomp their way over the Keeping Place, climbing up to higher ground, the apex of the ancient dune. When the first man reaches the saltbush summit, he hollers to the others on the beach with a jubilant cry. Immediately, the men turn on their heel and race back to the rowboat on the shore. In a state of frenzied glee, they start pulling the wood off the bottom of the gurrung.

I look to my kin in confusion. Whatever they have found must be priceless treasure to make them destroy their boat. But then I see the clubs and knives that had been hidden below our feet, and my heart clenches in a sinking spasm. Koormam. They have found more seals.

Dragging us along in their frenzied zeal, the men make us crouch behind a pocket of dense bush clinging to the headland. Below, a peaceful colony of mothers and their pups stretch out along the rocky platform in blissful ignorance of the fate that awaits them. The men plot their attack and one by one they peel away, taking up various positions downwind from the unsuspecting seals. One stays behind to guard us, club in hand, a reminder of the power he would wield without hesitation against seal and woman alike.

My breath catches shallow in my throat as I watch the men slowly sneak upon the mothers suckling their young. With one signalling gesture from the lead sealer, the men let out blood-curdling screams to confuse their prey. Panic sweeps through the clan of seals and they try valiantly to lurch their way back to the safe arms of Warrayin. But shock slows the senses of the young pups and an ancient instinct compels the mothers to protect their bubup. And then, the ngamudji are there, swinging their clubs with unmitigated force and abandon.

It does not matter to the sealers that these pups are the future of their clan. It does not matter to the sealers that these mothers would birth a baby each year for the rest of their lives to ensure the continuation of their kind. It does not matter that this is the way it has been for thousands upon thousands of years, the integral dance of all life in balance. All that seems to matter to these men is satisfying their immediate desire for unbridled gain and bloodlust. Before the newcomers arrived on our island of Korriyong, the bagarrook Elders would also hunt for seals. Careful selection of the right ones was an important choice. A choice that would satisfy our needs but also the needs of our kindred clan. This way, there would always be balance, the chance to thrive, for all of us.

Not anymore. Our koormam are all gone.

And now, winding all around us, Mornmoot carries the yapping cries of another family of distressed mothers and terrified pups. Punctuated only by the sickening sound of sealers' clubs indiscriminately smashing their skulls. Beside me, Borodanger and Naynar's bodies convulse with waves of nausea. Slaughter on this scale is unnatural, our murrup rejects it, and the dry retching of the girls makes all of our bellies churn.

It is not long before the sounds die away. Lifeless bodies litter the rocky cove, reddened with oozing blood. Our guard pokes at us with his club, motioning to head down to the carnage below. As flippers and tails are hacked off, some are set aside, but most are cast into the sea, a testament to the overwhelming waste of these warragul men.

I wonder with horror at the intention of these brutal men, capable of such limitless slaughter. It was not procuring food for their clan to provide sustenance and feasting, for they have no families. Not as some barbaric ceremony of ngamudji manhood, for no knowledge is imparted in these bloodbaths. And they enact them over and over again without gaining any wisdom or maturity. *Why*, I wonder, sick with repulsion at the carnage before me, *why destroy every last soul of a species?*

We are forced to drag the still warm bodies off the rocks and carry them up to the headland. Two long rows stretch out across the clifftop, a line of mothers alongside another of their pups.

The rest of the long afternoon is spent separating bodies from their skin. Keeping their knives close, the men do the cutting and flaying. The black woman passes around long shards of sharpened bone to peg the pelts, stretched and taut, above the ground.

For the briefest of moments, I imagine plunging the point of the bone into the eyes of one of the sealers. Over and over, thrusting it into his other eye, the soft dip in the base of his throat, the fatty rolls of his abdomen. I wonder if I could somehow send a message to my kin clutching their own bony knives and find a way to flicker the same thought in their minds of a combined uprising. All of us, at once, avenging the killings of our koormam kin, those nurturing babayin and suckling bubup, with the same sadistic brutality shown by their murderers. My breathing is shallow, palms sweaty, a rush of hateful eagerness spurring my body to action.

Then I see the shaking fingers of little Naynar, the stoop of her cowering shoulders, the unbearable sorrow on her pinched face. Nearby, her younger brother, Yanki Yanki, carries the same shock, wide eyes struggling to comprehend the vicious carnage laid out before him. He who, less than a week ago, laughed and played, boasting about kicking a marn further than any eight-year-old boy had ever done before, according to his own reckoning. Now hollow and numb. Small and scared.

Just like me. Just like all of us, young bagarrook and girls, lost in this cruel landscape, stumbling through it in shock and fear. Fighting to stay alive, fighting to stay sane, no fight left to stab the eyes of sealers. So instead, I let the tears fall as I push the bone peg through a mother seal's coarse haired pelt and tether her sacred remains to the ground.

Flints of sharpened stone, similar to the tools we have in our own Biik, are given to us to scrape off the residue of blood and blubber. As the sight and smell threatens to overtake me, I shift my gaze away, past the remnants of the seal nursery, trying to ignore the reddened stains on lichened rocks. Over to a distant headland, I notice the jagged cliffs of another island beyond a wide blue channel. It seems so close and yet I know the water between the two landmasses could be fraught with confusing currents, the patrolling children of Wiyagabul Darrak and possibly, some Koormamgarrook of another clan's Dreaming. Ones that might prefer bagarrook to kulin.

Yet those cliffs call me. I feel as if another people are watching me. Through an ocean haze, figures appear to emerge elongated, small but distinct, along the line of the clifftop, staring our way.

Goosebumps prick along my arms. Could this be the people who belong to that Country studying us, making their evaluations, waiting to see if we are friend or foe? I wonder what they think about the mass carnage wrought on their fellow kin, and the wanton waste of their bodies.

Scouring the contours of the island, I look for the tell-tale signs of curling smoke to see if any wilams are close by. But no smoke fills the air, only the mists of Warrayin. I shudder with a thought that maybe the figures watching us from the ominous cliffs are not people, but their ghosts, moorroobull.

In the radiant orange light cast by Nyawiinth as he wanes, we finally finish the pegging and cleaning of every last sealskin. It is only then the men offer up some small portions of meat to us, although they are careful to remove any tools that might be weaponised against them. After several days and nights of travelling over Warrayin on the ngamudji's vessel, eating morsels of their unfamiliar food, our churning stomachs are aching for sustenance that is known. But without the hearths made from our Biik's stones, the turrung primed for smoking, sheets of fragrant paperbark and flavourful bush herbs, we resign ourselves to a meal of basic subsistence.

Nestling into the folds of the shell-laden dune, we settle our makeshift wilam slightly separate to the sprawl of sealing men on the beach, but always under their watch. Behind us, perched on a higher vantage point, the long cylinder of a gun resting against his shoulder, sits another ngamudji. Back resting against a sheltering boulder, eagle-eyed, he inhales on a stick with a tiny ember flaring at its point. He is our guard for the night, fingers running along his gleaming metal weapon, languidly reminding us of the firepower he holds, the destruction he could deliver upon us if he so chose.

A flickering kuunh brings some comfort, along with the relief of being once again on land. The cool sand cushions our sea rocked bodies, offering a reassuring sense of familiarity.

It almost feels like we're home, Kardingarrook whispers hoarsely.

I want to go home, Borodanger's face crumples in anguished tears, her plea echoing the despair we all feel.

Me too, whispers Yanki Yanki

Me too, croaks Naynar.

Doogbyerumboroke cuddles her children tight. *We will find a way to get home. Sleep now, and dream of your favourite place on Biik.*

How I yearn for her words of finding home to be true. Reaching out, I grab the hands of my kin, Meendutgarrook on my left, Kardingarrook on my right. Like ripples across a lake, the holding of hands spreads around the circle of our fire. We bagarrook hang on tightly, the soft flesh of each other a soothing balm for our heartbroken souls.

From the beach below, a raucous laugh pierces the stillness of the night. The men are getting rowdy, bolstered by the firewater they drink greedily at the day's end. Night after night on the large boat, subdued by their leader's orders to leave his cargo alone, the ngamudji would pass between them a brown liquid, coloured like tannined water. Before long, their movements would grow looser, voices louder, punctuated with snorts, hollers and jeers. A rancid stench, like the rotting smell of over-ripened bush currants, filled the air, heavy on the sealers' breath. We would watch, wary, as a dangerous glint animated their expressions, base desires surging with each sip, controlled only by the knowledge that their captain carried a gun down below.

Now, Doogbyerumboroke and I stare at each other with an unspoken understanding. The captain is still on the large vessel, moored out in the deeper water. These men on the beach have a sense of freedom tonight, their first fall of darkness free from the confines of the ship. Stealing a quick glance at the sealer keeping watch on the higher ridgeline, Doogbyerumboroke rouses her sleepy children. Pressing her finger to her lips, she motions them to move to a different part of the sand dune, ducking down as they edge along the covering saltbush. I whisper to the older girls to leave the fire and follow the young ones quickly.

Is everything alright? Meendutgarrook whispers, concern creasing her brow.

Just in case, I murmur. Nodding in reluctant agreement, she follows the shadowy figures of Kardingarrook and Nandergarrook, moving silently across the dunes.

Under the low-lying branches of a coastal tea tree, Doogbyerumboroke urges them all to tuck under its canopy and use the leaves sweeping the sand as a cosy windbreak.

Huddle together to stay warm, I whisper. *And stay where you are.*

No matter what you hear, adds Doogbyerumboroke, for the benefit of the concerned munmundiik as much as her own drowsy children.

I miss my werrun, Yanki Yanki mumbles sleepily. *I wish I could cuddle her now.*

Look out for her in your dreams, I say, tucking his messy hair behind his ears. *She will probably come and visit you.*

My fingers linger, paralysed by the aching desire to be back at my family's side, stroking the cheek of my own boy, Yearl Yearl, in his carefree, spirited slumber. With an expulsion of held breath, I pull my hand away and nod to the older girls before following Doogbyerumboroke back across the dune.

Maybe we could swim to that other island? My voice is quiet and conspiratorial as we settle back at our fire. The older bagarrook presses a finger to her lips and glances up at the sealer keeping watch with his gun, lighted stick still smouldering near his bearded mouth.

Keeping quieter than the rumblings of the men on the shore, I press my point. *Tootkuningarrook did it. And our hands are free now. We just need to get closer to the water and see how the currents move through Warrayin.*

87

We don't know if Tootkuningarrook made it home, Doogbyerum-boroke whispers sharply. *And my three are much younger. The risk is greater.*

Behind her, the darkened face of the cliffs glistens in the moonlight. Again, I feel a presence on its uppermost edges beckoning me, searching for my responding answer.

There's something about those cliffs. Something calling to me, I murmur, fixed on the moving shapes I see in the dark.

It might be the call of death? Doogbyerumboroke's tone is stern, snapping me back to reality. *Because that's what would happen if I tried to swim with my children across an unknown sea to those cliffs. This is not our Country, we know nothing of its Lore.*

Light thudding felt through the sand stops our conversation short. Emerging from the shadows, the captain's woman squats down beside us, her white dress stained with the blood and fat of the day's slaughter. Immediately, Doogbyerumboroke turns her back to the bagarrook, rigid and resolute in protest.

Before I can follow suit, the woman gestures to herself and says, *Maytepueminner.*

You are a traitor, Doogbyerumboroke spits, making sure the meaning of her words is clear despite the language barrier.

The woman shakes her head pitifully, and for the first time I can see the markings of hopelessness and despair etched into her features. Placing her palm against her chest, she once again says, *Maytepueminner.*

An image presses on my mind. Of her standing at the bow of the rowboat as it came to our shore, arms outspread with strange and glittering treasures to draw the young ones close. I remember that teeth-baring grin, pulled wide by some unseen force and fixed there through undercurrents of fear and weakness. I want to hate her but somehow, I cannot.

Nannertgarrook, I say, touching my chest. Then I point to my countrywoman. *Doogbyerumboroke.*

Slapping my hand with a force that reveals her barely contained anger, Doogbyerumboroke spits again. *Traitor!*

Her whole body radiates hot with impotent rage. She glares ferociously at the captain's woman and looks her directly in the eye. *You did this.* She stands, cheeks glistening with tears. *Warragul! You and your men are warragul!*

Fists clenching, she fights back the instinct to lash out, then abruptly turns and disappears within the folds of the rolling dunes.

A weary silence hangs heavy between this strange woman and me. Awkwardly, I look towards the outline of the cliffs on the opposite island. Maytepueminner still squats, uncertainty restless in her body, unsure whether to stay or go. When she finally speaks, her tone is filled with sadness. Even though I cannot make sense of her language, I understand the gravity underpinning her words. As she complements them with gestures, I begin to make sense of their terrible meaning.

Pointing to the distant cliffs, Maytepueminner feigns crying as if to say that many tears have been shed on that Country. It is a place of sorrow, a Woorroowee. Forming a cradle with her arms, she swings them gently as if rocking a babe at her breast. I guess that she is showing me families gathered there, babayin with their bubup. In my mind, I imagine it like our Monmar, stretches of cliff rising from rocky reefs and plentiful shores. Headlands of warrak bush and green grass where kangaroos and emus feast. A place where men hunt their game and women gather bounty from the sea. And children play, collecting shells, digging for pippis, maybe even kicking a ball for sport like our marngrook.

Raising a straightened arm to the sky, Maytepueminner forces from her mouth a rumbling expulsion of air. Boom, like a gunshot. Over and over, she points her arm and repeats the sound. The final time, she aims her rigid finger in my direction and fires her makeshift weapon at my body.

Goosebumps flare all over my flesh as I understand her meaning. A massacre, perpetuated by the newcomers, using their deadly weapons. Remembering the splitting sound of the captain's gunshot piercing booroonth that first night on the boat, I realise spears and boomerangs are no match for the ngamudji's firepower.

In our Law, the rules on the right ways to do and be are clear and time honoured. Rarely will a kulin challenge the Old Ones and break the yulendji that governs our morality. If a man does, the sharpened points of our spears will teach the lesson, a throw to the leg, a cutting to punish, but never to kill. But this is not the ngamudji way. Without ancient Law, without honour and morality, their weapons are designed to destroy. Another check of the sealer on the high ground, and I see the metal of his gun gleaming like a warning in Meeniyan's shadowy light.

A shiver ripples over my skin and I look back at Maytepueminner. She continues her story, rocking the imaginary babe once more in her arms, becoming again the young mother on the cliff. Placing the bubup down towards the ground, the captain's woman moves her hand upwards as if the child has grown in height. She takes that imaginary child's hand, then reaches out to her other side for another phantom child. Families were on the headland. The message is clear. Children were caught in the carnage.

Once again, Maytepueminner forces the air from her mouth, a rumbling boom, and grabs at her side as if hit. Slowly, she points to the pinnacle on the distant island. With her other hand she touches her chest, then reaches for the child. Trembling at the very tip, her pointed finger slips off the edge of the cliff. Carefully, painfully, she traces a line down its jagged face to the boulders and crashing ocean below.

Dropping her arms by her side, Maytepueminner stands motionless staring at this place of Woorroowee. All air seems suspended in her body, all emotions drained, the burden of terrible knowledge hoisted on her shoulders.

Holding her outstretched fingers up in front of me, she touches each digit in turn. Over and over, she counts until we both lose track of the tally. Too many people, too many murrup, too much sorrow. I realise now whose eyes have been watching me from that cliff. Restless ghosts that cry out to be seen, to be acknowledged.

A girl's shrill scream pierces the night. Then a cacophony of more cries follow. Maytepueminner and I leap to our feet, and it is only then that I realise I haven't heard the men for some time.

Racing to the scrub where we had concealed the younger ones, I see one of the sealers gripping Naynar's ankles, trying to pull her free from the rescuing arms of her siblings, Borodanger and Yanki Yanki. Her small body twists and contorts trying to pull herself out of his vicelike grip. Wild with a fearsome rage, Nandergarrook pummels the man's back with closed fists, but he is immune to her blows. Numbed and emboldened by firewater, the man is focused on only one thing. Having his way with the youngest girl.

Nearby, another staggering man clenches the arms of both Meendutgarrook and Kardingarrook, trying to drag them down into the sand dunes. Kicking and screaming, the munmundiik try to wrench themselves free but, drunk as he may be, the sealer's rough hands are locked around the girls' slender wrists. Torn between helping the children or going to the aid of my cousins, I stand paralysed with an agonising choice.

Without a word, Maytepueminner strides past me towards the bushes, clutching a large boulder. One fluid movement, she raises it high, then thrusts it down upon the man's head. Knocked unconscious, he drops face first into the sand. Naynar scrambles to her siblings with a petrified whimper, one of her legs bending from the knee at an unnatural angle.

Spurred into action, I yank the thickest log I can find from the bush and race towards my screaming cousins. With all the force of my pent-up rage, I swing madly at the man's reddening back over and over again. Even when he releases the girls' arms and falls to his knees, I do not stop. I cannot stop. Not until the deadening weight of the log pulls down my trembling arms and I can lift them no more, do I reluctantly let my woman's fighting stick fall to the ground. As though numb to the pain but subdued nonetheless, the man half staggers, half tumbles back down the dunes to the sleeping sealers' fire.

In the shocked silence of the aftermath, punctuated only by rasping breaths and stifled sobs, I realise Doogbyerumboroke is not with us. Panic seizes me as I scour the surrounding dunes and scrub. Following in the direction where she left, I make my way tentatively in the dark, trying to remember the markings of this strange land mapped in daylight. Sweeps of sand meeting the rise of cliffs and their treacherous rocks below. I pause to sense my way.

Then I hear it. A rhythmic grunting. And I know immediately what it is.

A few steps away, Doogbyerumboroke lies unconscious. On top of her, a heaving beast of a sealer thrusts himself upon her.

A strangled cry escapes my throat. *Maytepueminner!*

Before the man has a chance to even turn his head, she is there, boulder raised, and I relish the satisfying thud of it cracking his skull. We pull my countrywoman free from under his slackened form and carry her to the warming fire. Closing around her in a protective circle, her bubup stroke her face and body, willing her to return to them.

It is then that I remember the sealer sentinel on higher ground. Surely he would have seen the attacks from his vantage point. Maybe he has fallen asleep, maybe he is no longer watching.

A racing thought grabs hold in my mind. Now is the time to escape. With the sealers incapacitated, and Maytepueminner on our side, we could launch the gurrung into the water and disappear into the blackened expanse of Warrayin. As I look to the boulder where he had been stationed, my heart beats an excited crescendo. Then freezes, in bitter awareness, when I see the telltale glowing ember of his smoking kalk. He was there all along. Awake and unmoved, watching it all.

Cold as ice, I turn back to the flames of our bagarrook fire and desperately grip my cousin's hands. A slow wail rises like messaging smoke from the base of my spine and the first phrases of a traditional song play low on my lips. Growing stronger, the chanting curls up and into the frigid night air, a call to our Liwik for their guidance and healing power. A plea for them to be with us.

As more kin join the yingali, Maytepueminner takes her leave. I watch her certainty on this Biik, as the moonlight follows her white-dressed silhouette down the dunes and across the sand to the rowboat beached on the shore. With a numb curiosity, I watch her remove three coils of rope and a ragged piece of cloth. As she pads her way to the men's dwindling fire, she lays down most of her supplies, holding onto one section of rope. In a well practised move, Maytepueminner deftly winds and knots the arms of an offending sealer behind his back as he sleeps.

Before she leaves, she adds to her collection of goods the vessel carrying the men's firewater. After securing the two other men still unconscious in the dunes, Maytepueminner makes her way back to our campfire. Without a word, she gently parts the hair on Doogbyerumboroke's head, matted with blood from a deep wound on her scalp. Wetting the piece of cloth with the liquid from the vessel, she carefully dabs at the injury. The acrid smell of the liquor ascends like heat from a fire, burning into our nostrils.

Still struggling to climb out from the depths of unconsciousness, Doogbyerumboroke winces groggily at the burning sensation on top of her head. Her hand reaches clumsily towards her injuries, but I take it in my own as I continue singing by her side. Blinking, she begins to arrive back in the present.

Yanki Yanki hovers in front of her face. *Wake up, babayin. Please wake up.*

Nandergarrook takes his hand reassuringly. *Let's give your mother some space, bubup.*

Just as she leads the young boy away, Doogbyerumboroke's eyelids flutter open. *I am awake, my bubup*, she murmurs.

Yanki Yanki rushes back to her side, finding a place between his sisters crowding their mother.

I am awake. You're not getting rid of me that easily.

As we laugh and cry, sing and stroke our countrywoman's bloodied face, Maytepueminner edges away from our circle, leaving her bottle and cloth behind. For the briefest of moments, she watches us from within the shadows, our expressions of relief, of love, of family, which leap and dance in the glow of the firelight. Then, she turns and shuffles back down the slope to the circle of sleeping men by their nearly extinguished fire. Her back to us, she sits rigid, staring out across Warrayin. A captive like us. But, unlike us, she is utterly alone.

Standing vigilant with his gun gripped by his side, the sentinel sealer flanks the captain who appraises the damage done to his cargo, the bruises, the cuts, the swollen twist of little Naynar's leg. Isolated at the far end of the beach, a sulking huddle of three outcast sealers stare at us, the brutes who attacked the children and violated Doogbyerumboroke. I realise they are to be left behind, exiled. A fitting punishment, I think, a flame of righteous anger making my fists clench. As fear flares in their ruddy features, the sealers' glares burn with hostility as if to say how can our worth be more valuable than theirs?

Loaded with a heavy pile of the slaughtered seals' skins, the rowboat sinks low in the shallow water. Held steady by two of the remaining men, Maytepueminner climbs on board to join Meendutgarrook, Yanki Yanki and Borodanger, already seated and flanked by two sealers clutching oars. The rest of us wait in line for our turn to embark, even though the prospect of returning to the open ocean makes our stomachs churn. With her knee swollen and leg unnaturally crooked, Naynar is wrapped in a blanket and hoisted by Nandergarrook and Kardingarrook onto the vessel.

Likewise, the girls help a limping Doogbyerumboroke, whose face is now purple and swollen. Unnoticed last night, the blows she endured reveal their ferocity in the day. The gaping wound on her head is covered with cloth tied around the nape of her neck. Determined not to show the depth of her pain, Doogbyerumboroke swings herself unsteadily into the boat and moves quickly to enfold her children in her arms. Kardingarrook is next and once she finds her feet, she gently pulls Nandergarrook behind her.

I am last. But before I go, I plant my feet once more into the comforting, cooling sand of this foreign Biik. At the tips of my toes, I notice a cluster of tiny shells, their fragile points catching the early morning sunlight. For a moment, I simply stare at them, as the face of my daughter fills my mind. I see her picking through the treasures of the tide line on the shores of our homeland, searching for her favourite shells. Her happy, peaceful smile when they are finally found.

Quickly, I bend down to collect the offerings at my feet, keeping them tight in my hand as I hoist myself over the edge of the wooden rowboat. Their curving forms press against the folds of my palm, buried safely in my clutches, as we move from gurrung to the larger vessel moored in deeper water. Yet another departure to a destination unknown.

Slicing through the white cresting waves of Warrayin, the captain's schooner pushes away from the island's jutting cliffs and the orange-flecked, tumbled boulders below. Surreptitiously, I run my finger over the sun-baked shells in my palm. Closing my eyes, I try to fool myself that I am back in the folding dunes of our burribarri. Teaching the younger girls how to strip string from kangaroo sinew. Piercing tiny holes in patterned shells with the bone of the kuyim. Watching nimble little fingers thread their precious finds onto the newly formed string. Seeing the pride in their faces as I wrap the jostling shell necklaces around their necks. Looking into the soulful, brown eyes of my Boyerup as she radiates happiness and love.

My eyes prick with tears, but I don't want to open them just yet. I want to hold these images, locked in my memory, at the forefront of my mind as if they were happening right now. As if it will be my manggip's sweet face smiling at me when I finally open them again.

Saltwater slides down my cheeks. I wish I could keep my eyes closed forever. But I know I cannot.

When I finally prise them open again, I find myself looking directly at the darkened cliffs of Woorroowee. And in front of them, the black ghostly bodies of children and mothers endlessly falling.

YARRADJINAN
NYILAM
A Bad Dream

I feel as if I'm moving in a dream, eyes open, but lost in the strangeness of fitful sleep. It is barely a day and night since we left the
exiled sealers on their deserted island and followed a winding span
of towering black cliffs along the coastline of an unforgiving Biik.
Only to arrive at yet another island, but one that reveals itself like
a fevered reverie.

At my feet, a scruffy creature stares up at me, panting mouth open
with a tongue lolling to the side, shaggy fur hanging over its face.
With the form of a werrun in its body shape and muzzle, the animal's
curling fur, mottled with dark and light patches, has some of the
texture or colour of a dingo. Expressive eyes and a curious tilt of its
head make me feel as if this creature is assessing my very character
and soul, waiting for me to reveal myself as possible friend or foe.

Dog, Maytepueminner names, brushing the animal on the top
of its head. Then she points to others of its kind, with various
colours and coats, lying in the shade of solitary trees. These too are
named dog.

Flanked by the sealing men both in front and behind us, my
kin and I wait while the captain huddles in conversation with an
old ngamudji from this foreign Country. Wide-eyed, we scan the
strange surroundings with a mix of apprehensive confusion and
uneasy wonder. This place is unlike any we have ever seen.

Trails forged by this landscape are unusually large and straight,
with all vegetation obliterated upon the paths. Wilams randomly dot

the valleys of gently cresting and dipping hills. Tall and straight, they are fashioned from the chopped-up pieces of felled ancient trees, the huge stumps of which eerily dot the ground as phantom sentinels guarding a now lost forest.

On the sides of every wilam, large holes have been cut, revealing glimpses into the inner workings of the camps. Shadowy silhouettes move just beyond the line of sight and a fluttering ripples in my belly as I wonder what or who these shapes are.

The captain's friend runs a roving eye over our group, lingering too long on our bare bodies. Once more, I feel that uneasy urge to cover myself from his prying gaze, to protect the swelling bulge of the bubup in my belly, so I press my arms together in front of my chest and angle my body away. The old sealer points to a large hut nestled within a few remaining trees at the base of a windswept grassy plain. Through pursed lips he whistles high and sharp, making the flopping ears of the creature at my feet stand erect. One last look at me and the dog follows his stooping master.

Straight lines of horizontal saplings are stacked in sections around the wilam. Penned within these barriers are still more creatures never before seen. Some have the girths of seals with rubbery, light pink flesh, protruding snouts and twisted tails. Others are covered in a thick pelt of shaggy fur, rounding out their bodies like fluffy balls on legs, as cosy as the coats of our wallert wallert. Both new creatures have hardened feet that pierce and trample the usually soft soil of Country. Nothing lives on the ground in their enclosure, no grasses, no yams, no orchids, all either eaten or trampled out of existence.

When we reach the entrance to the wilam, the captain's men give a small pile of sealskins to the old man waiting there, then peel away, heading back towards the penned animals. With his rifle pinned by his side, the captain watches as we are ushered inside the dwelling.

Emerging from behind a hanging row of tanned kangaroo skins, two women rush forward to embrace Maytepueminner. Running their hands over each other's faces and arms, tears welling in their eyes, the depth of feeling that moves between them is layered with unspoken loss, overwhelming relief and momentary joy. It is clear they are kin, but I wonder if this is their Country or if, like us, they were snatched from the bosom of their Biik. Even without words, a sense of tumultuous history is passed between them in a look, a touch, a tear.

Slight and wiry shadows duck and weave behind hanging pieces of cloth in a smaller area, tucked behind the main opening of the wilam. Pressing lightly against the compacted sand, a series of little feet scuttle back and forth. My straining ears catch the muffled whispers of high-pitched voices.

A burst of lightness warms my heart. Bubup are here. Hidden away for now, but their shuffling feet and muted murmuring bring a grateful smile to my face.

Easing out of their tender embrace, the women turn their attention to us. Comforting, kind smiles are darkened by the shadow of pity, a knowing of some of the horrors wrought upon us. Seeing Doogbyerumboroke's battered face and Naynar's twisted leg, one woman rushes to gather herbs, cloths and instruments of healing from a large tarnook. The other woman moves to a pile of ngamudji clothes, sorting through them and setting aside the ones that might fit our frames. All the while, the two sealing men talk low in their language, pointing out towards the campsite, the countryside and Warrayin, but always watchful of our movements within.

Scratching against my skin, the rough weave of the sealers' cloth hangs uncomfortably on my body. How I wish for the soft luxury of my possum skin cloak, warm and enveloping, grown around me since the time of my birth, always protecting me from the fierce rush of Mornmoot, the bitter cold of Perrin, the damp earth when laying my head to rest. There is nothing of comfort in the harsh texture of the ngamudji's coverings, nor do they stop the wind from whirling against me or the cold pressing into my flesh. They might, however, shield my body from the lascivious stares of uninitiated men.

I catch sight of Kardingarrook, surveying her new attire with disdain. Spreading her arms wide, the ends of the cloth stretch long, hanging limply over her fingers. Gathering at her feet, the material catches around her legs as she tries to step forward. Her puzzled eyes meet mine and we both try to stifle a sudden, bubbling laugh at our ridiculous new coverings. A bewildered Nandergarrook is dressed just as comically and as soon as she realises we are watching her, she begins to giggle. Cheekily, Meendutgarrook joins in the amusement, subtly flapping her arms in her huge garment, resembling a bedraggled bird caught in a net.

This tiny burst of levity sparks a flickering light back into my kin's eyes. Knowing we are walking this unknown, dangerous path side by side, carrying the burden together, brings a vital measure of comfort to our aching hearts.

Watching us cautiously, the other women allow themselves a smile at our playfulness. With a feeling of furtive connection, the woman dressing us steps closer, tucking herself behind us to make sure she is out of the line of sight of the men.

Quickly, she rolls the material up her arm to reveal long vertical lines of ceremonial cicatrices. Pointing at our arms and chests, she indicates she has seen our own markings. We are connected, she seems to say, glowing with pride and understanding. We all wear the scars of our sacred ceremonies, the indicators of our knowledge, the ancient rituals of our clans and Country. We are one and the same.

Around our women's fire that night, alongside the large wilam filled with ngamudji clothes, tucked-away children and peculiar animals penned in cramped confines, we speak in hushed whispers to each other, words that neither clan recognises, yet somehow, the meaning is understood. Dressed in the scratching clothes of our captors, lit only by the licking flames of our kuunh, our words merge into soft song, a welcoming yingali for each other. When our voices swell in volume, the other bagarrook quickly put their fingers to their lips as if to remind us to be quiet, to be contained, to not draw attention to ourselves. Maytepueminner points discreetly to the ngamudji gathered in groups around their own fires and wilams nearby. Stretching her arm out in front of her, she points her fingers, mimicking the long cylinder of the white man's gun. *As always*, she seems to say, *they're watching.*

Lowering our voices to a tremulous whisper, my countrywomen and I sing the songs of our sister bays, the glorious Munmun-diik, shining in their cluster of seven in the sky, Mother Whale and the Koormamgarrook, flanked by their steadfast companions, Barrunan the dolphin, Werrun the dingo, and the once bountiful seals. Even when we falter as a sealer staggers over to our kuunh, pulling a bagarrook to her feet and leading her into the darkened scrub, our new sisters continue to tap the rhythm of our songs on their knees. Willing us to persist in telling the stories of our yingali, they keep the beat with hand on skin, like a bittersweet substitute for the clapping of our daal kalk or the thrumming of our possum skin drums. In turn, when our song cycle finishes in a lulling taper, the island women continue the songline threads, singing low in their language, whispering what I imagine are stories of home and Creation beings, totems and heroes, right and wrong ways. Just like us.

Closing my eyes that night, the images of my clan's murndigar-rook, sitting around campfires past, float through my mind. Old, wise women, my grannies, my aunties, the warmth of my mother, Dindoo. Whispering refrains of that night's yingali echo in my ears, mingling with the memories of joyous ngargee on the shores of Warnmarring. Songs on a bayside sandbank calling forth betayil mothers and their curious calves. Songs of praise travelling far into Sky Country to the djurt of our Dreaming's beings. Songs of our ceremonies, celebrating the gaining of ancient knowledge, the growing of wisdom in all its wondrous complexity. These songs wrap themselves around me as I travel into my slumber, reminding me of who I am, anchoring me to where I am from, haunting me, now that I am adrift.

Yearl Yearl is a baby nestling in my arms, sleeping satisfied after his long feed at my breast. Next to me, Boyerup aligns a collection of colourful shells along the shore, arranging them in a design that pleases her. Only a toddler in this dream, her chubby cheeks beam wide at the beauty spread before her. Brown eyes shining, she looks at me for my approval.

You have found some beautiful shells, my bubup, I praise.

Suddenly, I am standing on a windy headland, Yearl Yearl awake and screaming in one arm, Boyerup clutching my other, tears streaming. Fear surges through my body and thunder pounds in my ears. Panicked, I search for a safe place to go but five steps in front of me is the edge of the cliff and a sea smashing on jagged rocks below.

Boom!

A shot rips through my side and I stagger forward with burning pain, still clinging to my children. Swaying so close to the ridge, I scream to the ocean below. Another shot fires behind me and I stumble, falling to my knees.

In agonising, slow motion, Yearl Yearl tumbles from the crook of my arm. But I manage to grab his tiny hand at the very last moment. One more shot tears through the air and I am thrust forward, suspended on the very edge of the cliff. Balancing precariously, the world spinning around me, I clutch Yearl Yearl and Boyerup. In front of us, a churning abyss. Behind us, a murderous rampage.

Time hangs paralysed for a long moment. My bubups' eyes bulge with terror. Then, my balance is lost. And we all fall.

I jolt awake, gasping for air. Shaking, I try to erase the image of my children's terrified eyes from my brain.

Nearby, the fire still burns with a freshly placed log and I stare into it for a long time, hoping the flames might cauterise the searing visions in my mind. Around me, the rise and fall of heavy breathing sets a soothing rhythm. In the rising pink hues of Nyawiinth's first light, I scan the sleeping bodies to make sure my kin are all accounted for. Some are restless, some almost completely still, but all are mercifully asleep where they should be, covered in the island women's kuyim skin blankets.

But I do not see Maytepueminner or the other sealers' women. Maybe they were gathered up as we slept, returned to rest inside the old man's wilam, or taken by other ngamudji to any one of the smaller wilams dotted along the wide paths of this flattened Biik. Keeping as still as possible, I scour the darkened landscape for signs of the bagarrook, or the ever-present stare of a watching sealer. Stillness hangs eerily in the chill of the pre-dawn air.

Carefully, I lift myself out from the clutch of my kin's bodies, my chest tight. Straining in the dim light, I keep low and move slowly to the edge of the clearing around the large wilam.

Suddenly, a shadow lurches towards me and I drop to the ground in panicked fear.

Tongue hanging out of a panting mouth, the shaggy werrun named Dog appears before me and sits, head tilted in a curious pose, as if to say, *Why are you awake?* I don't know whether to laugh or cry as giddy relief eases my tense body. In the creeping dawn light rising on Warrayin's horizon, Dog stands and trots to a path leading away from the camping place. Looking back, he appears to beckon for me to follow, like a spirit dingo promising a quest for hidden yulendji. Scouring the wilams one more time, I search for reassurance that all are asleep. With a hurried pulse, I take a gulp of air and pad quickly after the strange werrun.

Paths winding around the island emerge into shadowy view through the dim light of this newly born morning. Beyond broad tracts of coastal scrub, rising and falling with the sweep of the land, I see the rough, white flecked Warrayin, buffeted by frigid south-westerly winds. Shivering in the mornmoot's chill, I realise any passage to freedom would not be across those unfriendly waves.

In front of me, Dog keeps his nose to the ground and turns abruptly down a track partly obscured by a throng of overgrown tea-tree. Fresh imprints of feet lead the way through crowded turrung, until Dog and I reach a sudden clearing and stop. Winding through a plain of low-lying saltbush, a path leads up to a prominence at the very centre of this Biik, like a giant boulder thrusting up from underground, pulling the earth along with it. I imagine the hill holds some ancient stories, resembling the wizened pate of an old man, cruelly denuded of his hair.

Something stops me from travelling any further, and Dog senses it too. Instead, I stand still and let my eyes follow the line of the old mountain's forehead until I arrive at its apex. There, thick funnels of smoke curl into the air, rising with a singular purpose. This is not a random fire. I immediately recognise its true meaning as a call and answer to a kinship fire close by. Silhouetted in the gold rays of early sunrise, dark figures cluster around the signalling place, some tall, some small. *Am I seeing the moorroobull of those who walked this Country before?* I wonder.

Then I see the pattern of their smoke, so similar to the ways of my clan, the messages Dindoo sent back to Kullurk. Straight smoking lines paced in a particular rhythm, sending a question into Sky Country for family to read. *Are you there? Are you safe?*

My heart beats wildly with recognition. These are the bagarrook I sang with around last night's kuunh, the smaller shapes at their legs are their bubup.

Transfixed, I watch as hopeful minutes pass while the figures on the stony prominence wait for their answer. At last, it comes, and with the boughs of what scarce foliage is left on this occupied island, the women beat their own answering rhythm.

Scouring the ocean horizon around me, I search for the responding home fires. All is still on the distant jutting headlands to the south so I calculate their people must be beyond the other side of the hill. If they can see each other's fires, they must be close.

With a gnawing pang of yearning, I think how painfully tantalising it must be to know they are so close. From the vantage point of their signalling hill, they must imagine surrendering to the currents of Warrayin on these early mornings and trusting she will send them home before the ngamudji realise they are gone.

Like brave Tootkuningarrook. Seizing the opportunity of unbound hands and the calling shores of her Biik still in sight. But did she make it home?

A low growl rumbles from Dog, ears alert, turned back to camp. He swings back the way we came and I follow quickly behind. My mind spins as I picture this island's captured bagarrook seeing the fires of their family somewhere on the northern horizon. The torturous knowing that their clan is so close, the yearning to be free and by their side again. And yet, they are still here on this island with the sealers. No chance of escape taken. Like Doogbyerumboroke, maybe they fear the crossing of Warrayin with young children. Maybe it's the ngamudji's weapons that give them pause. Maybe one of them did try once and the cost of their failure was too great.

Back near the cleared Biik, dotted with the intruders' wilams, I wait in the concealing scrub with Dog. A barely perceptible thud vibrates through the ground and the werrun cocks his head towards its origin. At the far end of the camping grounds, past the patchwork of wilams and animal pens, towards the becalmed bay where we first made land, a lone sealer pulls a gurrung onto the beach. Satisfied that everywhere else is still, Dog looks to me then trots back to his own shelter. I creep to where my kin still sleep and ease myself under the warming kuyim covers. I lie listening to the waking chirps of the subdued birds hidden in the saltbush.

Then I feel a tremor in the sand. A flurry of footfalls. Women and children emerge from the scrub. Moving in swift silence, they slip back into the shadows of their wilams, as if they had never left.

WONGURRUNIN
Ignorance

We stand in a huddle beside our makeshift wilam, waiting to learn what will become of us today. The last few mornings, we have been tasked with menial labour around the camping ground. Stacking felled timber poles, cleaning out animal pens, washing bundles of ngamudji cloth, carrying piles of seal pelts from rowboats to wilams and back again. Today, the captain negotiates with a small cluster of island men, assessing the value of what he will gain for our labour.

Peering out through still swollen eyes, Doogbyerumboroke fixates on his every move. Like a mother tulum guarding her ducklings, Doogbyerumboroke's arms wrap around her three bubup like a pair of outstretched, sheltering wings. An agreement seems to be reached and Maytepueminner comes over to explain. Curving her hands near her chest, she jumps up and down on the spot then scratches at a pretend ear on the side of her head. Yanki Yanki giggles and breaks out into his finest rendition of kuyim, twitching hands like ears scoping for sounds on the breeze, chewing contemplatively on a tasty wad of make-believe grass.

Nodding, Maytepueminner grins at his clever mimicry. Then she elongates her arm and points her finger to indicate the white man's gun, creeping up on the boy as a hunter to prey. Doogbyerumboroke shoots out a protective arm, pulling her son back into her fold, as if to say *my boy will not be shot at*, even in a demonstration of kangaroo hunting.

Indicating both Doogbyerumboroke and Naynar's injuries, Maytepueminner motions the family of four to move to one side. For the rest of us, she points along a well-worn track and gives us some binuk of tools we recognise, to flay skin and peg down pelts.

Once again, a sealer leads the way and another one keeps to the rear as my countrywomen and I walk in a single line on an unfamiliar track over dunes of windswept grass. The women's signalling hill looms as a central beacon. At its sloping base, from this new direction, I see a lone tree, wide and gnarled, a marker of what may have once proliferated on this now barren Biik. Something about the shape of its trunk catches my attention and I slow my pace to get a clearer look. With a jolt, I realise what I am staring at.

A woman, skin as dark as ours, leans against the tree. Her arms are joined together, raised above her head and her face presses against the bark. As I pause, I see that her hands are tied, bound tightly to the upper boughs of the tree. More rope winds around both her waist and the trunk of the turrung, making it impossible for her to move, let alone leave. Exposed skin from the waist up, her back is patterned with dried rivulets of blood. Lacerations are etched into her flesh, obviously lashed there by a harsh whipping and someone's unbridled fury.

Blinking, I wonder if what I'm seeing is real or a ghostly vision. Glancing back to the tree, the woman is still there, sagging under the painful weight of her upheld, broken body. I turn to Meendutgarrook walking behind me and the horrified look on her face confirms we have witnessed the same thing. An urge to race to the bagarrook's side and loosen the cruel ropes, tend to her gaping wounds and shattered spirit, pushes my feet to step off the path. But Meendutgarrook whips me back.

Flanked between two grim sealers, guns resting against their shoulders, with strict instructions to get us to work quickly, there is no chance of stopping. There is nothing we can do.

Swallowing the impulse to run to her aid, I force my eyes back to the track in front of me. And as our cluster moves inexorably forward, the woman disappears out of sight. But the image of her brutalised body, tied to a roughened tree, left there for an interminable period of time, haunts my mind, torments my soul. *How long has she been there? Who did this to her?* Images flash on a loop before me. Such deep lacerations cut into her back, open and festering in the rising heat of the morning. Her tortured face, her failing body. *What could she possibly have done to deserve such cruelty?*

A question gets stuck on a repeating pattern, each word echoing with every step.

Did she try to escape?

Instinctively, my fingers spread out over my fluttering belly, reminded of the vulnerable bubup growing there. Over the four days we have been in this place, my countrywomen and I have mapped every part of the Biik we've walked on. Assessing, remembering, judging, imagining. Looking for a pathway that might lead to freedom. And now all I can see are the horrors inflicted on a bagarrook who is just like me. And all I can think is, *Will this happen to me if I try to escape?*

Freshly slain carcasses of kuyim are heaped in a pile before us. Once again, the ngamudji have exercised no restraint or discrimination in their hunting selection, just a wholesale slaughter of any bounding kangaroo caught in their bloodlust. Big boomers lay beside their smaller wives, and their even smaller offspring. Shaking my head, I look upon the bludgeoned body of a joey fresh from their mother's pouch.

What good is the tiny skin of this baby? I wonder to myself. *Not even big enough to stretch across a woman's drum.*

Konye! Nandergarrook squats on the ground nearby, a female kuyim lying at her feet. The kangaroo's pouch is swollen and peeking out from its folds is a tiny bubup's soft skinned face. Frozen in the rigor of death, the baby would not be more than four months old, still suckling milk in the safe confines of her mother's warmth.

Why do they kill a mother? Disgust courses through Nandergarrook's rhetorical question. *How stupid are they?*

Bulaadu wongurrunin, I offer.

Pulling the joey from its once cosy haven, she places it gently beside a tuft of long grass. *I better look out*, she snorts ruefully, *they'll probably beat me for not skinning it. Even though the poor bubup barely has any fur.* With a protective hand over her own growing form, Nandergarrook spits her disapproval. *Bulaadu stupid.*

Using the sharpened edge of a flint of granite, I begin the process of separating body from skin. On a rock nearby, I see one of the men reach into the folds of his clothes and pull out a small, shiny vessel. Surreptitiously, he sucks on it like it's his mother's teat. Firewater.

Those ngamudji, not much more intelligence than that little one there, I murmur, pointing to the dead joey. *No awareness, no knowledge, of how the world really works. Like a toddler, they just grab what they want, when they want, no thought for what comes after.*

But even one of our toddlers would know not to kill the one who brings life, Nandergarrook counters. *Stupid fools. Without the mother, there is nothing.*

I don't think they care. About anything else except themselves.

In my thoughts, I see clearly the knowing and wonder in my brother Derrimut's expression when he returned from his first ngargee for secret men's business. Etched on his features, fluid in his body, was a new and profound understanding. Of the mysteries of the world, his place in it, his obligations, duties, inheritances. He had left as a boy and returned as a man. Now initiated and ready for his wife, he married Nandergarrook, his love long promised. She who sits beside me now, their firstborn baby growing in her belly.

With his back resting against the warmth of a sunlit boulder, our captor takes another furtive swig of his firewater, then turns his face to bask in Nyawiinth's rays.

Soon they will learn their mistake, these boys. I tug at the bloody body before me. *When there's nothing left, when it's all been destroyed, that will be the white man's initiation.*

But their stupidity will destroy it for everyone, Nandergarrook spits, repulsed.

My grandmother's sage words, spoken at a long-ago campfire, a piece of the ngamudji's white cloth in her hands, whisper in the swirling mornmoot around me.

If the white man doesn't leave, it will be the end of the world.

Each day, on the walk back to the wilam, my hands blistered, back aching, from cutting and pulling the skin off too many kangaroos, I see the stark warning signs everywhere. Entrances to the burrows of mindalk the wombat, now grown over with creeping grass and wind-blown sand dunes. They are all gone. Bleached bones of barrimil the emu strewn across the scrub, skulls cracked, feathers blown away, the scrapings of nests long empty. They too are all gone. And with each full day of flaying and skinning, scraping and stretching, softening and tanning, kuyim after kuyim, it will not be much longer before the kangaroo will also be gone. All of them walking only as ghosts on this now desolate Biik. Only the wind to howl.

If the white man doesn't leave, it will be the end of the world.

MOONIP BA MANNIP
Embers and Ashes

Over the following week, swelling numbers of white men crowd the sparse wilams clustered around the harbour of our prison island. Ever-watchful stares keep vigilant focus on their cargo of black women and children. Prized workers, bonded in endless servitude to the demands of the sealers, cooking and cleaning for them, flaying seals for them, skinning kangaroo for them. And now, as an autumnal cold settles low over the dunes, the season of muttonbirding begins.

Long sticks laden with the hanging bodies of hundreds of birds are hoisted along the posts of the sealers' timbered huts. When we return to the camping ground in the late afternoon light, carrying yet more dried and tanned skins of families of kuyim, the pungent smell of moonbird hangs thick in the air. A flash of recognition lights up Kardingarrook and I wonder, given her intense expression, whether she is about to burst into laughter or tears.

Married into her husband's vast, rich estate of the Mayune Balak, Kardingarrook knows well the world of Bayadin the moonbird. Sometime travellers from across the seas, they flock in their thousands on the islands of Warnmarring when warm air envelops the earth. Journeying to Djouap in Mooderrogar's fire-shaped, stringy bark canoe, Kardingarrook would join his clan to collect the eggs of this sacred bird.

And then, as Old Man Sun shed his hot summer rays and the first crisp winds of autumn hailed from the West, the family would journey once more to select a sustainable portion of the fledglings, prized for flesh, oil and feather. Feasting on Bayadin joins the ancient estates of Burinyong Balak, Mayune Balak and Yallock Balak together again. Around roasting fires and the fresh waters of Koo Wee Rup, old stories are swapped and remembered, new relationships pondered and settled, knowledge shared, family celebrated.

These memories flicker across Kardingarrook's face, mirroring the ones moving across my own. We shared these gatherings as cousin kin and marital neighbours, around our young woman's fire, marvelling at our luck to be both born and married within our beautiful Boonwurrung Biik, thanking our murndigarrook for promising it so. Only six months ago, as the wattle reached full golden bloom, we had travelled to Djouap once again to collect the bayadin eggs. Not long after, we waded along the sandbank at Yellodungo, singing out to Babayin Betayil, our yingali calling mother whales and their babies to rest in our bay of Warnmarring. Again, not long after, the men dared to raid the sealers on Korriyong so the wirrirap in the north could save the blanket of Sky Country from falling down, while we women journeyed to the place of Ngargee Karralk, to hold in sacred ceremony the murrup of a little bubup, ready for their whale to take them across the ocean. Again, not long after, we gathered at Monmar as Wiyagabul Nyawiinth peaked high in the sky, weaving, telling stories, seeing our bubup grow in the safe embrace of their Biik. Watching a boat row onto our shores.

Now, merely one full cycle of Meeniyan later, Kardingarrook, my kin and myself stand on foreign soil, surrounded by warragul and the fear they raise in their wake, taking in the hundreds of fledgling bayadin they have commanded be pulled from their burrowed nests at numbers far greater than any Elder would allow. Staring at row, upon row, upon row of hanging moonbirds, the momentary flash of excited recognition quickly dims in Kardingarrook's eyes.

Evening descends and the circle around the women's fire is thickened with a new collection of bagarrook, strangers to us but not to each other. Tonight, our work continues as we pluck the feathers of the moonbirds strung by their feet, not for the ngargee of the people of this Biik, not to share throughout the clan estates, building bonds that would strengthen community and Country. Bayadin belongs to the ngamudji now, stripped of their feathers, squeezed of their oil, salted and shipped in countless thousands to the lands of those with insatiable appetite.

Assessing our skill with watchful eyes, these new moonbird women are quick to correct our unpractised hands, murmuring a steady encouragement. Only Kardingarrook flies through the assessment with her well-honed plucking skills, nods of impressed approval directed her way. I see an eagerness to please in her smooth, youthful face, a sweet softening in the glow of their praise. All of us feel it, the quiet happiness of teaching and being taught, of connection over shared purpose. Even though it occurs under the shadow of a darker world, teetering on the edge of destructive imbalance. Perhaps more so.

Subdued laughter passes between the women of the same language. Even though they know we cannot understand them, they try to engage us in their stories as best they can, mimicking familiar sounds, acting out recognisable movements. Louder than the rest, sitting directly across from me, a smiling bagarrook with tight curling hair and a mischievous light in her eyes, captivates us all with her quick words and expressive gestures. Laying down the moonbird she is meant to be plucking, the woman plays out her scenes with an ever-increasing complexity and bravado, a gifted storyteller no matter the language.

Stealing a glance to Nandergarrook, I wonder how our clan's storyteller is feeling about her new counterpart. With gleaming eyes and grinning lips, she watches the curly-haired bagarrook with a genuine, captivated attention. For a sweet moment, I look from one storyteller to the other, relishing the profound beauty of young women connecting over the celebration of their Lore, understanding, appreciating, even when they speak an entirely different language.

Mercifully separate from our busy circle, the influx of new island men mostly seem content to leave us to toil alone, communing indolently by their fires, no tasks in front of them, just firewater and the fruits of others' endeavours. Every now and then, one saunters over to claim a woman from her work, removing her for labour of another kind in a darkened wilam nearby. Only the occasional ngamudji stalks us in the background, checking on the growing pile of naked chicks behind each one, keeping tally of our industry.

As the self-designated bridge between the two clans of captive women, born out of a simple friendliness or possibly the residue of a guilty responsibility, Maytepueminner singles out each woman around the circle. Pointing to herself she says, *Maytepueminner.* Then, one by one, she points to the next woman in the circle, encouraging them to do the same. The one with the quick, easy laugh, curly-headed and wide-smiling, introduces herself as Worethmaleyerpodeyer. Nudging into the curving shoulder of the young girl next in line, the storyteller stretches her arm like a protective wing around the nervous munmundiik and calls her *Wottecowwidyer.* Woven by circumstance into a caring kinship, she adds, *Nawnta,* and a shy smile gleams across the girl's face.

More bagarrook state their names, and it begins to feel like some sort of reclamation, a tiny uprising against those who might insist on calling them something else, names with no meaning in an alien tongue. Arriving at a pair of women showing the rounded bellies of burgeoning babies, Maytepueminner smiles and says, *Pakata.* I see Nandergarrook pause in the defeathering of her bayadin to wrap an instinctive arm around where her baby grows. Our eyes meet and we share a smile of mutual recognition. Then the naming circle reaches our line, the row of quiet girls and women Maytepueminner enticed with white man's treasure, and I see a blush of shame rise. She stops and waits, unsure if we will choose to engage or not.

Enmity still etched in the energy between them, Doogbyerum-boroke chooses not to speak. Next to her, Yanki Yanki beams with a charismatic grin, declaring his name with pride. Beside him, his sisters murmur, flicking their eyes between their resolute mother and the new, curious women around them.

Nannertgarrook, I say at my turn, clear and proud. Knowing they do not understand my words but wanting to stand myself strong in the Biik I belong to, I make my declaration.

Born to Yalukit-Wilam Country, daughter to Dindoo and my father in Pindayi, married in Burinyong Balak. Husband is Bobbinary, mother to Boyerup and Yearl Yearl. Then, rubbing my ever-rounding belly, I whisper, *Bubup*.

Across from me, a profound kindness in her expression, Worethmaleyerpodeyer pauses from her endless task and, with a graceful dance of her fingers, blows a kiss to me with one hand and, with the other, a kiss to the baby inside me.

Tears sting my eyes at the beauty and love held in the gesture. Strangers to one another, each caught in our own microcosms of dislocation and pain, our worlds so different yet in that moment so profoundly connected, she still offers a brilliant speck of light, shining with a message that says I could be her nawnta and she could be my liwurruk.

And then it is gone. Because a sealer yanks Worethmaleyerpodeyer to her feet by her hair.

Looming over her with a dangerous rage, the sealer pulls her backwards out of the circle, their feet tripping through the small mound of defeathered moonbirds she had gathered behind her. Making her kneel before the tumbled pile, the man points at the other women's collections, then back to hers. A manic fury builds in his body and forces out through the fist clenching Worethmaleyerpodeyer's head. Utterly powerless, her body spasms under his violent stranglehold.

Beads of frothing saliva spit forth from the ngamudji's bearded mouth. Foreign words filled with furious contempt are hurled at her as she struggles to free herself from the man's iron grip. Ranting like an unhinged madman, the sealer pushes and pulls the woman forward and back, a vicious dance animated by the devils of savagery and sadism. All reason has vanished from his eyes, and the unreachable rage burning within him makes me churn from a sickness deep in my stomach.

The rumbling of men's voices from the other wilams has quietened now, and slowly their shapes move into view on the edges of our campfire. They have come to see the spectacle, to be the witnesses keeping watch in the shadows. I hope.

Feeling their presence, the sealer releases Worethmaleyerpodeyer and lets his ranting die. Silence hangs in the air, but not with the sense of relieved dissipation. No, this silence seems not to be one of completion. It builds, charged with a barely contained tension. I see the other island women shrink into themselves, an awareness of what this silence portends.

Suddenly, the sealer snaps his closed fist into Worethmaleyerpodeyer's downcast face. The sickening sound of knuckles thudding on cheekbone. The shocking sight of her head jolting backwards, her slender neck snapped to the side, like the fate of the fledgling moonbirds pulled from their vulnerable burrows. She stumbles before falling to her knees. Another fist slams against skull, and she crashes into the sand.

Turning to the silhouetted men lurking, I wait for their outraged response. But there is nothing. Not one among them rushes forward. Not one who will take a stand against this brutal punishment, the evil flourishing before them. No commands to stop, no words of horror. Nothing, but the sound of Worethmaleyerpodeyer's guttural groans and her kin's choking sobs.

Anger fires up my spine, righteous in its revulsion of the cowardice before me. My half plucked bayadin falls from my hands and just as I am about to launch to my feet, I catch Maytepueminner's deathly stare.

No you don't, her expression impeaches me.

424444444

Knowledge of savage experience fills her gaze with an awful apprehension, the force of which freezes me. We are all frozen, by the horrifying realisation that Worethmaleyerpodeyer's place could be any one of ours. Would be any one of ours if we attempted to make a stand.

Shifting in a daze on the now red-stained sand, the bagarrook tries to lift herself to her feet. Blood flows down the side of her temple but she brushes it out of her eyes, determined. Turning to her abuser, Worethmaleyerpodeyer's jaw tightens with all that she wants to say, to scream, but knows she cannot. Instead, she spits the blood pooling in her mouth at the face of her assailant.

That is when I see the gun leaning against the tree and I feel the world fall out from under me. *No.*

With one incensed stride he has it in his hands and aimed at her head. A deathly cry escapes her lips and terror ricochets around my body. Time bends slowly as I watch her turn and run. Every fibre in my being urges her to go faster. One step, two steps, faster, faster.

But I know she is too slow. I know she will always be too slow in those last dangerous seconds. That she could never be quick enough to outrun this white man's wrath.

The shot rings out. A seismic jolt rocks my being. I see it rip through the woman's nawnta sitting in front of me. I see it spin around our circle of stunned women.

And I see it tear apart Worethmaleyerpodeyer's body, splitting open her back, splintering the fragile bones of her neck. In an instant, she crashes to the ground, her murrup torn from her flesh, her lifeless eyes staring at her shattered mound of moonbirds.

Slow, shaking fingers pick mechanically at the calamuses of moonbird feathers, numb in shock, yet still beholden to an unfulfilled quota. Women's weeping ebbs and flows in choked whispers and, sometimes, when the pain of containment is too much, a thin, reedy wail ascends to booroonth, curling around the ribbons of smoke from a still roaring campfire. Flames lick hungrily at their logs, but I cannot feel their warmth. A hollow frost has infused into my bones, freezing them to their core, and not even the roar of a raging inferno could steam off its devastating iciness.

Still now, her crumpled form lies stricken where she fell just behind her nawnta's trembling outline. An old sealer stands by with two shovels, implacable, waiting until the very last moonbird is plucked. In Maytepueminner's steady hands, the final bayadin is quickly added to the piles and we are all released from the bondage of our toil and the heartbreak of watching a countrywoman pass without the touch of a loved one or the grace of her culture's ceremony and song.

With the shackles of a cruel, relentless quota finally released, Wottecowwidyer bursts forth in an agonising cry and stumbles over to her bagarrook's brutalised body. Quivering fingers with nails bitten down, sliced raw by the sharp beaks of fledglings and piercing calamuses, close the lids on her nawnta's perpetually staring eyes. Guttural, the young woman wails loud her mourning song, desperately trying to purge her unfathomable sorrow. Over and over, she punches at her left shoulder to honour her kin and signify the pain and suffering of her untimely death.

Giving the two shovels to Maytepueminner, the old sealer hesitates, then offers an almost imperceptible nod before shuffling away into the yawning anonymity of night. With another of her countrywomen, Maytepueminner heads solemnly towards a sheltered dune, its graceful curves protected by a rare gathering of saltbush. This will be Worethmaleyerpodeyer's place of rest. They start to dig.

Not much in the way of offerings grace these overtaken shores, but I search desperately in the dark to find whatever I can to lay in the resting place. Meendutgarook joins me, followed by Kardingarrook and Nandergarrook. We stumble around the sealers' piles of felled and forsaken trees, through the tufts of scratching grass, down to the tide line of a gently lapping Warrayin.

The hypnotic pattern of her endless cresting waves, their surging boom and retreating lull, washes our senses with its rhythmic balm.

Keeping our bodies close to each other, a pulsing need to feel the comfort of touch, we studiously fumble through drying kelp for whatever treasure we can find. My mind fills with my family, snapshots of so many images playing on the beach, whirling around in the dark, searching for a place of peace.

In the shrouding cover of booroonth, I let myself surrender to the yearning ache for those images to manifest. Sinking to my knees, I take a desperate pause, to rest, to breathe. Around me, my kin do the same, wordless, for what is there to say? Engulfed in shock, in revulsion, in sorrow. In the overwhelming realisation that with only one full cycle of Meeniyan the Moon, every tiny atom in our entire world has fundamentally changed. Pressing close to each other for solidarity, for shape, the only comforting axis to hold us steady in a wildly spinning world.

Only one full cycle of Meeniyan the Moon.

A gust of wind howls and I think I hear the tones of my children's voices, Yearl Yearl's joyous yelp, Boyerup's tinkling laugh. A sob crashes against my constricted throat. My babies' faces loom large, Yearl Yearl's dazzling grin, Boyerup's soulful eyes. In formless air, my fingers trace a trembling line, as if I were running a fingertip, ever so gently, down each delicate, sweet, innocent cheek.

I love you, I whisper.

And in my mind I ask, pray, beg Mornmoot to carry my voice on a breeze, back to my homeland, back to my beaches, back to my bubups' ears. So they will always know.

I love you.

YUWARRABUK
DJIDHU
Run Away

One by one, row by row, I release the dried kuyim skins from their stretched hold. After sorting them into piles according to their size, I take their pegs of sharpened bone to yet another clump of freshly skinned pelts. Our backs bent to the grind of monotonous routine, my countrywomen and I repeat yet another round of row building, pelt pegging, scraping clean and stretching to dry. At night, our toil continues, plucking bare the bodies of moonbirds, a wanton bounty of hundreds still being caught in the sealers' unrelenting plunder.

Yet the greatest burden descends on our weary shoulders in the subdued silence around our women's fire. Five nights have passed since the bright-eyed bagarrook, keeper of story, bringer of laughter, fell to the wrath of a warragul. On Maytepueminner's insistence, our kuunh was moved to the other side of the large wilam, but the wailing echoes of that fateful night still reverberate through the oppressive atmosphere. Looming over every one of us, the crushing spectre of grief stifles all sound, all light. And in the viscous darkness, as our trembling fingers strip all beauty from the bayadin, our collective anguish bleeds all life from our bones.

In daylight, the sorrow lingers. But away from the camping grounds, out in the open air, under the benevolent warmth of a kind Nyawiinth, breath comes a little easier. Resting my tools on the ground, I stand and raise my arms into the air to relieve my aching back. Reaching upwards to the sun's autumnal rays, I pull my bended spine straight and my rounded belly pops forward. Nearby, Nandergarrook brightens at the sight. Growing in parallel, we have both noticed a sudden shift in the blossoming of our bellies, skin stretching tauter, abdomens extending. Especially at night, when we finally sink our spasming backs into the cool contours of a sand-shaped bed, that's when the babies wake up to dance.

Readying myself for another round of scraping kangaroo skins, I sit down and feel a baby's wriggling body churn with sudden vigour. Gaping, Meendutgarrook points to my belly button with glee. Looking down I see what seems to be a tiny finger, pushing through my skin to point back at her.

Konye, Kardingarrook! Meendutgarrook cries.

Her finger still outstretched, she lightly touches the protrusion. For a few seconds, the tiny finger stays still, two points of tenderness touching. Then, it vanishes, leaving both Meendutgarrook and I with broad, beaming grins.

Kardingarrook smiles too, but I notice that the curling warmth playing on her lips does not reach her eyes. Brow furrowed, she shakily picks up a tool.

Liwurruk, are you okay? Meendutgarrook questions in a low voice, tight with concern.

Furtively glancing around, Kardingarrook pauses, hesitant, as if weighing up whether to answer her sister with truth or not. After some reluctance, she whispers, *I noticed Meeniyan was showing only half her face last night, so I wondered if the tides would be low like they are at home.*

Curiosity piqued by the secretive tone, Nandergarrook glances up from driving a bone peg through leathery skin.

With all the attention of her kin upon her, Kardingarrook hesitates again. Grasping her sister's hand in hers, the young bagarrook swallows and continues. *Which they are. Just like ours.*

How do you know? I query, unsure if I really want to hear the answer. Another deep inhale, then Kardingarrook's words spill out in a confessional rush.

I walked to the southern peninsula late last night, into the water and on and on. My feet could still touch for the longest time. And I got so close to those small islands of rocks. So close. Just a quick swim across to the next one. And the next.

Kardingarrook's desperate face turns to Nandergarrook and I, and she beams at us with an eager encouragement. *I know you could do it easily, even with your little ones in your bellies.*

My stomach tightens with trepidation as the young bagarrook continues breathlessly. *Especially with the tide so low. It would be so easy, so quick. Even for the kids, Yanki Yanki, Borodanger. Even Naynar could make it with her leg still healing. With the tide so low. Just one island to the next. And then we would be at those mountains we can see in the distance.*

Cloaked in a shroud of salt air haze, I imagine the cliffs of that Biik rising formidably like the ones we first went to, a headland lined with dark shapes standing on its edge, tumbling down its sides.

Who's to say there are not more of the ngamudji over there, I say. *With guns like the ones here.*

But it might get us closer to home, the girl pleads, her plaintive voice high with emotion.

Having listened quietly to our whispers, Doogbyerumboroke adds her wisdom to the conversation. *That is not the direction of our Biik, niece, however much I wish it was*, she teaches. *Look to mornmoot. Remember the direction of Mindayi's whirlwinds when he shaped the sand dunes over Burinyong Balak estate? Look to the signs in Country –*

But I am, Aunty, Kardingarrook interjects, begging. *The tides are so low, the passage through Warrayin so easy.*

Look to Old Man Sun, Doogbyerumboroke persists sternly, a lesson needing to be taught. *See the change in his pathway as the season cools, the movement of djurt in the night sky. All these signs tell us that our Country is above us, in the north. And remember the angry Warrayin we first crossed, over days and nights? Only our betayil could carry us home over that raging Sea Country.*

As the wind whips against my skin, I notice its cool whistling comes from the southwest and I nod in reluctant surrender.

I'm sorry, liwurruk, it's true. Those mountains are in the south. We would be moving in the wrong direction.

Bitter disappointment clouds Kardingarrook's face, and I see the glimmer of naive hope that had flickered, for the slightest of seconds, wane and snuff out.

We have to find a way! She flushes with an angry outburst, immediately followed by an uncontrollable, wracking sob. A tremor quakes through her hunching body and I see the depth of her fraying spirit, slowly pulled apart by the horror of what she has seen. *I just feel like I need to run*, she whispers.

A piercing whistle rings across the grass tufted field. In the distance, the tiny figure of a man comically flaps his arms up and down, waving for the attention of the sealer dozing on a rock nearby. Caught on the funnelling wind, his hollering finally rouses the ngamudji from a mid-afternoon nap. The shouting stirs Maytepueminner too and she stands attentively to her feet. Whatever message carries on the breeze, they wave an agitated ripple through the ranks of the other island women as well. On his rock, the dozy sealer claps his hands with a new and gleeful purpose, then barks a series of impatient instructions at us. In the barrage of his foreign tongue, I hear a word I have come to learn at the prodding end of a pointed stick.

Move! Move!

Copying the sudden bustle of the island women as they hurriedly gather their tools and pile their unpegged skins in a mound, we quickly finish scraping the pelts in front of us and wipe our oily, bloodied fingers down the backs of our scratching clothes. Pushed into a staggered, fast-moving line, dried kangaroo skins loaded on our backs, we march with Nyawiinth high in the sky in the direction of the cluster of timbered huts. Many of the island women walk so fast it's as though they are on the precipice of a run.

An unknown urgency propels them forward and their palpable tension sends our hearts racing.

Bilang full of tools bounce noisily against Kardingarrook's hips and I notice her shiver violently as she clutches the woven bags slung over her shoulders. Even when she tries to lace her fingers tightly in front of her, they rub and turn in an anxious, revolving spasm.

Primal fear begins to creep its way up my spine. As much as Maytepueminner and her kin seem to want to race towards whatever is happening at the camping ground, my feet are leaden with an impending sense of doom. Kuyim pelts grow impossibly heavy on my shoulders and hang dense, like our culture's fabled blanket of the sky. An insistent thought turns over in my mind.

Is this what it would feel like if the liyan holding up Sky Country were to fail?

A stab of yearning slices my heart as I picture my husband, Bobbinary, alongside his warrior brothers, ploughing through the waters of Warrayin in their bark canoes. Thick, strong arms push their paddles, steady and quick, eager to get home with the iron that would save us all. But was it all in vain? Could it be that the ngamudji's metal has proven too weak for the purpose of the wirrirap? Was his dream a literal premonition of Barrawarn the magpie's ancient props rotting away to nothing? Have the stories of our very Old Ones, the Murrumbunguttia, stooped in the time of shapeless nothing, begun to circle back around?

I see my children flash before me, as toddlers, as children giggling without a care in the world. Could it be they feel the same crushing weight of the falling sky's blanket on their bodies as I do now? This heavy, pressing, suffocating weight that speaks of the end of the world. A weight that speaks of a Fate worse than death.

Chaos erupts around us as we arrive at the edge of the wilams. Dropping the burden of their kangaroo pelts, the island women sprint to a huddling cluster of naked children standing beside a pen full of hooved animals. Their daughters and sons, nieces and nephews, normally carefully kept in the shadows, working in the vegetable gardens, sweeping the huts, washing the clothes, protected from prying eyes and wandering hands. Now, they have been pulled out into the open while their mothers were away, and ringed by an onslaught of new ngamudji. Burly, jostling men who encircle and appraise them, eyes fixed with a hunter's gaze as if the children were game about to be speared.

My knees wobble and bend, buckling as if hit from an unseen force, when I see the captain saunter purposefully towards us, the sealers from his schooner flanking his sides. Behind me, like an emu terrified into flight, Kardingarrook turns on her heel and races back the way we have come. But, as always, a guard is bringing up the rear and he grabs at her flailing body, pinning her arms and throwing her over his shoulder like a dead seal whose skull he's just cracked.

She should have run, I blink with blinding clarity. Last night in low tide, under Meeniyan the moon's half-veiled face, her Liwik showing her the way, she should have run.

I see Nandergarrook standing stunned, elbows tight at her side, hands pressing protectively against the bulge of her belly.

But she wanted to tell us we could make it too. Even with our bodies heavy with babies, there were islands we could swim to. That the children could reach. She wanted us to come too. And she wanted her younger liwurruk beside her.

Before any more of us can move, the men sprint to our sides. In a flurry of rough hands and ripping cloth, they strip every one of us and bind our wrists behind our backs.

Doogbyerumboroke is screaming in our mother tongue, twisting and contorting her body to stay within reach of her bubup. *Don't you savages touch my children!*

Gulping lungfuls of air, a panic-stricken Kardingarrook struggles against the sealer.

She can't breathe, you monstrous Buldjinganu! Meendutgarrook shrieks. *Let my sister go!*

In one sweeping movement, the sealer pulls Kardingarrook from over his shoulder, yanks the clothes from her trembling body and pushes her to the captain who binds her hands behind her back.

Lined up in front of the animal pens, it is all we can do to try to reach for the comfort of each other's skin, pressing into each other's side as the madness swirls around us. Cruel men grab unrestrained at our bodies, pinching our breasts, slapping our buttocks. An old ngamudji forces Yanki Yanki's mouth open to inspect his teeth, while at the same time grabs at the eight-year-old boy's penis. In an instant, Doogbyerumboroke throws herself between the letch and her boy and the old man moves away, a sly grin curling his lips.

Dog, he laughs, spitting on the ground in front of Doogbyerum-boroke's feet. Then he turns on his heel and points to another copper-coloured boy, younger than Yanki Yanki, and declares, *I'll take this one.*

In the circling cacophony of anguished pleas, more men come forward to do business. As I try desperately to keep a hold of Meen-dutgarrook and stay close to my terrified kin, the captain orders us to turn for his customers. We are poked and prodded, our ears and teeth inspected, our flesh pinched, scratched and slapped. With the obvious swelling of our bellies and breasts, Nandergarrook and I are singled out for special measurement.

Beside us, Doogbyerumboroke fights like a magnificent koon-warra, resolute in keeping lecherous hands off her children. Her spitting and snarling keep most away, but one has been watching from the sidelines. Indicating the entire family of four, the ngamudji pulls a small bag from around his neck and reaches into it, pulling out a collection of round metal discs. Slightly bigger than the shiny gold stones on the captain's cloak, these tarnished discs are dropped, one by one, into the captain's palm.

Seven pieces in total. Seven small bits of metal for four human beings. For a proud, strong woman and her three young children.

For our beloved kin. For Doogbyerumboroke, Borodanger, Naynar and Yanki Yanki.

Just like that, the sealer ties his captives to each other and marches them off to a waiting rowboat, bagarrook and bubup in stumbling shock. Eyes wide with confusion, a terror of the unknown that lies ahead, the family looks back at us as they are pulled away. Each other's safe havens in this treacherous new world, shattered now by the sickening realisation that we may never see each other again.

Spent voices ring hoarse with exhaustion, but the three children call out, over and over, *Bambun! Bambun!* We aunties force our lips to turn ever upwards in the hope that our grimaces might be seen as smiles.

Yannadhan! we sing out, our tones thin and scratched. One day, we will walk together on the path again.

Doogbyerumboroke is silent as she stares back at us, stooping under the punishing weight of this new burden she must carry alone. No sisters to sing with, to yarn around the campfire, to help her remember where she is from, what she knows and who she is.

At least they are together, I think.

From high on the hill where the island women smoke their signalling fires, three successive gunshots ring out around the island. Understanding its message, the sealers make haste to finalise their trade. A blur of men, grabbing bound arms, bodies being yanked away. Still clutching each other, we four kinswomen are dragged in a throng towards the waiting rowboats, their pointed faces turned to their parent ships, primed for a quick escape.

I see the captain nod his acceptance and another white man's silver treasure passes between them. Then, in one chaotic minute, cataclysmic in its reordering of our entire universe, our group of four bagarrook is torn asunder. Two men pull Nandergarrook and Kardingarrook in one direction, and another two men pull Meendutgarrook and me in the opposite. A blood-curdling scream sweeps from Kardingarrook as sister is ripped from sister.

Liwurruk!

Twisting and turning, wrists burning against rope, the girls battle to be free, to run back to each other, hold tight and never be prised apart again. But these slender, adolescent bodies are no match for the brute strength of grown men. So easily they are held back, subdued by a crack to the head, a palm around the mouth. Their searing heartache burns with an impotent humiliation. And a devastation so deep it threatens to destroy the tender soul.

I am too numb to wail, too stiff with shock to even breathe. I float above my body, standing and rocking, yet again, on the hard deck of another floating gurrung. My murrup does not want to stay, not here, not in this body, wracked by seizures of compounding, torturous pain. Not in this vessel, stinking of blood and guts, slaughter and rape, greed and plunder, the malevolent sins of the ngamudji.

So, I let my paralysed spirit swirl above it all, my mind too, in its hopeless struggle to comprehend, find meaning, to understand. Relying on my stricken hands to be my only anchor to this boat, I watch, with the feeling of a hollow ghost, as the boats disperse far and wide. In the distance, a tall ship glides into view, its erect, white masts like a three-finned beast patrolling its shores. This is what those shots were heralding, what the pariahs of the islands are running from.

As a gusting mornmoot blows us back into the endless expanse of an untamed Warrayin, the last thing I see is a young girl on a boat. Her sunken eyes and wretched face speak of a soul drowning in sorrow.

It is Wottecowwidyer. And standing beside her, a possessive grip on the nape of her neck, is the sealer who murdered her kin.

MARRAMBAYIK
I Am

Seven days on the open sea and any sense of footing I held in this world is lost. Far, far away, shapes of Country loom hazy at the very edge of Warrayin, promising a stable shore, blessed relief from this fretful rocking. Each glimpse of rising earth sends my mind to my Homelands and I fantasise it is my Biik peeking above the horizon, that its headland is Monmar and, standing as sentinels, my family are waiting.

I fashion all of the giant forms of land into Boonwurrung Biik, even as we travel further along a changing coastline, day after day. Even as the sealers' vessel follows the early autumn path of Nyawiinth, tracking with Old Man Sun's daily descent in the West, I choose to ignore the truth of this direction. That we are travelling away from where my Homelands truly lie. Instead, I continue transforming far away contours of earth into the cliffs and valleys, beaches and streams of my blessed Biik. *Soon*, I whisper to the misty outlines of land across the sea, *soon, I will be home.*

Hours I endure against the side of the boat, with Meendutgarrook beside me, fingers interlaced, searching the long blue line of the horizon for the wisps of our mothers' and aunties' smoke. Turning our ears to the wind, we try to catch their voices in yingali, singing out the threads of a songline to guide us back to them. Even though we know the truth of the cries we hear on mornmoot's gusts, plaintive calls of gulls, bayadin, sea eagles, we still turn to each other in willing delusion and ask, *Did you hear that? Was that the song of our murndigarrook?*

Seven days since our kin were ripped from our safe embrace, yet we stay resolutely anchored in the same place on the slaving sealers' boat, standing tall, fierce, facing out to the ocean.

Meendutgarrook and I steady each other with linked arms, turning our backs on the brutal reality behind us. We choose not to acknowledge the bustle of foreign men on the deck, the stench of their sweat melding with the reeking remnants of blood and rotting animal flesh, seeped into every crack and furrow of the splintered deck. Following the arch of Nyawiinth across Sky Country, we know we have a span of light to keep the gathering shadows at bay. At least for the time of Old Man Sun's journey from one side of Warrayin's expanse to the other. In this dome of sunlight, we find some comfort. Light bears witness, light sees the truth. And when it slips below the edge of the world, everything changes.

Each night he comes for me, the sealer who bought me. Darkness is his friend. He uses the cloak of booroonth to hide his reprehensible acts. To cover the swell of my belly where the rightful man's baby grows, the fire in my eyes when I fight against his aggression, my disgust when he violates me. Darkness is his accomplice. Keeping the crimes of his weakness, his shamefulness, his pathetic immorality, a shrouded, dirty secret.

Only when he is done does he light a tiny flame, flickering like a fragile flower at the tip of a stem. In this dimmest of glows, I hold my stare and let contempt crease every resolute line in my face. I will make sure this lambent light bears true witness to the iniquity of his actions. That it lays bare the rotting weakness at the core of his character. I see the truth of who he is. And he knows.

Jabbing a filthy finger at my chest, he growls, *You are mine.*

My gaze is steady as I see the staunch women of my clan flash through my mind, lining up in a formation ready to fight. *I am Nannertgarrook.*

A derisive chortle sputters from his lips. *I name you Eliza.*

My kin shake their heads in my mind and I do the same, standing tall, like a mighty turrung before a storm, deep roots grounding a towering canopy. *Nannertgarrook.*

A fist slams on wood next to my head. Air gusts from his mouth, nearly snuffing out the candle's flame.

No! Eliza.

Implacable, I feel my bones harden like a woman's clay tool baked and forged in fire. The strength of my Liwik, the Old Ones, surges through me. The very cells of a long line of murndigarrook who have come before me and course through my blood still, pulse in my flesh.

I am Nannertgarrook.

Striking with the full force of a pitiful coward caught in the exposing light, the sealer's fist hammers the side of my head. I feel my brain thud against my skull and a high-pitched ringing envelops my ears. Staying centred as I sway, I make sure my feet stand firm on the steady shoulders of my Ancestors.

You are no-one, I hear him spit as he turns to leave. *Eliza No-one!*

Staring into the flickering flame of the candle as it settles and grows stronger, I watch its white-hot fire reach into the air, burning brighter as it ascends. I let its light seep into my cells, reshaping every fibre in my being, cleansing, healing.

I am not Eliza, I whisper, a certainty steeling my tone. *I am not No-one.*

As I close my eyes, I picture every woman and girl in my clan. I picture each shell stacked in the thousands of lines of our Keeping Places. I picture the world spinning in a vortex of time, traveling through thousands upon thousands of years, and the women who thrived over those epochs. I picture my body, my heart, my spirit, my murrup, composed of a fragment from every single one of these women since Time Immemorial. Yes, they are me and I am them. Yes, I know who I am.

I am Nannertgarrook.

BARRING DJINANG
Footprints

Cracks on my knuckles divide more with every shovel of salt I haul into the sealers' bags. The windless autumn day burns hot on yet another island our captors have brought us to. Midday Nyawiinth bakes my arms, cooled only by the beads of sweat dripping from my forehead. Leached from every pore, water drains out my body, leaving my cells parched. A yearning gnaws at my bones, to drink from the fresh, sweet waters of Langwarrin, to dive into the cooling arms of Warnmarring on the shores of my Biik.

But I am here instead. On a lonely island distanced from the mainland, once belonging to another invaded people, hauling daily the salt from their dried lagoons, bag by heavy bag, along interminable lengths of sandy track to the waiting ngamudji boat on the bay. And when each wearisome day finally closes, the nightmare continues, caught in the wilam of the sealer who calls me No-one.

Quicker, the red-faced man barks as he scrapes every crystal of salt he can from the lagoon into stretching rows of gleaming white mounds, lining up to be bagged by a disparate collection of countrywomen, all taken from their Homelands and imprisoned here. *Quicker, you lazy dogs.*

I know some of their words now. I know when they call us their dogs, when they tell us we are too slow or too stupid or too weak. My ears can hear the meaning of their words now but my tongue refuses to shape them. My lips hold onto my own language, speaking it in whispers to Meendutgarrook as we trek our weary bodies back and forth along this relentless track.

I keep my language close for the baby growing rapidly inside me. Our words sing the rhythms and tunes of Country, songlines that tether our spirits to culture, to Biik and to each other. This little one taking shape in my body will know their mother's tongue so they can speak to their Country when we at last return. As I keep close an image of my bubup's tiny feet buried in the sands of Monmar, the baby tumbles in my belly, eager to be out and running with those quick feet along the shore.

Lifting the now full bag over my shoulder, my legs tremble under the load of both the salt and my swollen body. Meendutgarrook shoots out a steadying hand until I regain balance. Together we set off on yet another five-mile march to the coast, our voices low, using what little breath we have to sing the songs of our Old Ones, the prop of their ancient stories keeping us upright.

We sing too of the Biik underneath our feet. Five days on this salt laden island and we know most of its curving contours. Mapping as much of the land that we can see on our trudge over sandy dunes and scrubby ridges, Meendutgarrook and I sing its songlines to remember as many of its pathways as we can. Tracks that lead to strips of placid beach, or wind blasted boulders, or sheltered rock-pools that tantalise with the bounty they may hold. Trails that we will remember to return to when the lagoons have been stripped of their salt, and our long daily labour of sack carrying is done. But we haven't yet seen any barring that might show us a secret path of escape. Ngamudji know well how to imprison, choosing only those islands that one cannot leave, too far away from any other adjoining land, with a wild and unforgiving Warrayln in between. Still we sing the maps of this Biik, for one day we might find a pathway which will lead us to our freedom.

Ahead of us on the salt trail, a gathering of bagarrook huddle under the dappled shade of a moonah tree. Drawing closer, we see a woman lying on her side, face creasing in pain, the flesh of her backside exposed between the coarse folds of ngamudji cloth. A scar gapes across her buttock, red and inflamed, trying to heal but weeping at its edges, made angry by the relentless movement of stride after stride under salty weight.

Sealer knife, explains Kalungku in the white man's tongue, slicing through the air with a deliberate gesture to show the callous carving of the woman's flesh. *Too slow clean kangaroo skin.*

Her dark eyes flash with barely constrained rage. Fierce this one. Proud. Sharp gaze always watching, calculating, clever. We joined her and her kin on the salt trail the same afternoon the sealer's gurrung rowed ashore, the ngamudji wasting no time in putting us to work to replenish their bags of round metal discs. On that first day, while we stopped under a leafy turrung's shade, Kalungku placed her hands on my belly and sang a welcome song in her language to the bubup and us. Travelling together on the main trail, she would point out the tracks branching off and gesture how long each one was, describing with her hands as best she could, what we would find at the end of it. Then, at the apex of the winding path leading to the bay, Kalungku stopped and stared at a hazy shape rising just above the distant horizon. Land, a long way from here. Slowly, deliberately, she pointed to the tantalising glimmer of Biik, then placed her hand on her heart. Tapping on her chest, she sung an acknowledgement, hoarse with emotion, then indicated back to the mainland. We understood the agonising meaning. Her heart belonged there. That glimpse of sea-misted Biik was her Country. So achingly close, so achingly far away.

Kalungku!

An older woman calls the bagarrook to assist, passing her a strip of clean cloth. This slender murndigarrook, black hair streaked with a sweeping line of grey, thin fingers adept with the nimbleness of a healer, retrieves bush ointment from the inside of a conical shell, kept in the pocket of her ill-fitting clothes. Dabbing at the old wound, she speaks soft words of encouragement in her own lilting language. Little by little, the medicine forms a slick shield over vulnerable flesh but it could never heal completely such a permanent maiming. *Too slow*, was the white man's argument and yet, in forever scarring his enslaved, he ensures that is all she can be henceforth.

Bulaadu stupid ngamudji, Meendutgarrook murmurs as if reading my mind. *Small minds only thinking of themselves.*

Nodding in agreement, I add, *Quick in base emotion, slow in considered thought.*

Bulaadu wongurrunin, we mutter in unison.

Once the murndigarrook has covered the wound in her healing ointment, Kalungku winds a band of clean cloth around the weakened woman's waist and backside. And then, knowing the deadly consequences that await from being too slow in our labour, we stand as one, a bonded flock of burribarri picking our way over the endless path once more.

In the monotonous rhythm of step after step, my mind leaps between memories, replaying them over and over with every stride. About the ghostly vision of Wottecowwidyer, her small frame shivering under the vice-like grip of the sealer who murdered her kin. I remember those fateful minutes before her world spun off its axis. The dancing eyes and ready laugh of her protector, her nawnta, Worethmaleyerpodeyer. A natural storyteller, who, if left in the peaceful continuum of the life she was born into, would have taught her clan's children the first intriguing layers of knowledge, opening their shining eyes to the wonder of the world around them.

Anguish hammers in my chest as I remember Worethmaleyerpodeyer, only a few weeks ago, setting the moonbird down in her lap, freeing her expressive hands to gesture the story, helping us understand its essence despite the differences of tongue. Fateful, fleeting minutes when feathers were not plucked and a stalking shadow of evil lurked behind, counting the seconds and keeping his deathly score.

If only, if only, if only. If only she had kept plucking that bayadin she might still be alive today.

Worries flicker about my own countrywomen. I imagine Nandergarrook's belly swelling as quickly as my own, the bubup within tumbling in preparation for their arrival, and I wonder if my liwurruk has the soothing arms of other women by her side to help her when that time comes. I wonder if, I hope that, one of those is Kardingarrook, as kin still tethered to each other. Sweet, playful, sensitive Kardingarrook, whose cries in the chaos of separation echo around my ears like a mournful mornmoot trapped in an ever-spinning whirlwind.

If only hammers my mind as the midday sun burns the sand under my feet. *If only* she had followed the whispers of her Liwik, beckoning her across Warrayin to each island haven, like giant stepping stones, forming the only possible path away from an enslaved fate of perpetual servitude. *If only* she hadn't waited for us.

The memory of Doogbyerumboroke pierces my mind with her blazing rage, aflame in all the righteousness of a koonwarra defying any odds, to fight each and every monster coming for her young. Soft hands, that should be holding necklaces of shells, the reeds of partly woven binuk, the taut skin of a marngrook ball, instead clinging fearfully to each other. Shoulder to shoulder stand the children, Borodanger, Naynar and Yanki Yanki, with Doogbyerumboroke's desperate arms around them, a whole family swept up in a tumultuous, treacherous tide that threatens to pull them all under. *If only, if only, if only,* those girls hadn't followed the lure of the strange, gleaming trinkets dangling from Maytepueminner's arms.

I blink back the stinging rush of tears as the images of my own family crowd my pulsing mind. Pictures of Bobbinary's smiling eyes, Yearl Yearl's cheeky grin, Boyerup's soulful gaze. Stuck now on an unbearable loop is that excruciating scene. My son racing down the sand dunes towards the beach, my husband close behind with spear raised. The wide, panicked eyes of my daughter staring at me from behind a rock sentinel on the shore of my once peaceful Monmar. My family, my clan, my Country. If only I was still with them.

One step falters, then the next and I come to a shuddering stop on the trail of this isolated island far away from home.

If only, I whisper, an agonising ache throbbing through every limb. *If only that boat had never come.*

Our wall of salt-stuffed bags, built over countless five-mile journeys from lagoon to coast, lines a makeshift platform of tree trunks and rope. Tethered to this, a floating pathway leads out to a small collection of masted vessels and their rowboats, anchored to Warrayin's ocean floor by plunging arrows of iron. Many men gather here, most not staying for long, taking their pick of salt and skin, kangaroo and seal, and sometimes women and children, before striking back out into the deep blue.

Ngamudji travelling through this place are marked in the different colours of their Ancestors' lineage, evident in the tones of their skin and hair, shocks of red beard or flaxen yarra on their head, like the sun-bleached sands of Wamoom's coved shores. Some have brown or black hair too but always a pale skin, sometimes tanned by the sun or flecked in red dots the same as their flaming hair.

Not just ngamudji pass through this meeting place but men with skins of darker shades. Some wear designs drawn in lines of permanent ochre, others show jagged scars that speak of aggression, not knowledge, purpose or ritual. Sometimes countrymen come to shore but they are not from our clans, nor our allied confederacies, and often, it appears, not under the sail of their own free will.

Regardless of what version of man steps upon these shores, and even though their labours on the ocean may be long and arduous, it is always us black women who do the greater share of work on this prison island. It is our legs faltering under the weight of leaden bags of salt, our broken backs stiffening as we bend to peg, scrape and stretch carcass after bloody carcass, our hands blistering after day upon day of cleaning, cooking, shovelling, scraping, sewing.

And it is our bodies, taken at whim, whenever it pleases the ngamudji, that lay bruised and aching in the night with the repeated damage of violation.

The sealers who bought us, from the captain who stole us, for a handful of round metal discs, spend their days in languid ease. Sitting on platforms carved from felled trees, patchwork rugs of kangaroo skin, sewn by our hands, stretched across their knees, looking out to sea, occasionally pointing to the shapes of ngamudji vessels on the horizon. Packing a pipe tool fashioned from clay with their pungent, dried, from far away plant, the men bend the tool to the fire and light its top, sucking the smoke into their bodies, then releasing its heavy cloud back into the air above their heads.

No great learning, no ceremony nor ritual accompanies the imbibing, aside from picking up the tool whenever they are compelled to rest. Which is often, their bodies proving to be weak from an inability to run and hunt with a spear, wasted by the lazy hours watching others work. Instead, they talk over and over again about the smashing of their prized vessel two nights after we arrived. Of the careless idiots who anchored it in a treacherous bay on the wrong side of the island. The surging of the southern tides throwing the boat against the rocks like a child's tarnook.

Moaning about their bad luck, being forced into isolation against their will on this island, the men suck their pipes, blow their smoke and spit on the sand, all the while plotting ways to gather enough of the ngamudji's prized treasure to buy their way out of this forced layover. As each bag of salt we countrywomen carry is given to the passing vessels moored by the shore, the sealers dig up a secret box buried in the far corner of the wilam that holds their bags of metal. Money, they call it. Even greater worth are the thin pieces of a strange feathered bark, carefully rolled and bound by leather ties. Money, they call this paperbark as well, unwrapping it carefully, adding a new sliver when enough bags have been taken, counting it over and over again, then burying it once more in the corner of their wilam. A treasure valued above all else. Their money.

I cannot understand it. Prized more than everything that is relentlessly taken, slaughtered, felled and sold, all for the flimsy material in the sealers' box. Often, I wonder what would happen if, one fine day at the end of my time, I picked up that box and threw it into the fire. Watching, smiling, as all their schemes and plans are consumed by smoke, reduced to powdered ash in minutes. A few stunning moments in the fire would reveal how foolish their treasure is, how pointless. But look at how much rampant destruction they wrought to get it.

Wisps of paper-thin bark in return for the plunder of all that Country offers. Boundless bounty taken, not to provide sustenance, nor eat, nor warm, nor share among their clan, but to pass from one to the other for money. But one day, I think, as I picture that box engulfed by flames, these ngamudji will see. When all has been taken and slaughtered and felled, when there is nothing left but emptiness and death, only then will they realise they have nothing. Except their money. *And I'd like to see them eat that*, I smirk.

Meendutgarrook lifts the lid on the ngamudji's metal pot, releasing the succulent aroma of stewing kangaroo tail into the sheltered confines of the sealers' wilam. Piling up their flat, metal bowls, she ladles a generous portion of cooked kuyim onto each, then gives the plates to me. From under smouldering coals and earth, I pull a risen mound of damper made with the white man's flour and seasoned with wattle seed collected on our travels between lagoon and coast. I break two large portions for the men and set aside what is left for Meendutgarrook and me.

In between filling the sealers' plates until they are satisfied, we snatch what scraps we can. As we watch the ngamudji fill their cups several times over with firewater, we know we might be pulled to lie in their beds tonight if they so desire. It is only when Meeniyan the Moon is high in booroonth, and the Seven Munmundiik

Sisters have begun their slide across a shimmering Sky Country, do Meendutgarrook and I take our hardened pieces of bread away from the snoring men in the wilam to our own secret fire, nestled between dune and saltbush.

This aloneness, when the ngamudji are finally asleep, like the slow exhaling of long-held breath, is what fuels us through the endless days. Our moments of stillness, of togetherness, bodies warmed by fire and cloak, the whispering of our language in song and story to each other. In the erasure of darkness, hearing the rush of ocean onto mornmoot-swept shores, we pretend we are sheltered in the dunes near our women's Keeping Places, safely ensconced in the sacred places of our Biik, and surrounded by our people as has always been.

Most nights, we reminisce about memories from home, stories of swimming races in the bay of Nerrm, dolphins joining in to show how it's done, the moment when Meendutgarrook did her longest dive and found her very first wurrdin shell. Laughing over our long lists of questionable sightings of koormangarrook at a multitude of tidal rockpools along our women's songline tracks. That time when Bobbinary raced Barrunan up a gigantic wurrun to see who could reach a wallert wallert drey first.

Tonight, though, Meendutgarrook is quiet. Nibbling at her bread, she stares into the fire, lost in a daze. It is not until a tear slides down her cheek that I understand her stillness comes from a shroud of grief, mantled heavy on her shoulders.

What's wrong? I ask.

I know there are so many possible answers to that question in our current existence. But she understands what I mean and when she replies, her voice is that of a little girl, pained and high-pitched, strained under a hopeless sadness.

I haven't had my bleed. Stifling the upswell of emotion threatening to burst, Meendutgarrook chokes on a rising sob. *I wanted to have Barrunan's baby.*

Heaving with suppressed sobs, lines of despair creasing across her face, confusion mingled with naive disbelief, Meendutgarrook's whole body trembles with all this means. In that moment, I see the child she still is. The young, fourteen-year-old girl who, not so long ago skipped along the forgiving shores of our Homelands with the other munmundiik.

Not so long ago, that gaggle of girls would giggle, collect shells, weave small binuk, work on their emu feather skirts, and whisper among themselves about who might be the first to pass through the ceremonies that teach of womanhood. And still, after Meendutgarrook's small munmundiik body had shed her first blood only a few months ago, after she had swum with the dolphin at the base of the women's ngargee cliffs, after she had endured her first bagarrook scar, donned her dilburnayin and had the initial layers of ancient knowledge opened to her, still Meendutgarrook had to wait until the murndigarrook decided.

Even though she had been promised to Barrunan for some time and they had shared glances and secret smiles, even though she had started to dream of when they might be able to finally hold hands and walk together, maybe brush their lips and bodies against each other, Meendutgarrook still had to wait until her mother, aunties and Elders decided the time was right for her to be married. Until her body, her heart, her mind and her murrup were truly ready.

Those summer days, just a few months ago, as Old Man Sun climbed high in the sky and the hot, dry days stretched long, Meendutgarrook learnt the art of lasting the long dives the fishing bagarrook made for abalone and crayfish. She watched other women with swelling bellies carve out their cradling tarnook and stretch out the softest wallert wallert skins, all in preparation for the soon-arriving bubup. And she waited for the Elders to tell her it was now her time, that she was ready for her marital ceremony and all it would mean.

Those last evenings, around the murndigarrook's campfire late at night, I sat with my mother and the other old women. With the hypnotic loop of Warrayin surging over the shores of Monmar, lulling all else to sleep, we mended the long funnels of yurok nets to trap the season's travelling eels, and the Elders talked. In murmured agreement, they finally decided it would be Meendutgarrook's time. Old knowledge demanded that close attention be given to the girl's body and spirit. Readiness must be whole, the entirety of the being, before the munmundiik could truly ascend into womanhood and the roles of wife and mother.

Around that fire, the murndigarrook decided that when the chill descended over Country and autumn began to slow the pace of life, when the first rains fell and the slow burns prepared the grasslands for greening, when the kangaroo and emu began their feasts and clans could reunite around the ngargee gurrubayin of Wonga, that is when the marriage would be planned.

A message stick bearing the joyous news would be carried to the other clan estates to join us for the marriage of Burinyong Balak, Waa man Barrunan and Werribee Yalak, Bunjil woman Meendutgarrook. Giddiness filled me that night thinking of the jubilation my young cousin would feel when she learnt of the news she had waited so long to hear. And then, just a few days later, that rowboat arrived on our shores.

Two full turns of Meeniyan the Moon since that fateful day and we sit in the sand of a new island prison. Nights are growing colder, days becoming shorter. Ants build the mounds of their nests higher in anticipation of rain to come. The wintry chill of Perrin is soon to descend. And, in another Time, around the fires of our murndigarrook, nestled in the sheltering dunes of Kullurk, a message stick bearing the news of Meendutgarrook and Barrunan's marriage would be carved. To herald an occasion of excited anticipation, celebration, and knowledge earning ceremony. In a Time that once was, but not now.

Instead, rocking back and forth before me, this not-quite-child, not-quite-woman, convulsed with a singular agony. All she had dreamed of was gone and the path before her, bound to a foreign captor, to the ngamudji devoid of our people's ancient knowledge or understanding, was inexplicable, even in nightmare.

In our late-night solitude of stories and songs from home, we both fanned the flame of hope that it would not be long before we were back in the arms of our Country and culture. With the black cloak of booroonth hiding the real world around us, we could imagine that soon we might wake up and discover we had been sung back to the life we were meant to be living. Back to a sacred wedding with Barrunan, and maybe, if the Ancestors decided the time was right, a piece of djurt would manifest as a Boonwurrung bubup in the making.

But we are where we are. And all I can do now is grab Meendutgarrook's writing form and hold her tight.

I have something to show you, I whisper.

From behind a stack of firewood only a few short strides away from where my captor sleeps, I pull a stuffed hessian bag from its hiding place. Back at the fire, I show Meendutgarrook the collection of soft scraps of kangaroo skin I have saved and hidden over these past few weeks. Dried kangaroo sinew is pressed between the strips, alongside the pointed knob of a kuyim's incisor tooth and three small fingers of bone, ends sharpened, ready to sew.

I have enough for both of our bubup.

Tears flow unimpeded down Meendutgarrook's grief-pinched face.

We may not have our family, our ceremony, possum skins, the songs and stories we have yet to learn. We may not ever learn the knowledge that is our birthright, I say, my eyes likewise brimming over. *We may not see the songlines of the lives we imagined we would walk.* I place strips of kuyim and sinew in her lap and mine. *But we have each other. Bellies that might yet grow babies. Little cloaks we can sew to keep them warm. The very cells of our Liwik to pass into their bodies, strong and continuous, no matter what else mixes in their blood.*

Biting her lip, Meendutgarrook nods, inhaling the crisp night air into her lungs. Long breaths out slowly ebb the tide of her heartache. Shakily, she clutches a length of kuyim skin and a sharpened bone. I thread the strings of sinew, and together we start to sew.

MARDAN MARDAN
Crying Crying

Over the next few days, we trudge the long track from lagoon to sea, carrying sacks of salt on our backs, again and again. Late each night, when the snores of the ngamudji drone in the air, signalling a blessed respite, my cousin and I sew strip after strip of fur into two tiny makeshift pelts to wrap warmth and culture around our babies. As the patchwork strips slowly grow into blankets, we talk about the designs we will carve into the threads of skin with the kuyim's incisor. Bunjil the wedge-tailed eagle soars in the sky as our moiety guardian. But our men belong to Waa the raven, protector of the Kulin clan estate of the Burinyong Balak, and so too our children are covered under his ebony reach. Clever one is Waa, and so his intelligent eyes and shielding wing will begin our bubups' stories etched on their cloaks, hovering over the contours of the bended-knee peninsula of their true Biik.

When our embers burn low and we grow tired, it is time to fold the prized kuyim cloaks and secret them away behind the stack of firewood. Before we can sneak our weary bodies to rest in the sealers' wilams, the low rustle of saltbush catches our attention.

In the pale light of the slivered moon, a pair of dark eyes shines through the shadows of the wilam, staring at me. It is Kalungku.

Stepping into the waning firelight, the woman holds a finger to her lips. Then, she points to a barrel of firewater tucked behind the sealer's timbered trunk of ngamudji treasure.

Immediately, I shake my head, knowing that if we were caught stealing this revered elixir, it would be lashings of knotted rope to the back, or knives carving pieces of flesh at a wronged sealer's whim. Meendutgarrook stares as well, the same dreaded thoughts travelling through her mind.

Pointing this time to me, Kalungku shakes her head too, and then rests it against pressed hands to indicate that I should go to sleep. I laugh silently, rueful in the knowledge that it would not matter whether I was truly asleep or not, if the firewater was stolen, I would still get the blame.

But it is clear the bagarrook is resolute. I turn to the barrel and notice the grubby jug the sealers use at night to hold their firewater over dinner. Could there be anything left in that?

Ever so cautiously, my breath holding tight in my chest, I pick my way over to the trunk. Slowly, I lift its lid just enough to get my hand inside and avoid the creaking I know will come if I push it any higher. My fingers feel for the small metal bowl tucked in the corner, placed there after washing up from the sealer's dinner. I pull the cup painstakingly from the trunk, then lower the lid.

Body tense, I bend to the jug of firewater, and delicately wind loose its grooved stopper. A waft of acrid vapour hits my nostrils. There is liquor in here still.

Lifting the jug, I try to weigh the leftover firewater and calculate how much I can syphon for Kalungku. A tremor runs through my fingers and I steady them before pouring as much of the liquid as I dare into the cup. I set the jug carefully back in its place and wind the stopper closed to the position it was originally in.

Satisfied that the scene appears undisturbed, I tiptoe back through the wilam, cradling the bowl of dangerous liquid in my trembling hands. With Kalungku and Meendutgarrook following softly behind, I head to the sheltering dunes. Once again shrouded by darkness, I turn to Kalungku and demand an explanation.

Why?

I show you, she whispers, her voice grim, eyes sombre.

Seeing an eager Meendutgarrook, I shake my head and tell her she is not to come. *It might not be safe, and you need to get some rest now.*

Before she can disagree, I turn her around and firmly send her in the direction of our women's wilam, positioned beside the camp of the snoring, wheezing sealers who bought us.

Dotted around the docile bay where ngamudji ships moor and a collection of coves, ridges and beaches on the calm side of the island rest, a disparate assortment of shelters are scattered. Black women and their children live in these, captives like us, torn from Homelands near and far. Some, like Kalungku, can see their Biik just beyond the treacherous Warrayin. Others, like us, come from a great many days and nights away. What we all share in common is the warragul who keep us here, trapped on a prison island, to work for their money, slave for their wants, submit to their every whim.

Often, in the early rise of morning, a bagarrook from a distant wilam might use her breakfast fire in the old way, sending a covert signal if something is wrong, or a new ship is coming, or a warning that storms are rolling in. Sometimes, even earlier, before Nyawiinth has peeked his fiery head above the eastern horizon line, a bagarrook might steal away to a different part of the island, to a favoured rockpool, a hidden pocket of women's bush medicine, a special quarry of sacred ochre. Often a clandestine cluster of other women might join her on these trails, sometimes even Meendutgarrook and me.

Tonight though, Kalungku leads me in a different direction, well past any wilams or trails, down to a windswept smattering of isolated scrub. Wedged between dune and rock, a makeshift wilam, barely two pieces of crumbling bark and branches, is surrounded by a huddle of weeping women. Despite the lateness of the hour, the campfire still burns bright. Above the fire, hanging on a crossbeam in the tradition of the sealers, a handled, metal tarnook dangles precariously. Water steams and bubbles within it and, every now and then, a woman dabs a piece of cloth into the liquid then moves away.

Motioning for me to come quickly, Kalungku hurries over to an older woman kneeling on the ground. Her hunched shoulders rock as if buffeted by unseen currents of sadness. When she looks up at me, her shadowed eyes speak of a desolate grief. I offer my metal cup of firewater to the bagarrook. She takes it, but rather than drinking it herself, she shuffles towards a small, blanket-covered mound lying on a large cloak of kangaroo skin.

A shocking wave of realisation crashes over me when I see the reason for the stolen firewater. It is for a young boy, barely eight years old, his brown skin sallow and beaded in sweat, the hues of the desperately ill. He is curled up on his side like a baby, and even though he is covered by the thickest blanket while the campfire burns close by, he shivers as if pummelled by an icy wind. A moist piece of cloth lies across the side of his head and I realise it is like the one being dipped into the tarnook of water simmering over the fire.

The older woman tends to him with the desperate focus of a grieving mother. Kneeling by his side, she places the cup of firewater close to his face. In her other hand she holds a bleached white pipi shell, the inside curving like a tiny bowl, cleaned and honed for a particular purpose. Dipping the shell into the cup of firewater, she pools a mouthful of liquid into it, then moves the muryok to her boy's lips. With painstaking care, she tucks her hand under the side of his face and lifts it gently.

The boy whimpers, a high-pitched, exhausted bleat that pierces my heart and floods my mind with images of my children. In this little one's face, I remember my own yanyean, Yearl Yearl, his spark, the wondrous innocence, the mischief. That is what I should see in this boy now. Running along the sands of these new shores, splashing in Warrayin's shallows, chasing minnows in the rivulets, climbing trees, collecting treasures, shouting, jumping, playing, laughing. Pulsing with the unashamed, vibrant joy of a little boy.

Instead, he is curled tight around himself, trying to conserve what minuscule spark of childhood murrup still flickers through his body, as his desperate mother raises a shell full of firewater to his lips. My mind races with questions about what afflicts him, an accident, some strange illness from the ngamudji, an evil sorcery or the workings of this island prison's bad spirits. Only something terrible would force a mother to pass the white man's burning firewater through her child's lips.

Behind me, a young woman dips another cloth into the steaming water of the metal tarnook. Using a sharpened stick, she lowers it in, then pulls it out several times before letting the saturated cloth hang above the tarnook, steaming in the chill of the late-night air. When it is cool enough to touch, the bagarrook cups the cloth and carries it over to where the boy lies. Studying the mother, the young woman waits for her signal. Dipping the pipi shell once more into the cup, the babayin holds her son's head up to drink another mouthful of the sealer's firewater, then gently lays his head back down.

More settled now, the boy murmurs sleepily as he rests once more against the soft kangaroo fur. In a soothing, raspy whisper, his mother sings him a lullaby in their language. Some of the other women join in, Kalungku too, and the purity of their tones in unison momentarily lifts the heavy desolation that hangs in the air. Sedated by firewater and the sounds of his murndigarrook's love around him, the bubup drifts off into a numbing slumber.

It is then that I see the full horror of what has happened. With a quick nod to the young woman holding the clean cloth, the mother tenderly pulls away the covering over one side of the boy's face, and the bagarrook lays the clean piece in its place. Even in that split second, I can see, too starkly, the gaping, festering wound where the boy's ear should be. Bone and mottled blood, pus and jagged pieces of flesh are all that is left. A queasy revulsion rushes from my gut, threatening to burst out of my mouth in a wail or a scream or hurling sickness.

They cut off his ear. The thought, like a question, like a condemnation, like a howl, ricochets around my mind. *They cut off his ear.*

Digging my feet into the sand with every step, I hope that Biik will keep me steady as I stagger back to my captor's wilam. Pounding thick in my ears, my heart hammers blood through my shaking body and whirling mind. Twenty-nine steps I count, away from the makeshift wilam hidden in scrub, away from the weeping songs of the bereft babayin and her countrywomen. Twenty-nine steps away from that poor, brutalised boy whose crime was apparently so terrible, so unforgivable, that his punishment warranted the severing of his tiny ear. Twenty-nine steps around the rise of a dune endlessly shifting in a southerly wind, and I bend over with a sickness that hurls out in a vicious, retching groan. Every fibre of my being in rictus, clenched in a nauseating horror that rolls through me over and over.

They cut off his ear.

For the next three nights, he lingers. Each day, with every trudging journey hauling salt bags through the sand, I think of him. I think of his mother, watching her child suffer and slip away, and how her soul will be forever lacerated with irreconcilable cuts, never to be seen but an agony always to be felt. And I think of my bubup, my Yearl Yearl and Boyerup, and I desperately try to erase the image of a sealer's knife at their heads.

Each night, with Meendutgarrook by my side, we cook and serve, clear and clean, and wait for the middle of the night to arrive. While the men eat and drink, smoke and laugh, plotting their fortunes by the fire, I pour as much firewater from its barrel as I can fit in my cup. When all is finally still, we steal over the dunes to the boy's wilam. On the fourth night, we arrive to a low burning fire and an empty camp. Faintly, on a fleeting mornmoot, we hear the women's cries, mardan mardan.

He has departed.

As I try to sleep that night, I think about all I know of the journey our murrup continues when we leave our bodies. riding on our whale to Karralk, climbing the golden pink rays of the setting sun to reach Pindayi in Sky Country and the starry djurt of our Creation Beings and Liwik. I wonder if that is the journey this little boy will take, if those are the stories this disparate band of country-women and their children carry with them from their culture. Do they revere the whales who travel such long distances to carry a soul across the sea? Or do they have some other Creation Being of their Dreaming as guide and protector?

Like us, do they paint the kalk of their beloved bubup in the red and orange hues of love and blood and ngargee? Do they circle their eyes in white ochre, following the contours of that bony cradle that holds the mind and the window to other times? What songs make their mourning yingali, wishing the murrup well on their journey, asking their Liwik to show them the right path to Sky Country? And is that Karralk for them? Do they ascend, like us, on the rays of the setting sun or is it a mountain they climb or the stretching boughs of an ancient turrung?

I remember Bindergarrook carrying the sacred remains of her bubup in her tightly woven binuk. Preparing for ceremony at our time-honoured bay, flushed with the sweet water of the Burrabong, carrying life-giving sustenance through the clan estate of the Barinyung Balak. This sanctuary, flanked by towering rock sentinels formed as Mother Whale thrashed her tail, cushioned by the sandy folds of our embedded Keeping Place, held the memory of countless cycles of ngargee. And on that day, it was a sombre ceremony to farewell a precious babe which called us together.

A group of wise murndigarrook led the bereaved mother with her sacred bilang around Babayin Betayil's rock that afternoon, the keepers of revered knowledge earned through years of ceremony, years of walking the ancient songlines of sacred women's business. My hungry eyes followed their every move, yearning to know what they knew, desperately hungry to understand the layer upon layer of mysteries of our Old Ones, our spinning worlds, our long stretching times.

But I thought then, I must be patient. A teacher has to be taught first, must wait and watch, listen and absorb. But a restlessness taunted me. An urge to race around the rockpools and follow the murndigarrook, through the passage of the ocean rocks, the dangerous caverns of the Koormamgarrook, around to Mother Whale's sacred ocean platform.

How could I know that, soon, it would all be taken away. How could I know that, soon, I would be on a foreign shore, untold distances away from my Biik, searching, questioning, wondering what happened in those last stages of our mourning ngargee. So that I might share this yulendji with a desolate mother and help her grieve her beloved child, so cruelly snatched from his babayin's embrace.

But I didn't run to the murndigarrook that day. I didn't see, I didn't hear, I didn't learn. And now, trapped in an alternate Time, a wrongful place, devoid of yulendji, I can't bear to remember that beautiful day. Because now, I realise I may never know.

YADABILING
Beloved

Early morning mist rises like vapoured spirits over the lagoon, stripped clean of its dry salt crust, now filling again with water from replenishing winter rains.

We leave early this morning, with only a glimmer of pale light seeping into the darkness to shepherd our trek for fresh water. Fashioned into pliant rock, the shallow wells that we bagarrook have carved collect the overnight Perrin rains. Animal tracks crisscross our trail, marking the busy pre-dawn rush of communing creatures, feasting and travelling, not accosted by two-legged predators. Every now and then, smaller indentations in the sand speak of the tentative steps of young kuyim taking their first hops in a new and uncertain, yet infinitely intriguing, world.

Scouring the budding green Biik as we walk for signs of herbs, medicinal plants, growing tubers, orchids, berries and grasses, Meen-dutgarrook and I relish the quiet of the emerging day, when peaceful purple hues colour the contours of Biik. My pregnant belly is full now, stretched skin wrapping a wriggling baby tightly inside. *We are both ready*, I think wryly, perching on a lichened rock to catch my shallow breath, *to be separate from each other.*

A rustling in the thickened tea tree belies a wandering kangaroo, herself pouch-heavy with a growing bubup, whose tiny face peeks out from its cosy cocoon, shy but curious. Following a trail of freshly sprouted, sweet grass, the mother hops languidly over our path and it is not until her delicate nose picks up our scent that she quickly

153

whips her head up from the ground to stare at us. Sensing the rush of its babayin's tension, the kuyim joey snatches its head back into the warm confines of a seemingly safe, dark pouch.

Not here, I whisper to the kuyim. *Find somewhere else to feed, far away from this end of the island.*

Feeling a kinship to this young mother, growing her baby in a dangerous world, I want to warn her that it will not be safe when daylight comes, as rows and rows of pegged kangaroo pelts attest, just over the rise of the adjoining sand dunes. Three turns of Meeniyan the moon on this island, and with her own belly beginning to blossom, Meendutgarrook feels the connection too.

Go, she commands, low but urgent with empathy. *Go, find a safer place.*

Deliberately, she moves forward and, in an instant, the kangaroo bounds away into the wattle, the power of fear making her and her joey immediately light, fleet of soft foot and bounding tail.

With a cheeky grin, Meendutgarrook laughs and turns to me. *Did we just chase away breakfast?*

What have you become, I snort with feigned horror. *A ngamudji's woman who would butcher a mother and baby?*

No, don't say it, she wails, covering her ears with her hands. Then she looks at me, a sudden seriousness clouding her expression. *Push me off the highest cliff into the roaring Warrayin below if I ever, ever, become that.*

I laugh and haul my swollen body back up to my feet. *I was joking, cousin,* I reassure, turning to go.

But Meendutgarrook grabs my arm and locks me in a penetrating stare. *Please, I mean it. If I ever do that. Forget our Liwik's teachings, ignore the right ways. If I lose me . . . me.* Her fist presses fiercely against her chest. *If I ever lose myself in all of this . . .*

Fading into a whisper, her words hang suspended as phantoms in the air, haunted and gaunt, like her fallen face, so wise yet still so young. Bereft, Meendutgarrook is quiet, like a bewildered child suddenly realising she is lost and alone in a strange Biik.

Grasping her hand, I squeeze it and pull her beside me, the touching of our skin giving comfort. *Let's go to the rockpools*, I whisper conspiratorially.

We won't have time, she shakes her head, eyes wide with hesitant glee. *They'll be awake before we get back.*

We will if we hurry!

I point in the direction of Galinbarriam, where a vast reddish light is starting its slow rise.

Nyawiinth is still waking, I smile encouragingly. *We can make it.*

Reaching the pock-marked limestone cliffs in record time, we breathe in the salty spray of Warrayin. Below us, a rock platform stretches along the beach, promising bounty from the sea, hidden abalone and crayfish, maybe the flick of a Koormamgarrook's tail. It is not often we can steal away to this spot, slipping out from under the watch of the captors, but when we do, our exhilaration catches in our throats, hearts thrumming in our chests.

For in this place on a foreign shore, the meeting of Biik and Warrayin looks so much like our Homelands. Rugged cliffs of cratered ochre, yellows and pinks and white, are majestic in their wind-blown forms, and if I allow my mind to reshape them slightly, I can see the jutting outlines of our beloved Munmundiik. Fecund platforms of tidal pools teem with whelks and crabs, kelp and urchins, a plethora of treasures like our generous Sea Country, if only we had our own time to explore them. Standing at the highest ridgeline, merging the Country before us with the one in our hearts, we inhale deeply. And, for a few blessed moments, the blood in our bodies sings once more in the harmonies of our Liwik's songlines.

Red hues flush with orange as the burning crest of Old Man Sun shimmers on the horizon. Bathed in golden light, Meendutgarrook's shining eyes reflect my own wishful ones. I squeeze her hand and turn back out to sea, exhaling in a slow, calming release.

And then, just as I take another lungful of briny ocean air, she is there. Mother Whale. Magnificent, wondrous, breaching up from the dark blue. Levitating magically in mid-air for the longest of moments, before falling back upon Warrayin's surface with a booming crash. An eruption of spray hovers around her receding body, then rains down where Babayin Betayil has disappeared back into Sea Country's depths.

Gasping in delighted awe, I turn to Meendutgarrook and see the same wonderment. *Our Liwik is with us still*, we say without words. Our Mother Whale still sees us, telling us that we are not alone and lost, that we are tethered still to our ancient songlines. Throwing our arms around each other, we weep with relief. We weep with a yearning to believe that yes, there still can be joy, hope even, yingalis that call to be sung. But even so, in the clutch of each other's consoling arms, the ache of a droning bass note still hums underneath.

We want to be home.

Taking one last, long look, we scour the placid, gold-flecked water for one more sign of flipper or fluke. All is still.

Intertwining our fingers with each other, we turn to go. Just one step and a searing, contracting spasm grips around my abdomen.

I falter.

Meendutgarrook's mouth drops open. *The baby is coming.*

Under the gnarled arms of a comforting moonah, a gush of water breaks between my legs. Steadying myself against her bark, I turn to the young turrung for strength.

Meendutgarrook races ahead for help, hollering for country-women to come quick. The contractions return in ever tightening cycles, heightening more with each new revolution. Squatting down, I rest my aching back against the ribboned trunk of the moonah and take my anxious mind to the story of the turrung's mother. A girl in love with the wrong boy, stupid, brave and ultimately immortalised as a warning beacon for all those who may be seduced by wrong ways.

Here that Old One's child is now, her spread of fragrant green canopy always bending towards Warrayin, reaching to the ground, feeling for the shore, like outstretched arms desperate to reach into the sea and hold their drowned lover once more.

As much as I am grateful for this moonah's strength, she is not the one my murndigarrook, and the endless line of those who came before, have spent generations raising to be our sacred birthing trees. Mighty turrung, at least ten times the size of my moonah's sprawling shelter, chosen as saplings, a long, long time ago. Then, each year, before the first rush of spring growth, the old women would light a small fire within a groove at the young turrung's base. A gentle, ceremonial fire, embers burning just long enough to transform a thin layer of bark into charcoal. Every season, the fire grows, spring after spring, with the wurrun herself. Until many cycles of generations later, that same turrung is a giant, thrusting into the sky, anchored with a sheltering cave at its base.

Closing my eyes, keeping my breaths deep and full, I imagine I am enclosed in that warm certainty of our women's wurrun at Kullurk again. My first girl was born there, Boyerup. It did not matter that the mornmoot hurled cold and harsh over Warnmarring's sand dunes. Nor did it matter that the rain drove from the djurt above. For I was wrapped in the loving embrace of a gentle giant babayin. She would keep me safe as she had done for so many mothers before me. Knowing this in my heart, feeling this flood through my murrup, my bubup came into the world with peaceful ease.

How different my world is now. Ancient birthing trees gone, the songs of my countrywomen no longer in my ears, the certainty of millennia-long knowledge and experience lost to me on the other side of the horizon. And for the first time a maternal fear creeps up my spine and wraps an icy hand around my heart. Will my baby be safe? Can I do this alone, without my Elders, my aunties, my countrywomen by my side?

Without my mother by my side.

Pricking with a sharp sting, my tears spill.

My babayin. I see her, like a moorroobull appearing before me. Once more, her dark eyes peer into mine, full with love and wisdom, holding me in an unbroken gaze of tenderness and strength. And it is as if I am a bubup again, safe in her arms, rocked to a somnolent calm by her soothing embrace.

My eyes flutter open and she is gone.

The tears spill faster as the child's voice inside me cries out, *Help me, I've lost my mother.*

A rush of women's sounds echo along the path snaking beside the grove of moonahs. Strange calls, foreign languages, but the unmistakable song of countrywomen and kinship nevertheless. Rising above them all is Meendutgarrook's.

Nannertgarrook! Urgent, gasping from exertion, she calls again. *Liwurruk! Nannertgarrook!*

Summoning all the shallow pockets of air left in my panting lungs, I answer back. *Kye!* My trembling legs saturated with birthing water, bulging belly constricting with the bubup's pushing, I lurch out from under the moonah. *Kye!*

From around a bend on the winding trail, a determined mass of countrywomen hurry, a bustling sisterhood, calling, singing, smiling, laughing. Leading the charge is Meendutgarrook, and when she sees me, she shouts a joyous *Kye!*

Arms open wide, she flings herself towards me, catching me just as my knees melt under the rush of searing relief that floods through every cell in my body. In an instant, I am raised by the strength of many arms, Kalungku and her kinswomen, lifting me up and carrying me to the safe embrace of the moonah tree.

Over the next unknowable passage of time, I am encircled and held by a disparate collection of women who are tethered together, both in spite of and because of the apocalypse quaking around us, and by a profound spirituality. That which is risen from our own separate, yet the same, custodianships of Biik, our ecstatic adherence to Ngargee and Lore, and the fundamental, inexorable connection to the sacred business of women. In this arcane understanding of each other, I surrender.

As I shift into full connection with my body, the women prepare around me. A fire is lit, filling the moonah cavern with warmth and flickering light. On the fire, fresh green leaves smoke scents of eucalyptus and peppermint through the air, at once invigorating and calming our senses. A metal tarnook of water hangs over the flames, clean cloths in a binuk at the ready nearby. Meendutgarrook, directed to collect whatever is necessary, watches curiously as the murndigarrook move in and out of the makeshift women's ceremonial gurrubayin.

Finally, as the gaps between the contractions ripple ever closer, a birthing bowl is sculpted in the sand and layered with supple grass and soft balls of moss. An older bagarrook, wearing the proud knowledge-marked scars of her clan's yulendji, comes forward bearing a small tarnook filled with a fine, red paste. Images of my Country's red ochre cliffs flash through my mind as my panting grows sharper. My Biik's ancient sentinels of sacred business, scenes of countless ceremonies, the drawing of blood, the learning of knowledge, bodies smeared in their vibrant colour of love and life.

I weep as she rubs her red paste over my stomach and legs, marking me for initiation. I weep as her voice rises in the mesmerising chant of ritual, echoing in the sacred space, its resonance wrapping around me as my body prepares for the final push. And I weep when I see the collective of shining eyes watching for the peeking head of my bubup bravely entering this new world. Held upright by Meendutgarrook, I squat with trembling legs over the birthing bowl. One more push and he arrives.

The world swirls around me in a haze as I stare down at the suckling babe on my breast. I am vaguely aware of my body moving with an ancient instinct, delivering the afterbirth into the sand bowl, soon to be buried as an offering to the moonah for her sheltering grace over this warp of time. A flurry of movement cutting the cord binding our bodies, wiping the residue of birth from my tiny bubup's wrinkled limbs, pressing the nourishing, fragrant tea to my lips. All this beautiful movement in my periphery.

But always, foremost in my mesmerised view, is him. My little one's sweet, contented face. Velvet skin as dark as booroonth, full lips drinking greedily, tiny perfect hand wrapping around my finger.

Bobbinary, I whisper. *Named for your father.* Love closes around us in an impenetrable cocoon and all else is forgotten. *I love you.*

WIRRAYIT
Far Away

One week old and Bobbinary is swaddled in a crisp, white ngamud-ji's blanket. Meendutgarrook and I wear pristine cloths of fine texture and delicate detail, our bodies scrubbed and scented, our hair brushed and coiled with metal pegs.

That morning, the sealers had prised their hidden timber box from under the floor of the wilam and counted the shining discs of silver they hold in such high esteem. Depositing the coins in two leather bilang strapped to their chests, they piled a wheeled platform with their stash of kangaroo skin and salt, then set off along the trail to the calm bay where visiting boats harboured. Just as Old Man Sun had reached his highest point in Sky Country, the men returned, pleased and purposeful.

Now, we stand as a huddle of three, Meendutgarrook, Bobbinary and I, on the shores of the island's most sheltered inlet. A giant ship appears from Warrayin, great swathes of sailing cloth flapping in a sleepy breeze. More men in red coats, gleaming gold discs running up and down their lengths, gather with the sealers, occasionally glancing at us with appraising eyes. Around them, their subordinates bustle, loading the rowboats full with stacks of salt and piles of kuyim pelts, and shuttling the cargo back to the bowels of the looming vessel.

A fluttering rises in my belly as I sense the shifting mornmoot of change threatening to blow us away yet again. Meendutgarrook feels it too and she clutches at my hand, a desperate uneasiness closing in around us. I tighten the knot of Bobbinary's swaddle secured around me, pulling him close, finding comfort in the touch of his smooth cheek against my stiffening neck.

Amidst the flurried activity of the men in fine coats, a battered rowboat sidles in to shore at the opposite end of the curving bay. A small group of three rugged sealing men climb out of the vessel, their eyes trained on the actions at our end of the beach. The oldest ngamudji barks commands and the two younger men hasten to follow them. One has darker skin but wears features not like our countrymen. From another place yet again and doing the work bidden by a sealer, whether willing or unwilling it was impossible to tell, but he works hard all the same.

Meendutgarrook and I watch as they surreptitiously haul two bundles from their boat, one small and the other twice the size. When the men set them down on the sand, the bundles suddenly stand, each one elongated with a pair of slender black legs.

People, Meendutgarrook murmurs.

And as I fixate upon the figures, I realise she is right. A woman and a child. Turning our way, I can see, even at this distance, that particular expression on the young bagarrook. I recognise it all too well. One that tells the story of numbing shock, worlds ripped apart, the foundations of all you know decimated. Also there, but almost hidden behind the fear, is a valiant spirit fighting off desolation. I have seen it in Meendutgarrook's eyes, and those of Kalungku and every countrywoman entrapped on this island. In my own if I could see them, the desperate battle of a once serene body, mind and murrup, now in a fight against the relentless anguish of brutality.

The older man stands behind them, his broad body pressed against the child. Goosebumps prick along my arms. A knee-weakening ripple of revulsion surges up my spine. Something about the way he stays there, crowding against the small girl. Him, quadruple her size, thick waist pushing against her back, heavy hands clamping her shoulders, long fingers snaking around her slender neck, her lean chest. His smirk is grim as he watches the other men offload supplies from the rowboat.

I can barely look at the child. I do not want to see the truth of what is etched on her baby face, what is held in her tiny bubup's frame. My stomach churns in disgust, in conflict, at once wanting to run to her and wrap her in the safety of a mother's arms, and at the same time, wanting to turn away. To pretend I did not see. To try to erase her stricken expression from my mind. Tiny nub of a nose, delicate bones in a fragile face, and those eyes. Those eyes, which should be sparkling with the light of a child in play, immersed in a world of wonder in the cradling arms of her Biik, curious and mischievous. Happy. The simple, rightful happiness of childhood.

Instead, those eyes are huge with terror. Staring, trying desperately to make sense of the nightmare she has been forced to wake to. Searching to find the way out. Hoping to sleep then awake in a new morning to find it was all a terrible dream. Just one of her clan's warning stories told around the campfire, made real in a drowsy night-time realm, about Toorradin the Bunyip or Buldjinganu the Devil. But somewhere in those fretful eyes, this bubup knows she is in a horror story made real, with every moment now a waking, visceral manifestation of the very worst things that can happen to a little girl.

Under the weight of the ngamudji's overbearing body, a desperate fear swirls like a phantom cloud around her small body. Hunched inwards, her thin, rigid arms push forward, trying to cover her chest and the wildly beating heart housed there. Fastened together in a white knuckled grasp, her tiny hands are locked in front of her private, should-be secret, places. Using the only defence she has, every part of her turns in on itself, shoulders, arms, knees, legs, toes, trying to galvanise her own body as a shield. As if that might make him stop.

Except it will not and she knows it, yet it is all she can do. A valiant but hopeless attempt of a child to protect herself when no-one else can or will.

Once the men finish emptying the rowboat, the older sealer directs each one to carry a portion of the cargo. The bagarrook is loaded with heavy rugs and blankets and she sways under the strain of it. Next, hoisting a sack onto the child's back, the ngamudji ties it with ropes to her. Knees buckling under the weight, the bubup manages to stay upright and the sealer pushes her to walk in front of him. Solemnly, the procession trudges up the saltbush hills of the furthest sand dune. One by one, as they reach the dense wattle blooming with golden dust at the top, they disappear into its folds, the dark man first, then the bagarrook, flanked by the younger ngamudji. Lastly, the bubup, still lugging the sack nearly as big as she is. And right behind her, shadowing her every move, the sealer controlling them all.

As stealthily as they had arrived, the group were gone.

Involuntarily, my feet shuffle forward as if to follow and I feel the scrape of a small shell lodging between my toes. A blessed distraction, a desperate way to stop myself from drowning in the breakwater crashing through my body.

I pick it up and focus on its curious shape, trying to obliterate the blazing image of the little girl and her terrified eyes from my mind.

It looks like a tooth, I muse. A bubup's tiny tooth, and I think of my children, Boyerup and Yearl Yearl, how they are both still losing their baby teeth.

And I am back there again. On the shores of Monmar, the boys whooping as they play their marngrook, the girls weaving binuk as they listen to stories of the Moonah, the youngest ones paddling in rockpools and collecting treasures. Walking up to a rowboat. Then, the splashes and screams, the force of the ngamudji's arms, my wrists bound in burning rope. And peering out from behind a rock in front of our ochre cliffs, Boyerup, terrified, staring helplessly at me. The eyes of my daughter merge with that of the little girl who just faded away, like a moorroobull, into the scrub.

Crashing back to the prison island beach, I clutch the tooth-like shell in my fist and it cuts into my flesh. A rivulet of my blood streaks the white shell. Like a tooth fallen from its socket.

She would be losing her baby teeth right now, I think as I stare at the patch of golden-yellow blossoming kurrun the child disappeared into. I imagine her having a shy sweet smile, seeing the gaps where the missing baby teeth once were and the minuscule ridges of new teeth breaking through.

Stop! The word spills out like a wish. *She is just a little girl*, I whisper to Meendutgarrook, my voice failing.

Gazing over Biik, into the clouds of Sky Country, across the swell of Warrayin, I whisper again, *Liwik of this place, help us. She is just a little girl.*

I wait for the mighty flap of an eagle's wings, a screeching Bunjil launching an attack from high, soaring from his place alongside the djurt in the sky. Or the battle cry of a fearsome raven, waiting to witness Waa spearing his pointed beak into the sealers' flesh.

But no help comes. On this island, Biik is still, ambivalent, and whatever Old Ones are watching, stay silent. No vengeful Creation Beings take up the honourable cause to rescue the bubup or the bagarrook. Or indeed, any of us.

Still staring at that patch of wattle, gripping the bloodied shell in my palm, the soft touch of my baby's cheek against my neck, the sealer pushes against the small of my back and leads me to Warrayin's edge. In an overt show of feigned chivalry, he lifts me over the water and into the polished rowboat. The other sealer does the same with Meendutgarrook. Pressed side by side, we sit on a timbered bench opposite a row of gaping, red-coated men. I listen to the methodical slapping of oar striking sea, propelling us to the waiting ship.

Once again, Meendutgarrook and I, baby Bobbinary still strapped around my body, stand against the timbered edges of another departing vessel, watching the shores of another Biik stretch further away. This time, the faces I catch are Kalungku and her countrywomen, watching us leave from a windswept headland. Jumping up and down, they throw their arms high into the air. We wave back secretively, hoping they can see, and a wash of strange regret sweeps my chest, the foaming tide of another cresting loss. These women, bonded in our suffering, enjoined in our rituals of womanhood, who had mid-wived my baby into the world and held me in sacred women's ngargee, had become our countrywomen. Sharing not blood, but kinship, profound and abiding.

A sudden hope takes hold and I wonder if they might find the young bagarrook and the child. Maybe, somehow, they might be the ones who rescue them.

Fading from sight, merging with the haze of the horizon line, the women on the beige and grey island slip away, back into the turning of the sea. As Warrayin's waters grow ever deeper, I hold my baby tight with one hand and clasp Meendutgarrook's hand in the other, wondering when might be the time of our rescue. Is it at the end of this journey? Could this ship be taking us home?

Light on the edge of the world turns bright orange and golden pink. A rich red permeates then deepens into purple hues tinged with blue as Nyawiinth slips away to lay his old flaming head to rest. The dark rises to claim us, still standing in the same spot. And as it does, the small girl's face looms in my thoughts.

He would be coming for her now. I shudder, trying desperately to shut out the hideous thoughts of the old sealer and the damage he will inflict on that bubup's vulnerable body. And her soul, her sacred murrup.

Someone help her, I sing out silently, into the clustering shadows of a moonless booroonth. Then, fingers like pincers enclose my elbow and my captor steers me, with my suckling babe at my breast, down into the stinking bowels of the ship.

Part Three

MUYIIPNALLOOK
Hell

**(Continuous descending through a narrow
opening and never stopping)**

NYALINGGU
Return

Saltwater envelops me and I glide through it like a silver-scaled wirrap. Shafts of sunlight pierce through Warrayin's shimmering skin, illuminating the collection of treasures sparkling along the ocean floor. An array of beautiful shells sway with the rolling tide, their designs hewn on brittle edges telling the stories of their journey from wild open ocean to the placid shores of Nerrm. Schools of multi-hued wirrap brush past me, quick and curious, showing off their brilliant colours and patterns against the backdrop of my black skin. Slowly expelling my held air, I wish I could stay under the waves forever.

It is impressive how long you can hold your breath, my mother smiles as I surface for air. *You're a true Bubup-Warrayin, child of the sea.*

Maybe I'm a Koormamgarrook, I laugh, performing my best mermaid dive back into Sea Country.

Lying with arms outstretched on the sand, Old Man Sun's light floods me with a grateful warmth. Overhead, flocks of kwiyup soar and spin, squawk and sing, aerial dancing their way from turrung to turrung. Sheltered in the dune of our Keeping Place, my aunties tend to the herb-encrusted wirrap roasting over the fire for dinner, singing as they sort through binuk full of rockpool delicacies and juicy fingers of murnong yams. Surrounded by the sun, the salt, the smells and the songs, I drift into contented sleep.

Then, free of my body, spirit manifest, I soar like the wind over Biik, a mischievous mornmoot surveying the estate. Myself lying there, blissfully unaware on the beach, the shimmering bay lapping the lips of the shore. Giant turrungs, full of blossoms, birds and Biik's children busy with the labour of life. Wetlands link their reeded tannin shores to each other. A river of mists rushes over her waterfall, ochre cliffs of all colours, beckoning the songs of ngargee.

On I soar, to the mighty rocks tumbled from jagged ocean cliffs, the great swamps swirling around the thrust of Wonga, the crash of betayil flapping flukes in response to our song.

I do not stop. I cannot stop.

Frantic now, higher and higher in the ether, I spin over and under. From stretches of shimmering sand to rising mountain peaks, valleys of green flanking grooves of cascading water, I see it all. But I am careening now, launching towards the sentinels at the very end, the betayil rocks of Wamoom, faster and faster until suddenly, I am swallowed by the starless cloak of booroonth. Into nothingness.

My eyes snap awake and Meendutgarrook is there, concern etched in her troubled face, furrowed brow contoured by the flickering firelight.

Another dream of Country? she asks.

I nod, slowly adjusting to the reality of the space around me. *Did I wake anyone?*

Meendutgarrook grins as she surveys the brood, five of mine and two of hers. *Not a peep.*

Clustered in the corner of our large wilam is a bundle of bubups, lost in a dreamy haze. On the edge of the snug of small bodies is Bobbinary, only six but ever wise and responsible. The role of elder brother weighs on his slender shoulders, guarding his siblings even in sleep, arms flung above his head in a stance of somnambulant readiness.

Pushing down a sudden rising sob, I am struck with how much he resembles Yearl Yearl. Spirited brothers alike, animated even in the deepest sleep with a restless, perpetual motion.

I try not to picture my first son too sharply in my mind, try not
to count the years and imagine him at twelve, a blossoming young
man eager for that sacred journey with the men to his coming-of-age
reckoning. I try not to think of these two boys together, emulating
their father, Bobbinary, playing marngrook on a bountiful stretch of
beach, cloistered in the loving encirclement of their Biik, cousins and
community, play and place, of birthrights bestowed in a continuous
line over millennia.

Instead, I concentrate on the heap of soft limbs and sweet faces
before me, a bevy of seven koonwarra cygnets. Brown-skinned
babes tucked under kuyim blankets, chests rising and falling in
harmonious rhythm. Their innocence, their immediacy, wills me
to stay in the present, to focus my spinning psyche on their world,
their needs, their smiles. But an insistent restlessness hisses in
my limbs.

Knowing it will be impossible to get back to sleep, I stand and
stretch, looking out past their slumbering bodies to the rocky landscape beyond our women's wilam.

I won't be long. Turning to my kin, I try to reassure her. *I just
need a quick walk, some air.* My laugh is low and hollow. *Mornmoot
to blow through my mind.*

Please be careful, cousin.

Her dark eyes are shadowed with worry and not simply because
of the treacherous terrain that awaits me in the dark beyond the
light of our wilam. Reading the signs in my taut figure, Meendutgarrook knows I am struggling under a brooding weight. One that
threatens to push me from an already precarious perch on granite
cliffs, sending me reeling into the jagged rocks below.

Don't leave me. Her voice is a gentle, low bleat and I am reminded
she has only just turned twenty. Still young. Still locked in a place
of stasis, having been stolen away from her rites of initiation and
womanhood, all crucial, early layers of yulendji hidden from her,
possibly forever.

I will never leave you, no matter what. Wrapping my arms around her, I hold her like a mother would a child, for we are all things to each other now. *Go back to sleep, liwurruk.*

A well-worn track leads me to a stand of giant boulders, great shapes looming in the gleam of starshine. Above me, the familiar, slow-rolling wave of twinkling djurt floats its way through the darkened Sky Country. Still watching from high above, the Munmundiik orbit in their cluster of seven sisters. Once, I dreamed they might fly down from their place in the distant realms if they could see their children in grave danger. Then, as each season wheeled through another cycle, over and over and over, I learned this would never happen. And I wondered, over so many nights tracking their travels, again and again, maybe it is because the Munmundiik simply cannot see us. Perhaps we are too small, hidden by the trees, the boulders, the sealers' ships. Or perhaps, too insignificant. Maybe they do not care to see us, like the passing parade of the ngamudji who glance our way, then furtively turn their heads, deciding it is easier, better, cleaner, not to see.

Perhaps the truth is much simpler. It does not matter what is happening to us, because we do not matter.

I sit motionless on the jutting boulder until a gradual light begins to bleed out from the horizon line at Galinbarriam and up into the night sky.

Slowly, as dawn rises, the prison reveals itself, a gigantic, rocky beast thrust up from the depths of Warrayin. Beachless, bayless, riverless, dangerously steeped on all sides, punishing most who try to come close and condemning any woman or child who tries to leave with just the protection of their bodies against hurling waves and ragged rocks.

Small pockets of flat land exert every effort to encourage life, and some brave turrung murrup have heeded the call. Twisting limbs of a smaller kind of moonah hug low to the ground here, as always reaching for their drowned lover in the sea. The golden powdery bloom of kurrun and the sweet spikes of the warrak blossom flavour our bread and sweeten our teas. Grasses grow stout offering up their stalks for our binuk and bilang. Old Man Saltbush crowds the ground for courageous, travelling kwiyup-kwiyup to shelter and build their nests in. Not much more than that.

No markings of a symbiosis of People and Country on this stony Biik, no rolling dunes woven with a Keeping Place, no grinding basins crushing the seed of bread for djambanna, no bagar-rook tended fields of murnong or scarred turrung used to make tarnook or gurrung. Not even the echoes of a long past yingali reverberate around the perennially impassive boulders surrounding me. This has always been a solitary Biik, alone since antiquity. Until six turnings of the seasons ago.

Mornmoot is likewise quiet on this not-quite-night, not-quite-morning. Warrayin is still as well, the rocks that had fallen a long, long time ago around the base of this giant island boulder, just visible under the clear saltwater skin.

Staring out across the expanse, I picture a gleaming rise of land a quick swim away. On it, figures come and go, some standing, some dancing, some fanning wisps of curling smoke with a message just for me. I see women, shapes and faces emerging and merging, over and over, Maytepueninner, Kalangku, Nandergarrook. But I shake my head when I see the faces of my kin because I don't want to see, don't want to remember. And yet, they persist, gather-ing on the mirage of a tantalising strip of sandy Biik, one long dive away from my rock honed prison. Doogbyerumborokc holds hands with her children, entwined in a circle, squishing their feet into the beach, laughing. Curly-haired bagarrook join in, the nawnta Worethmaleyerpodeyer and Wottecowwidyer, reunited and vital, the singing women from the island of salt, smeared in the red clay of joy and birth, all together in a shimmering gurrubayin of dance and life. Then my mother emerges, cuddling my bubups, my Boyerup, my Yearl Yearl.

A strangled wail hisses from my lips. My head pounds with a punishing thought. *Am I seeing a reverie of ghosts?*

Stinging tears blur the vision and I rub them away fiercely. Steadying my swaying body, I force my eyes open but the mirage is gone. In its place, a still sea, like a yawning chasm, waiting to swallow my lonely murrup.

I miss them, I whisper to the indifferent Warrayin. *I miss them so much.*

In this place, Time revolves on a repetitive loop, the cyclic daily motion of two bagarrook and seven bubup. Alone. Stripped of the skin of kin, the comforting reassurance of a communal embrace, of family, whether it be born of blood, of pain, of plucking moonbird or carrying salt, of a shared yulendji from a new, nihilistic world. Just us now.

Mostly.

For there is always the sickening coming and going of the sealers who bought us for a few pieces of metal. Cunning choice of a prison on this bald island, where they can leave and return as they please, knowing we will always be stranded, trusting that the babes at our breasts will prevent our wilful plummeting from sheer cliffs. Their return brings fresh slaughter to skin, koormam and kuyim in ever dwindling numbers. With long-practised diligence we tend to their wilam next to ours and the rough sating of their base desires at night. During the day, we hold our breaths and quieten the children with stern frowns. Finally, when they leave again on their revered gurrung, there is a flooding release of tension and a fervent wishing that their rowboat will never return.

As a pervading glow of pink and gold paints Sky Country from the east and the autumnal chill of a changing season eases in the light, I stand and take one last shuddering inhale before trekking back to my soon-to-be stirring children.

Just as I turn to go, I see her dark shape glide across the surface of the water. Soundlessly, secretively, the betayil breaks the surface then recedes once, twice, three times, and I know in my jubilant heart she has come to see me. I stand on the very tip of the precipitous edge, half wanting to take that extra step and plummet down into the sea to be with her. But a primal surge in my breast, where my newborn baby will soon be suckling, stops me.

I see you, I whisper.

And ever so slowly, ever so guarded, she raises her fluke in an acknowledging wave. Tears swelling, I bend my knees and push my arms out to the side, flicking my hands up at the wrists, mimicking her tail like the old days on that glorious sandbar in Warnmarring. Humming our sacred song, twisting my body side to side, I stare straight at her, hoping she understands.

A moment later, she disappears under the glassy sea and I let my stance drop. Then suddenly, the betayil bursts into the air in front of me, launching in full glory from the stillness, suspended on ether for a breathtaking moment, then crashes back down in an exultant uprising of foaming water.

She sees me too.

On the rocky trail back to the wilam, my feet are light and my legs young. As the orange flaming head of Nyawiinth awakes from his rest, I see the island in a rare golden light. This Biik, a harsh mother, sometimes cruel, at best ambivalent, revels in a strange beauty today. I remember to be grateful for what she does provide, seeds from the bush, eggs from the birds, skin and meat from the small, rock hopping kuyim, wirrap from Warrayin. Fresh water too, from the perfectly round, wind carved bowls on her ledges that capture and contain the parnmin when it falls.

Thank you, I acknowledge as I lift the woven mats we use for covers to help keep the well water clean. As I scoop water to my mouth, a holler reverberates around the solemn rocks.

Babayin?

I brighten at the sound of young Bobbinary's voice, sleepy but insistent, and loud enough to wake his siblings with a jolt.

I hurry back to our wilam, a gentle regeneration propelling my step, a renewed choosing of this present, the family of two koonwarra and our seven bubups. Meeting my cousin's searching stare with a reassuring smile, I say, *Babayin Betayil is with us today and Warrayin is sleepy.*

Meendutgarrook's beautiful brown eyes light up gleefully and she shines with a wide, dazzling grin. Turning back to our drowsy brood, she rallies them into action. *Wurrdin!*

Perched happily on our favourite rocky ledge, we all dangle our legs in the placid swell that fills and falls around us. Crystal clear, the saltwater is alive with darting wirrap and climbing crabs. Restless fingers point to the quickly disappearing creatures, or twist strands of dangling kelp into headbands and armbands, or pick slow snails from their stony homes and place them in shallow rockpools to race. All the while, their eager ears listen to our tales of the Koormamgarrook.

Shapeshifters, you see, they can be seal or girl as they choose, explains Meendutgarrook as she fastens her bilang around her body, ready to dive for the abalone shell.

They can even blend in perfectly with the kelp, I add, warm with the memory of those days on the beaches of Euroyoroke, listening to my babayin tell me the same. *The Koormamgarrook become as one with their rhythms, making sure the kelp never gets wrapped around a diving bagarrook's body.*

Nodding in agreement, Meendutgarrook fills her lungs with air and slips below the tranquil water. Briefly pausing in their endeavours, the children turn to where the bagarrook's shape dives down into deeper water in awe, offering a wave of their tiny hands in recognition.

Standing tall and important, Bobbinary is on lookout, scouring Warrayin for the dorsal fins of patrolling darrak. A puzzled frown creases his forehead.

Why do the Koormamgarrook eat boys?

I snort with sudden laughter and try to offer a quick clarification on the ancient mysteries of Boonwurrung women's Lore.

It's not that they eat boys, my mammam! But Sea Country is women's Country, and if a boy or a man swims where they shouldn't, or takes from Warrayin a bagarrook's bounty, then the Koormamgarrook might punish them. They might pull him down to their underwater home below the giant rocks and keep him there forever.

The young yanyean ponders the teaching, but still the frown on his forehead remains. He hesitates before asking his next question, spoken softly like a quiet wish.

I wonder why they haven't taken the sealers then?

No easy answer comes to my lips. Yet, the stillness that fills the next few seconds hums with layered meaning, broken only by Meendutgarrook's gasp as she pushes through the surface of the saltwater.

To the cheers of jubilant children, a clinking bilang is hoisted onto the rocks, a modest bounty of wurrdin within. Pulling herself up onto the ledge, Meendutgarrook sprawls against a sun-heated boulder, letting Nyawiinth evaporate the chilly water from her skin. I watch as a languid ease loosens her body and relaxes her face, revealing the youthful radiance of the girl I used to teach to hold her breath, so many years ago, in the benign bay of our Biik.

An excited shout from Bobbinary draws all of our attention. Suddenly, shooting upwards in a display of vigorous beauty, a frolicking fraternity of barrunan leap gleefully from the sea.

Meendutgarrook gasps and turns to me in wonder.

Without thinking, I blurt out, *Here comes your husband to say hello!*

Do you think? Her words are choked, tears already gathered.

I nod, as the sting of both happiness and sorrow burns in me too. *Barrunan for you. Betayil for me.*

Down here, in the cool pressing depths of Warrayin, breath held, body floating, time seems to hover. I carefully prise the wurrdin from their rocky shelters and thank our Liwik for their gifts. Not long and my bilang is full, but I don't surface yet. I wait. *Time is suspended,* I think. Light dissipates in the depths, blurring the lines of the world underwater. *Place is suspended too,* I muse. *I could be anywhere. Beside the reefs of home. Sinking into a Koormamgarrook's abode.*

I feel the oxygen seep from my body, my mind spins lighter, a comforting haze wrapping its tendrils around me. *I could be nowhere. Just here. For all Time.*

Above me, I see the distorted outlines of bodies beyond the surface of the serene sea. Muffled sound falls around me and I sense an urgency in the tone but everything moves in a daze of slow motion.

Babayin!

Ripples made from small tapping hands on the water overhead break through the mist clouding my vision. Again, the muffled sound of a child drifts down to me.

Babayin!

A face pushes through the surface, searching. My Bobbinary.

Sudden panic fuels a rush of blood around my body. In an instant, my mind is clear and I thrust upwards through the numbing swell, launching myself onto the rocky ledge with a surge of dread.

Is everyone okay? I pant, breathless and rasping.

A bewildered Bobbinary shrugs then looks past our rocky ledge to a jutting headland beyond. There, an excited clutch of young children crowd around Meendutgarrook, all craning their heads to see the commotion below.

Hearing me, Meendutgarrook turns to reveal my baby Isabella nestled against her shoulder and a stunningly wide smile on her surprised face. She shouts, partly cheering, partly crying.

Kardingarrook!

All day we wait, our bodies bubbling with untold excitement, churning questions, tears and laughter, but we contain it all in a bursting silence. All day we follow the sealers' commands, trudging the stores from the rowboat up and down the treacherous cliffs, me with a newborn swaddled to my back, just like Kardingarrook, whose little one's shock of sandy hair bobs up and down above his blanket with each stride she takes. We fortify the neighbouring wilams, collect firewood, clean fish, prepare bread, keep the children quiet and out of sight.

That night, we tend to the ngamudjis' needs, keep their fire burning, steam their water, cook their dinner, clear away the detritus, replenish their firewater. And when their desire rises, when they grab us by the arms, shove their hands under our clothes, force their fingers between our legs, we give our suckling babies to our countrywomen, tell our children to go to sleep, and close our minds and eyes to the ngamudjis' flushed skin, stinking breath and rutting bodies.

When, finally, the night is still and our time, our bodies, our choices, are returned to us, we light our own bagarrook's fire and sit down for Kobin Koolin, the ceremony for embracing the one who has returned. All day we have held inside the galaxies of feeling, thoughts, words, love, spinning like sparkling djurt between us. Hour by hour, we have dutifully performed our slave woman's work, all the while aching for our ngargee to begin. How long it has been since we have seen her beautiful face. Our Kardingarrook, brave one, who had the courage one night to swim those foreign channels between islands and hopefully find her way home, but who's loyalty to her kin made her wait. A devastating mistake.

For that very next day, hordes of ngamudji descended on the island intent on enslavement. Lined up, inspected, pushed, yanked, the frenzied market for our bodies tore our unified sisterhood apart. The last time I had seen Kardingarrook, she was fighting like Koonwarra to get back to her sister. Howling and screeching, biting and scratching, she was valiant like the swan, blood-soaked and stripped to the core.

But it made no difference. Two boats took us in opposite directions.

Now, seven turns of the chilly winds heralding Perrin later, and like an apparition of a loved one long departed for Karralk, she has arrived unexpectedly before us, a glorious lambamurr. Salvation climbing the jagged boulders of our rocky prison. Now, after so long, she sits silently, patiently, ready to be welcomed in the old way at our women's kuunh.

A choking howl bursts from Meendutgarrook in her desperate rush to kneel by her kin's side. Falling on her knees at Kardingarrook's feet, she presses herself against her sister's breast and unbridles the upswell of emotion that has amassed in her body from the moment she saw her liwurruk. Barely able to breathe, vast, convulsive sobs shuddering through her body, Meendutgarrook clutches her sister's hands and presses them to her cheek. When finally she can gasp a pocket of air, she whispers her profound love for her sister, over and over, every word a strangled cry.

Kardingarrook sits as still as she can, as the ritual of Kobin Koolin demands, letting the full force of her sister's heartbreak, grief, unabated love, crest and crash around her. Impossible to stop, tears slide down her cheeks and merge with the flood of her liwurruk's deluge. Long, aching minutes pass as she is held tight in her younger sister's embrace, any doubt at how much she may have been missed and mourned irrefutably erased in the overwhelm of Meendutgarrook's emotion.

When the last fervent waves of feeling have surged and receded, Meendutgarrook kisses her sister's hands one final time and stands unsteadily, spent, purged, free, in the knowing that she has let her liwurruk truly see, hear, feel, understand the profound depths of her love for her.

My weeping is next, the ritual of Kobin Koolin allowing my murrup to open and liberate the cascade of terrified balambalam who have long resided and proliferated there, keepers of the panicked, fluttering desperation in the depths of my soul. Finally, I can let free the haunted image of Kardingarrook's stricken face as she is torn from us on that fateful day, fighting, kicking, screaming, her body, heart and soul shattering, an anguished vision that has played over and over in my mind since, waking me in the dark of night and rendering sleep an impossible dream.

Finally, I can release the throbbing agony of not knowing, endless questioning about where she might be, who she is with, how she is treated, if she is alive. And finally, in a crescendo of weeping regret and choking whispers of *I'm sorry*, I can release, at last, the hollowing guilt of letting her be taken. Of being one of the kin she refused to leave without, when she might have otherwise followed the voice of her Liwik and swum to some sort of salvation. Of knowing she may be enduring the horrors of her captivity alone, while I am able to balance the burden with her sister.

One last kiss of her small hand and I rise wearily to my feet, hollowed out, exhausted, yet ever grateful for the expulsion of deeply held grief. I return to my place by the fire and wait for the ritual of Kobin Koolin to curl its ancient custom around Kardingarrook. Between steadying exhales and sobbing inhales, she speaks, cries, whispers and sings the story of her songline since we lost each other.

Same as ours in too many ways. In a hushed tone straining with the task of voicing the unspeakable, our countrywoman retells the mindless savagery of the ngamudji we have all come to know, their beatings over the smallest things, their rampant violations, the slavery their laziness encourages. She talks of circling the islands with Nandergarrook and their captors, near to where we were all ripped apart, the two bagarrook constantly searching the disparate women strewn in these places hoping to find us again. Reuniting with Doogbyerumboroke and her bubup Naynar, whose splintered leg had never healed, leaving her permanently maimed. Discovering that Yanki Yanki and Borodanger were gone, taken by sealers to places unknown. In a whisper she speaks of the profound joy of helping bring Nandergarrook's bubup into the world, and the bitter desolation of the baby taking her last gasp merely weeks later. Then, not long after, being ripped away from a grieving Nandergarrook and the steady wisdom of Doobyerumboroke, and with that, the snapping of her tenuous tethering to kin, to culture, to the life she once lived.

Sobbing now in desperate waves of grief, I see how close her murrup was to breaking. But she gathers herself, straightens her shoulders and forces out the rest of her story. She speaks of the finding and forming of kinship with women from other Countries, all trapped in the maelstrom of the same fate. Birthing her three bubups in a conflicted eruption of joy and fear, yearning for the comfort of mothers and aunties, to be wrapped in their promise of safety and wisdom, to receive the endowment of ancient yulendji along the sacred places of the Warrayin we once knew. But, when the bubup arrives, being overtaken by that powerful surge of love that only a babayin can feel when she gazes upon her newborn babe suckling at her breast.

Finally, Kardingarrook's story reaches the arrival of her boat at the stony shore of a desolate rocky island. How her heart pounded with exhilaration when she looked up the slope to a ledge and discovered her sister staring back down at her. Meendutgarrook's strangled cry ricochets around our ngargee fire and once more, we all succumb to a flood of unfathomable emotion.

Throughout the night, we cling to each other, not wanting to let each other go in case it is all just a dream. Awake when the first gilded rays begin a new day, we stare at each other in the golden light and laugh with wondrous relief.

This is real. We are together again.

BARNDANA
Message Stick

Nimble on his feet like his father, Bobbinary leaps down the steep boulders of our island prison with agile grace. I place my feet more carefully, carrying a sleeping bubup tethered to my back, and the fishing implements of bone kalk and timbered line in my clinking bilang.

Swelling in the hues of first light, Warrayin calls us to her depths with saltwater clear and calm. Below her surface, schools of languid wirrap take shelter in the curves of submerged rocky inlets. The burgeoning summer air carries an easy warmth, and I inhale deeply, savouring these peaceful early mornings when Warrayin is gentle and the breeze of mornmoot is kind. When, higher up, sheltered in the understory of a dense Moonah grove, the sealers are still asleep in their wilam.

Behind me, Kardingarrook descends the sloping pathways slowly, her own growing infant bundled in kuyim skin on her back, with two other children, barely three and five, clutching at her hands. Cautious and awkward, still adapting to life upon a forever slanting shoreline of granite, the family moves nevertheless with the particular lightness that comes when surrounded by kin.

On a flattened ridgeline, Meendutgarrook is busy ensuring our morning fire stays warm and strong, as well as keeping a bevy of babbling children engaged in the soaking of warrak blossoms for a sweet drink at daybreak.

My eldest daughter Martha practises threading lengths of bobad into string, her concentration only broken when Kardingarrook's oldest manggip sits shyly beside her. Passing over a fistful of poa grass, Martha smiles and the two cousins sit in companionable silence, tender fingers synchronised in their rhythmic braiding. I stop mid-step as I stare at the two girls, heads bent, shoulders touching, hands weaving. A catch in my throat, the stumble of my feet, as the image of another two young girls shoots through my mind. My firstborn bubup, Boyerup, sitting on the white sand of Monmar, pressed against her cousin Barebun, youngest daughter to Doogbyerumboroke, with the same dance of their small hands plaiting dried kurrawan into string.

Another image electrifies the air around me, the desperate memory of them clutching each other as a gurrung pulls onto shore, me stumbling across the sand screaming, *Run!*, my Boyerup's terrified eyes as she pulls her younger cousin away to the safety of the boulder-strewn rockpools.

My heart seizes as if it happened yesterday, not seven cycles of the seasons ago.

Nannertgarrook? Meendutgarrook calls cheerily, oblivious to the ache searing my murrup. *Do you have the fishing hooks?*

Forward I move, keeping focussed on the gathering of bagarrook and bubup before me, step by step, until I am back in the present day, sitting on the stony flattened ridge, pulling tools from my bilang, with an eager Bobbinary at my side.

Using the metal blade of a ngamudji's knife, I carefully sharpen the ends of an elliptical wedge of bone from the small kuyim that flourish on the island. Knotting securely at the centre of the linganlingan, I attach a long line of cordage made from stripped fibres of fallen and dried bark. I give the fishing hook to Bobbinary and he threads morsels of worms and grubs onto the spiky points.

Before he can pass it back to me, I say, *Your turn, mammam. See how far you can throw it.*

A broad grin beams across his lips and he turns his attention to the task with gusto. Throwing his arm forward in a sweeping arc, Bobbinary hurls the linganlingan out past the swells pushing against the island's bouldered body.

Monameit, I say, nodding my approval, and he straightens with a bashful pride.

Beside us, Kardingarrook's toddler jumps up and down eagerly. *Me too*, he demands. *Me too!*

Not yet, bubup, Kardingarrook scolds lightly. *You must watch and learn first. Konye!*

Placing her snoring baby in a rocking tarnook by Meendutgarrook's fire, Kardingarrook picks up the linganlingan and juggles its weight in her skilled hands. With a well-practised throw, she launches her fishing line straight into a patch of glassy sea and it is not long until the wirrap start to bite.

Nyawiinth has barely begun to raise his head above the edge of the world when my bilang are full with cleaned and gutted fish. Murrup still aching, I feel the familiar pang of homesickness hitting my chest as I think about wrapping this generous bounty from Sea Country in a fold of paperbark, letting it smoke and roast over the hot coals of our women's fire in the old way, along a beautiful stretch of beach bordered by our women's Keeping Places.

But there are no towering paperbark turrung rising from the banks of wetlands on this stony Biik, no sandy shores or mounds of millennia-old shells, and I quickly push the yearning from my mind. Forward I move, step by step, forcing the ache back down into the numbed pockets of my blunted murrup.

At the flattened apex of the sloping ridgeline, the hustle of curious bubup crowd around my legs, peering into the bags of many coloured wirrap. The succour of their sweet faces washes over me and smiling, I shuffle my way to Meendutgarrook. The morning fire still blazes and the hearthstones are hot. Sitting beside her, I pull the fish from my bilang and she begins the selection of which ones to skewer over the coiling smoke and which ones to roast on the oven rocks.

Just as each child settles in a circle around the kuunh, a cry from Kardingarrook brings us all to our feet.

Below, in the tranquil sweep of the island's north-westerly point, a large, masted ship sidles into view and stops. In mere moments, a rowboat drops over its side and a group of men make haste towards us.

Swiftly reeling in their linganlingan from Warrayin, Kardingar-rook, Bobbinary and her toddler clamber hastily up to the top of the ridge. As if sensing the sudden anxiety flicker through me, my bubup squirms restless on my back, and I swing her to my breast. Keeping the children close, we stand as a huddle near our women's fire and watch the ngamudji navigate the treacherous rocks at the least imposing section of the rocky shoreline. Luckily for them, the usually tumultuous ocean is still drowsy this early morning and in a few deft strokes, the men manage to reach the island safely and fetter their boat to a berthing rock.

A flutter of panic ripples through us. As the strange men pick their way up the rocky slope, another feeling rises too, swimming within the current of nervous anticipation, not quite hope but the faintest rivulet of possibility. For these men were clearly not sealers. They were the other kind of ngamudji we had witnessed gliding past many times in their gleaming ships, surveying the contours of the new, beckoning land across from our island outcrop, calculating, assessing, then moving on. Vessels under their command that could cut across the vast expanse of Warrayin with ease, if mornmoot blew a hasty wind in their favour. Back in the direction from whence we had come. The direction of our Homelands.

My mind reels through a varying set of outcomes and glancing at my countrywomen, I can see they are having similar thoughts. Would this encounter herald more of the same or could we dare imagine something different? A ship pointed in the direction of our Biik that just might be able to take us home.

Up on the higher ledges of the island, the sealers would be starting to wake. As the light shifted from the pinks and golds of dawn to the brighter yellows of the burgeoning day, they would rouse from their firewater slumber and search for us to order the provision of their morning meal. It could be any minute now. If ever we were to summon a foolish courage and make a bid for possible freedom, now would be the time.

Hello, the leading man calls, in the tongue of the sealers we had all, unwillingly, become accustomed to. Dressed in crisp, clean clothes made of delicate thread, dotted in buttons of glossy gold, the telltale signs of the particular clan this white man belongs to is evident. Scrambling up the last lengths of the slope, he motions to our fire, offering a reason for their approach.

Fire. Speaking slowly and loudly, as you would to an unruly child, or someone who has difficulty hearing in their wirring, he points to us and asks, *You speak English?*

Raising their eyebrows, Meendutgarrook and Kardingarrook turn to me, questions in their eyes. *Should we engage with these ngamudji? Should we dare to trust them?*

Despite the uneasiness fluttering in my stomach, I grasp tight to a thread of frayed bravery and speak quickly back to the older man. *Yes, English.*

As the other men arrive at the top of the hill carrying various objects, we all stare in awkward silence, taking the measure of each other, calculating the risk. I watch the captain carefully as he studies my kin and me, taking in the clothing on our bodies, the collection of children clutching at our legs. Questions accumulate in his curious expression as he observes Bobbinary standing alert behind me, his dark skin like mine contrasting starkly against the cream-coloured clothes the sealers make us wear. Roving across the younger bubup, the captain's eyes narrow at their paler skin, their lighter irises, the tufts of sandy hair on a swaddled baby nestled in a tarnook beside the kuunh.

After a few minutes of deliberation, the captain barks a command and one of his crew rushes forward with a tanned leather bilang. Finding a flat portion of rock to sit on, he pulls from the bag a white feather, its calamus chiselled to a point, and a small glass vessel filled with black liquid. They are implements I have seen the sealers use to draw designs on paper. Bound in a flap of thin leather, a collection of paper is stretched open, and dipping his gangan in the cup, the captain begins to scratch out a series of markings.

An instinct eddies in my belly, to try to make him understand, to compel him to use the drawings on his paper to tell our story, as if somehow, somewhere, someone might find them and decide to help us get home.

I step forward, heart hammering, blood rushing to my face, tapping my chest so he will comprehend.

Me, Nannertgarrook.

The feather hovers mid-air as he fixes his gaze upon me. Shallow breath makes my voice tremble as I try to explain who we are, words tumbling out in a combination of my Boonwurrung tongue and the smattering of English words I have learned.

I am Nannertgarrook. Turning to my countrywomen, I point to each of them in turn. *Kardingarrook and Meendutgarrook, liwurruk, friends. Boonwurrung bagarrook, you say lubra. My Biik, land, Nerrm, Warnmarring, Westernport. Boat, long, long way. Many days, many nights. From there east, there Galinbarriam.*

I pause, waiting for him to scratch at his paper, write down my story in his pages.

I am Nannertgarrook, I repeat, gesturing for him to write. *I am Boonwurrung bagarrook, we Boonwurrung bagarrook.*

But he doesn't pick up his quill or move to scratch in his book. Just a fixed expression of confused blankness, a furrowed brow, the slightest hint of frustration.

Again, I impel him to write, gesturing the movement with my hand in the air. Urgency fills in my chest, an insistence to tell it all, for it to be known, for the savagery to be held to account. And it all tumbles out, thick and fast in the language of my Homelands. How, on a perfect late summer day, nine of us were ripped from our beloved families on the peaceful shores of our Biik, the terrified eyes of our bubup watching the horror unfold. How we were bound, brutalised and violated, and tried desperately to protect our too young daughters from the sealers' hideous lechery. How Doogbyerumboroke was very nearly beaten to death and her child of ten forever maimed by a sealer trying to steal her in the night. How we have seen cruelty beyond the capacity for words to describe, in any language, women viciously battered, stabbed and killed, nawntas sold to their kin's murderer. Bagarrook and bubup tortured, children dying slow hideous deaths with wounds that no living thing should have to endure. Little girls, no older than seven, violated by old men.

Still, the ngamudji's feather does not move, the black liquid drying on the point of its calamus. I know he cannot understand my words but I had hoped he could intuit their meaning from the surging emotion in my tone, the trembling in my body, the nodding heads and stricken faces of my countrywomen in solidarity behind me.

We want to go home, we want to see our families, I plead, desperately searching for words that he will recognise. *Friends, Westernport.* Pointing to the ship idling on the docile sea and then back to our group, my kin, our children, I repeat, slowly and loudly, willing with all my heart for him to comprehend. *Boat to Westernport. There, friends.*

A flicker of comprehension sparks in him. Finally, the captain dips his quill in the glass bottle and presses its calamus to paper. Relief washes over me and the tiniest seed of something like hope plants itself in the recesses of my mind.

Casting a calculating glance over our brood of bubup, he points to Meendutgarrook and asks a question in the tongue of his kind. Puzzled, she bites at her lip, pulls her children close and looks to me.

Meendutgarrook, I say, pointing to my cousin. *Nannertgarrook.* I touch my chest. *Kardingarrook.* I gesture to my countrywoman who has rescued her baby from his tarnook and cradles him protectively against her chest.

Once again, the man blinks at us blankly, unable, perhaps unwilling, to understand my words, acknowledge the names our wise women Elders, our Murndigarrook, bestowed upon us at the time of our births. Names carefully considered, holding connection to our Biik, tying generations long past with the living, revealing the songlines walked, the beginnings of our sacred rites of passage through womanhood. It becomes clear to me that the only way to have our story told, our existence validated on this barren, isolated rock countless passages of time from our Homelands, is to use the words the ngamudji understands, the names the sealers have branded us with.

Ugly on my tongue, remembering the sneering way the sealers speak them, the smirks, the eyerolls, the sense that the names might hold a derisive meaning, or perhaps no meaning at all, just thought-less words, nevertheless I try to form the sounds in my mouth.

A voice rises in my head, insistent, screaming, *Nyudha!* It should be our true names recorded in this white man's way. How else will our families recognise us, our husbands and children remember, our murndigarrook know where we are and somehow sing us back to Country? How else will our Liwik, whose voices have grown dim in our world as it spins further and further away, carry us back on a mornmoot to where we truly belong?

Taking a measured breath, I quieten the raging voice, soothing it with the consolation that having some names recorded is better than none being written at all. I repeat my gestures, pointing to each one of us in turn, deliberately identifying us both with our true names and in the foreign sounds the sealers have labelled us.

Meendutgarrook, Mary. Nannertgarrook, Eliza. Kardingarrook, Julia.

Animated now, the captain scribbles lines and curves on his paper. Pointing again to Meendutgarrook, he affirms the sealer's name. *You, Mary?*

Mute with trepidation, Meendutgarrook nods, pulling her two bubup close to her side.

Your children? He holds up two fingers, indicating to the little ones gripping their babayin's hands, trying to disappear behind the curtain of her rough clothes.

Meendutgarrook nods again.

Satisfied, the ngamudji turns his attention to me, calling me Eliza. Counting the toddlers clustered at my feet and the baby pressed against my breast, he holds up four fingers.

I shake my head vehemently. If this is how the sum of myself and the breadth of my experiences is to be defined by this ngamudji, then at the very least I will have *all* the children born from my body acknowledged in his white man's book.

Holding up my hand with fingers splayed, I tap each one as I speak the names of my bubup clearly, proudly.

Boyerup, Yearl Yearl, Bobbinary, Martha, John, Robert, Isabella.

The captain analyses this information, seemingly unable to reconcile the woman standing before him as a mother of seven children. Not without raised eyebrows and a palpable air of disbelief, he finally marks my testimony on his flimsy pages.

Just as he is about to turn his attention to Kardingarrook, a shout echoes from the rocky ledges above us.

The sealers are awake.

Turning to the sound, the captain passes his book to one of his crewmen and extends a waving arm in greeting to his fellow ngamudji, who saunter purposefully down the slopes towards us.

A knotting fear twists in my stomach and I see in my countrywomen the swelling of the same anxious thoughts. What will the captain tell of our story? Will the sealers distort or deny all that we have said? Will they punish us for speaking at all? Most insistently, a thought like an admonishment, a warning, a regret, lingers.

Have we missed our one chance at freedom?

I take a small step forward, pulse pounding around my body, sweating palms pressed against the swaddle of the bubup at my breast.

Please. Back to Westernport, friends.

But the captain's attention is now directed to the sealers' arrival. Our three captors stand before us, imposing, exuding a mock congeniality that makes our stomachs churn, animated in their conversation with the captain. Back and forth, questioning and answering, a narrative is woven of which we have no comprehension, no control. Every now and then, the captain adds to his notes, sometimes raising his eyebrows in wonder, sometimes pursing his lips in contemplation. Eventually he turns to us again, a sudden remembering of our existence, and checks the markings on his papers. Pointing to Meendutgarrook, he repeats the name Mary and the sealer that bought her jumps forward.

More scribbles, more stories spun in a language we cannot understand. Kardingarrook's captor likewise steps forward, volunteering unknowable information, weaving the yarns of their shared story into whatever tapestry he so chooses. Only my enslaver doesn't speak, a careful withholding of information, a reluctance to reveal too much about either the circumstances or himself.

It is not until the captain points to me and asks, *Eliza?*, does the sealer look me directly in the eyes and mutters.

No-one.

A white-hot rage burns through my bristling body. If I were not encircled by innocent babes, relied upon by younger kinswomen, half the size of him, so far away from the strength of my Biik, I would have flown at him like my spirit bird, Koonwarra, a fearsome swan charging at the hideous bunyip who seeks to destroy all that she has and all that she is.

And he knows it, a malevolent glint in his eyes as they trail up and down my body.

Glancing up from his writing, the ngamudji repeats what he believes he heard, a questioning clarification. *Nowen?*

Still keeping his stare fastened to mine, the sealer smirks. *Yes.* Turning back to the captain, he shrugs nonchalantly. *Nowen.*

Against the warning call ringing in my ears, a furious voice erupts from my lips.

I, Nannertgarrook.

Unbridled by my anger, a vicious desperation, fuelled by my cruel impotency entrenched in this imprisoned world, I spit out the words in the only tongue the men care to know, emphasising them with vehement pointing. *Boat. Friends. Westernport.*

The sounds echo through the ether like a shout, like a sob, at once carrying the force of a command and the desolation of a begging lament.

One long, breathtaking moment stretches, suspended, between the captain, the sealer and me. A kaleidoscopic warp of time where myriad possibilities spin before us, glimpses of other pathways sliding back and forth, opening and closing, waiting for that one definitive decision to set in motion the chosen direction. One glorious moment when anything is possible. When a choice could be made which sees us on a boat setting sail for our Homelands.

But then, the captain decides.

Without another word, he wipes the black ink from the calamus of his quill, blows on his paper to dry the wetted markings and closes the book on the stories he has gathered. A glance in our direction, a hasty sweep over the ragged collection of three black women and their brood of young children, and he nods to the three white men standing shoulder to shoulder as imposter ngarweet on their stolen outcrop of granite Biik.

As quickly as they arrived, the band of well-dressed ngamudji slide back down the rocks and into their waiting rowboat.

Easy strokes over the glassy ocean and they arrive at the side of their ship.

Subdued, Meendutgarrook and Kardingarrook sit back around the fire and resume skewering fish to char over the remaining embers for the sealers' breakfast. I stay standing, Bobbinary resolutely behind me, watching the big ship glide out into the depths of Warrayin, setting off in the direction I yearn to go.

Feeling his glare bore into me, I know the sealer will come for me later. Using his fists to try to convince me that I am no one, trying to beat out of my very bones any thought of self-possession, of my Boonwurrung woman's worth. For he is too ignorant to comprehend the abiding strength of the ancient line of bagarrook who stand solid behind me, stretching over scores of millennia, reaching into Time Immemorial. For he is no man, but a coward, a thief, a rapist, an idiot. So far beneath me that he has to scrape and claw, grab and pull, just to stop himself from sinking into his own abject filth.

That night, with storm clouds closing over Meeniyan the moon and a howling mornmoot writhing up from the icy Gurriin, with my bloodied face aching, my numbed body pinned underneath his brutish thrusting, I let that tiny seed of hope find a nourishing ray of sunlight. Maybe that white man, weak and indifferent, in his fine clothes and buttons of shining gold, might search for the place named Westernport. There, he might be brave enough to speak to the people on that beautiful stretch of Country, my people, and show them his barndana, a message stick of scratchings on ngamudji paper. And when they do not recognise the sounds of the sealers' names, he might remember snippets of the real ones. Even just Nannert.

And maybe that might be enough.

Maybe then my koolin ba bagarrook will know we are here and they will find a way to us.

My face is so swollen it cannot move, yet in my mind, I smile. Thinking about my husband, Bobbinary, arriving at these rocky shores in his gurrung, flanked by Barrunan and Moorderrogar. Thinking about the match between our men and these anaemic, drunken fools whose strength relies on the subjugation of women and children, and the anaesthesia of firewater. I play out these imaginary scenes over and over, long after all have fallen asleep, long after the wind screams and subsides, the rain falls and dries, and Meeniyan slips away and Nyawiinth takes her place to spin the day around again.

Over and over, Meeniyan falls and Nyawiinth rises. The sealers come and go, week in, week out, while we remain on that monumental rock, waiting. Waiting for the barndana to reach our kin. Waiting for the salvation that never comes.

Once bathed in a promising prism of sunlight, that seed of hope, sprouted with a solitary, pale green stem, freezes in time and place, slowly drained of life as the world revolves around us and we stay locked in our prison. Not long, and that little shoot withers away. The seed shrivels and hardens, and that one small space, naive and hopeful, tucked furthest into the recesses of my mind, goes dark and quiet, closing into itself.

And stays that way as the seasons roll inexorably over our unchanging island prison. Persistently dormant while we find ourselves falling, faster and faster, into the relentless hellscape of Muyiipnallook.

KULMUL
Blood

Bending under the gale force of a roaring mornmoot, the moonah trees cower over our wilams, their rugged, woody backs braced against the wind, holding us safe inside their leafy arms. Around us, shards of icy rain hurl upon the bald heads of boulders. Gushing waterfalls cascade down their faces, and the giant rocks become small like crying children, terrified in the wrath of a storm darkened Sky Country.

Huddled together, we three mothers and our gasping children wrap ourselves in our blankets of kuyim and wait. It is all we can do, tiny in the majestic awe of a ravaging gurriin, to wait and wait, and watch for the signs that the storm is easing.

Dolls made of woven grass and dried kelp stare out blankly from our toddlers' fists, their nutted eyes mirroring the dazed expression of their young owners. Gently prising them from rigid fingers, Meendutgarrook sits the dolls in a line.

Ignoring the whistling mornmoot snaking through the wilam, she starts up a song, telling the story of the burribarri scratching their nests in flimsy sand. As she sings, she picks up each doll, one by one, flapping their arms and kicking their legs in a funny dance, their eyes bouncing up and down comically. Slowly, surely, the bubup start to laugh. Grin growing, Meendutgarrook revels in the play, daring us all to smile in spite of the maelstrom surrounding us. Before long, all the children join in, the older ones twisting the toys into ridiculous shapes, each trying to outdo the other.

Late that night, bubup finally asleep, we all press close to each other under the warmth of a patchwork of kuyim blankets. Eyes closed, I listen to the Country's rage. As each thunder of colossal waves crash against the cliffs and the force rumbles through the rock beneath us, an image pushes into my mind like a beacon in the bellowing storm. Of a flimsy boat carrying three sealers, buffeted by a vengeful Warrayin, tossed like a child's toy against the jagged teeth of rocks and smashed into uncountable pieces. I picture the submersed silence of their underwater grave and it is like a soothing salve, cold and calm. I watch as three shadows, the broken bodies of the unredeemable ngamudji, sink into the booroonth of a bottomless ocean.

The next morning breaks tranquil, a collection of pacified clouds smattered across a now clear Woorwoor. Emerging from our moonah cocoon, we survey the damage wrought on this resilient Biik.

Long accustomed to the ferocity of south driven gurriin, the island has cleverly evolved. Hunkered down vegetation remains intact and the myriad of creatures seeking harbour within their sheltering kalk emerge unscathed to resume their daily business.

Travelling along the well-worn trails on the upper ridgeline, we can see from our high vantage point the tumbled rocks below and a now subdued Warrayin. Several lengths above the ocean surface, a tide line of driftwood and kelp hang precariously from boulders and ledges.

I hold my breath, last night's wishful image of a rowboat pummelled against the rocks still fresh in my mind, as I search the beached debris for signs of wreckage.

There is none.

I exhale, slow and surrendered, most of me knowing it was a fanciful wish, but clinging to the delusion for as long as I could anyway. Later that afternoon, with the stormfront spent and the sea remaining appeased after its violent bluster, the sealers' boat returns.

A whistle signals for us to make our way down to the berthing bay. Piles of uncleaned kangaroo pelts are hauled from the boat and, skin after skin, we trudge them up the soggy slopes to the wilams, where we will scrape and dry them by the campfire late into the night.

Just before dawn, a rasping cough echoes around the boulders and Kardingarrook dutifully rises to tend to her captor. Throughout the day, the congestion thickens until it seems the sealer's very insides might expel on his next wheeze. Piling the fire near the ngamudji's wilam with fresh green peppermint leaves, we infuse the air with a healing smoke to try to clear his chest. Kardingarrook also uses the leaves boiling in water to flavour the sealer's tea, hoping to stave off the strengthening infection and prevent the cough from spreading. Along the string of islands used as our various prisons, we had witnessed firsthand the devastating effects of the white man's illnesses on countrywomen and children.

Three days later and every bubup is afflicted with the deathly illness, their tiny bodies heaving with the same wracking cough. Kardingarrook too, and no amount of smoking or steaming, tea or balm makes the slightest difference. Helpless, Meendutgarrook and I try to keep some light shining in the little ones' eyes by flailing the arms of dancing dolls, humming the tunes of ancient lullabies, telling the stories of cheeky baby whales and mysterious Koormamgarrook. But, as the blanket of Booroonth descends, the illness worsens and an icy fear begins to crystallise around my heart.

Please make them well, I murmur to our Liwik, over and over.

Wheezing in shallow gasps, my youngest, still a swaddled babe just past her first year, is barely able to feed at my breast. Instead, she slumps against my chest, skin clammy, body battling an unseeable assailant. Stroking her smooth forehead, her velvet skin feels danger-ously hot to the touch, in spite of the chilled winter air flurrying around the corners of our camp. All night I lie awake, holding her tiny hand, trying to coax her to suckle. As the darkness draws on and her wheezing rasps louder, it is all I can do to keep willing her to breathe.

Please let her live, I whisper in the dead of night, not knowing if anyone or anything is really listening now. *Let her live.*

But, by the first light of morning, she is gone.

And then one by one, the others fall. So quickly after Isabella, young John and Robert are swept away. Striking Martha with a lessened ferocity, she clings to life across the night and makes it through to morning, the tiniest speck of light beginning to glow again in her eyes at sunrise.

But then, before the day is over, it takes a hold of Bobbinary. Ferocious in its attacks, my boy's lithe body is no match for its savagery. I lie beside him through the aching night, begging the Liwik to let him live.

Take the ngamudji, I plead in my mind, watching his chest barely move with an agonising labour. *Let him live.*

But the Old Ones are silent. His body is cold by the morning.

Fists clenched, I stand on the very edge of a steep, wind battered cliff, staring out at a vicious Warrayin.

Why didn't you take them! Why didn't you take the ngamudji! I scream, furious, heartbroken. *Why my bubup, my innocent babes? My Isabella. My John. My Robert. My Bob . . .*

I falter. I cannot speak his name. No, no, no. Unspeakable anguish pounds around my head. No words, only sobbing. Then, the primal urge surges again and I am screaming once more.

Why them?

Wailing once more into the ambivalent ether until my throat burns, taut and tearing, and I can barely breathe.

Collapsing to the ground, I convulse in a retching spasm, empty stomach churning in the sickness of unutterable grief. I pound my fists against the dirt, trying to shift the pain away from my wounded heart.

But I cannot, and once again, a scream gathers force at the base of my spine and rips its way through my body, careening out of my mouth.

Why didn't you take them instead? Why didn't you take them instead?

Even in the cacophony of my cries, I am acutely aware of the silence surrounding my questions. No answers come from Woorwoor, no signs from Biik to explain, to justify, to make sense of the endless cruelty. Only silence.

And it is then that I truly know, we are alone. Too far adrift from our Homelands, all tethers severed, unreachable by our Liwik, or any songlines our murndigarrook might sing. We are alone. Our murrup abandoned on this hostile, stony beast squatting in an uncaring Sea Country.

I pick up the nearest rock and, with as much force as I can muster, bring it down upon my chest. Under this ngamudji's cloth, the scars of my earned rites of passage rise up to remind me of all that I used to know, Lore and Law wrapping around me, culture and knowledge weaving through my skin. I had it all for a sacred, blessed stretch of time.

And now it is gone. Along with three innocent babies and the child of my true husband. My little Bobbinary. A living, walking, playing, laughing, beautiful embodiment of his father, the one who kept the tethering of my soul to the life I had before. Gone.

Over and over, I strike at my chest. Around me I hear a ghastly wail, and I know it is coming from me, but I feel nothing in my numbed body. Nothing at all. Blood seeps into the creamy hues of my captor's clothes and I rip them away, baring the tears in my flesh to the uncaring ether.

When my arm falls to the ground weak with exhaustion, when my flesh has split into gaping wounds, when my throat is swollen closed and no sound can be formed, I stare up into Woorwoor, helpless as a child. Shaking my head, I know I will never understand. I know that no yulendji will ever arrive to ease my sorrow.

A bitter chant loops relentless in my mind.

Why didn't you take the ngamudji instead?

As the sinking sun hits Warrayin's edge and brilliant shafts of light pierce up through the clouds, the passage of Karralk lights up in a golden glare. I stare at it, on my knees, paralysed.

Until one strangled word is expelled from my lips in a shattered, bewildered gasp.

Why . . .?

BALDU
Fall

The last grave holds two small bodies, one wrapped around the other, the protective embrace of an older brother forever watching over his baby sister. It is nearly impossible for me to look at their sleeping forms, but I force myself to, knowing this will be the last time.

Bobbinary's face is peaceful at rest, his velvet skin dark like booroonth on the night he was conceived, a glorious, long-ago night when I was wrapped in my husband's sheltering arms and staring at the blanket of Sky Country above us. And just like those dazzling djurts, my mammam's eyes shone as twinkling points of light illuminating the world around him. Closed now, the light extinguished.

Resting in the curve of his arm, Isabella sleeps, the bubup still enfolded in her swaddle of patchwork kuyim pelt. I stare at them both for an age of time, willing their eyelids to flutter open, their chests to rise with life giving air, for something, anything, to change. But they are motionless in the folds of each other's too young bodies.

For me, there is no comfort to be found in this vision, no hints of peace, not for a long time yet. But, looking down on these two children together, held in a cradle of earth and soft leaves, I find the beginnings of an unwilling, yet inevitable, acceptance.

This minuscule seed of respite does not prevent my body from quaking as I place a small square of woven mat over Isabella's tiny face. Threaded through strands of poa grass are strings of my braided hair, cut when I felt her murrup leave me, and blossoms of as many flowers as I could find on this barren island. I place it gently over her infant cheeks like a small blanket of protection, a shield, serving to hide that which pierces my heart to see.

Another woven covering rests at my feet, same as Isabella's, grass threaded with babayin's hair, and rings of fading blossoms in hues of yellow and red. But resting in a line along its centre is a string of delicate shells, collected a long time ago from the beach of another island prison. Collected for another bubup, my Boyerup, when my naive younger self still held a flame of hope that it would not be long before I saw her again.

Time has not offered kindness to me. It has been a cruel master in the years that have passed by since, no realisation of hopeful fantasies, no pathways leading back to the arms of Country and Kin. Just a relentless marching away from where we all should have been, the life we should have lived.

Even this mammam lying before me now, who was just a growing shape held in my body when I first picked up those shells. As was his birthright, Time should have forged him a pathway back to the shores of his Biik, to flourish in the blossoming of who he was meant to be, wundul to Boyerup and Yearl Yearl, third born of Bobbinary and Nannertgarrook, a child of Waa, heir to the mighty estate of the Burinyong-Balak. Yet here he lies, so far away from all he was promised as a murrup entering his mother's body.

Placing the woven covering over his precious face, a shriek of grief wails against the walls of my skull.

No.

Too exhausted to howl, it spins instead in a dizzying mindayi around and around in my head. Steadying myself with knees planted on the ground, I fill my fists with soil. Scoop by scoop, I place the earth carefully on my children's slender limbs and let Biik slowly disappear their bodies, until the ruffled land is level again and they are gone.

Beside me, Meendutgarrook and Kardingarrook stare at the small mounds of unsettled ground in front of them. In their hollow forms

I see the same collapsing grief. This should never have been. No mother should ever have to lay a child to sleep in the cold cloak of the earth. Let alone whole families of them. For in this small stretch of rocky Biik lie most of our once thriving brood of bubup. Four of mine, two of Kardingarrook's and both of Meendutgarrook's. All lost to the disease of the ngamudji.

Only Kardingarrook's youngest, with the shock of sandy hair, and my five-year-old manggip Martha, gently rocking the fretting one-year-old to sleep under the boughs of a nearby moonah tree, remain. And once again, that bereft question thundering in my head escapes my lips as a strangled whisper.

Why?

A week later, we stand in a pressing huddle, shoulder to shoulder, hands intertwined, on a flat, stony headland at the northernmost peninsula of our island prison. Time after time, when Nyawiinth's rosy light made this Biik beautiful, my countrywomen and I, a bright bevy of little ones gathering around our legs, would come here to fish. If Warrayin allowed, two of us might even slide into her icy depths while the third played and watched over our children. Diving like we did long ago in another time and place, our breaths held calmly over stretching minutes, we would swim like the Koormamgarrook to the kelp beds below. Boonwurrung women in our saltwater element, diving long to pull abalone from the depths. A feast for babayin and bubup only, when the sealers were away.

So many times, we would sit around the campfire, rocking our babies in tarnooks, telling boisterous toddlers to keep away from the ridge's slopes, twisting the arms and legs of reeded dolls in silly dances, laughing at their nutted eyes swinging up and down in a joyous bounce. With balls made from stretched kuyim skin, or thick leathery leaves of washed up kelp, we would play catch with the bigger ones. Testing their agility, imagining them playing marng-rook with their cousins on the pristine shores of a distant land. And sometimes, for a short while at least, their play would soothe the heartache for that distant kin. Tiny legs running, peals of laughter ringing, their flurries of life would sound large enough to make a whole clan estate here in this place. A new collective of family, three liwurruk together, joining their bubup as a clan, making our own women's circle as best we could under the boughs of another kind of moonah on shores of hardened stone.

But that was yellinguth, many yesterdays ago. Today there are no sounds of play, laughter, women's fires, or saltwater dives. Our children are gone, our circle is ruptured. And now, after the turning of two winters, Kardingarrook is being taken from us once again.

Swaying beside the rocks below, listing on a swelling sea, a rowboat is packed with belongings. Sealing men gather in clumps like barnacles on the ledges of jagged cliffs. Some skinned pale, another whose flesh is blacker than mine, yet another like that one on the beach years ago, brown skin with large cheekbones, who helped an old lecherous ngamudji vanish away a petrified girl of no more than seven into the bush.

Beside me, Kardingarrook shivers uncontrollably. Strapped in a kuyim blanket around her, resting his head peacefully against her breast, her youngest bubup, now her only child, is mercifully oblivious to her tumult. But Meendutgarrook and I feel every quaking tremor, as they ripple back and forth through all of our bodies.

Gripping her hands in mine, I turn to her with as much reassurance as I can muster. *He says he is taking you home?*

Biting her trembling lip, Kardingarrook nods doubtfully.

Then that is what you must hold in your heart. I squeeze her fingers, trying to infuse into her very cells, somehow, a sense of resolute strength, of courage in the midst of yet another unknown future. *He said you are going home. He promised.* My voice carries the steeliness of determination. *And when he forces his way into your bed, you should remind him. Remind him that he promised to take you home.*

Stroking her beautiful face, trying to etch its contours into my memory, I feel my own bravery beginning to falter. Under my touch,

Kardingarrook senses it too, and everything about her crumples. Sadness sweeps through all three of us and we are weeping again, *mardan mardan*, as we have so often in the past, too many times, too many tears still left in our weary bodies to spill. Yet another *warrana wurrba*.

Promise me, you will get home, I whisper. *For all of us.*

In a succession of forceful pulls on the oars, the rowboat lurches away from the island. With both arms wrapped tightly around her still-sleeping *bubup*, Kardingarrook is planted, unmoving, against the side of the vessel, stare locked, unblinking, with ours. Heaving strokes send her further away, and as she grows smaller and smaller in our view, I try to send her my message again through the ether.

Promise you will get home for all of us.

Steady in the undulating, open sea, the boat glides out from under the giant boulder island's shadows, and suddenly I see a bundle move in the very far corner of it.

Illuminated in the late afternoon sunlight, a pile of stacked *kuyim* skins rolls upright, elongating into the silhouette of a *bagarrook* and I realise I am looking at another countrywoman, much like the women we once befriended on other prison islands years ago. Like Kardingarrook, she has a bundle strapped to her chest, a tiny infant at the breast, yet another *babayin* trying desperately to keep both her child and herself alive in this brutal world.

How many?

My brain reels with the sudden, splitting thought. How many of us are out there? Countrywomen ripped from their *Biik*, their husbands, their children, their mothers, everything that they know and are. How many of us have they stolen, enslaved, trapped on barren islands over uncountable fathoms of *Warrayin*? How many of us in this agonising state of loss and fear, yearning and despair?

The gentle tugging of a small hand upon my trembling fingers breaks my gaze on Kardingarrook and the other woman in the departing boat.

Face pinched with worry, Martha's tone is plaintive. *I don't want Aunty to go.*

Even though her six-year-old legs are long now, I still lift her up high and sit her gently on my hip. Holding her close, I whisper, *Me neither, bubup.*

Where is she going?

Mustering as broad a smile as I can manage, even though my liwurruk is leaving us, even though I might never see her again, even though my heart shatters once more, I touch the tip of her delicate nose and say, *She's going home.*

BERRENBERREN
Flee

My body glides between enormous shapes as if I am one of them. Their song fills the water around me like music floating on a breeze from afar. Each note holds more meaning than a string of words ever could and somehow I can understand its every nuance. Songs of family enjoined, mothers shepherding the young through a vast saltwater world, communities uplifting each other over the journey of epic lifetimes. Songs of obligation and antiquity, duties to carry ancient lines of yulendji through Countries and Dreamings, dimensions and eons, knowledge that cuts across the fabric of time itself. There are simple songs too, of greetings and curiosity, sung as I pass between them, these magnificent bodies of the betayil, at once massive yet weightless in the buoyant arms of Warrayin.

Reaching the sandbank at Yellodungo, I see the thin black legs of my countrywomen standing, stork-like, in the shallows. I hear their song too, hovering in the sky above, different sounds, the hum of human voices, clapping sticks and beating drums, but the sentiment is the same. Mirror images of each other, the songs are a conversation between bagarrook and betayil, back and forth, spanning species and generations and epochs. I want to float here forever, enfolded in the liquid blanket of Warrayin, wrapped in the vibrant melodies of woman and whale, effortless in the water like a Koormamgarrook.

Until I am not. Until the water grows denser around me as a snaking ribbon of red winds its way towards me. I know immediately what it is. Blood. The kulmul of the whale beside me, gushing like a waterfall until I am enveloped in its clinging viscosity. More rivulets cascade around me and, with an inexplicable heaviness, the glorious betayil beside me begins to sink to the bottom of the ocean, streams of red curling upwards as she falls. One by one, each whale plunges, blood seeping from their beings, until not one remains swimming in the vast sea.

And all around me is silence. Deafening, pervasive silence.

Eyelids flickering open, I make out shapes looming in shadows. Curves of our women's wilam, sheltering two mounds of blanketed bodies. I'm not ensconced in the saltwater of Warrayin, back in the Warnmarring bay of my Homelands.

Instead, I am where I have been for so long now, lying on a bed of stone, barely cushioned by layers of leaves, pelts and the ngamudji's rugs. A stabbing pain spears into my heart and I clutch at my chest with a sense of dread. Movement nearby tells me that Meendutgarrook is awake. She has felt it too.

Wrapping our cloaks of kuyim around us, we pick our way over to the windswept and salt-sprayed, southern cliffs of the island, perennially bare from the pummelling force of Warrayin and Mornmoot raging from Gurriin. Even though it is not yet first light, we know every inch of this prison Biik, having trudged up and down its rocky slopes, season after season, year after year, until we can, like now, traverse it under booroonth's inky darkness.

Dread hangs heavy in our limbs with every step. We know what waits for us out to sea. It has happened before, and as each season rolls ever onwards, the destruction grows more and more.

Carrying the daal kalk we have fashioned from the limbs of moonah, we arrive at the furthest jutting headland and sit looking out to the ocean. The howls of men in the distance twist like wraiths on the wind, so we bring our women's sticks together with a mournful clap and offer up a counterbalance. Funeral songs are what we sing now, merging the chants of our Old Ones with the laments that rise from our wrenching bellies. Somehow, we hope, somehow these sounds, sent with love, with sisterhood, with the hum of our ancient connection, will drown out the raging of all others.

Even as Meendutgarrook and I sing, I wish Nyawiinth would not wake this morning. I don't want to see what his light will show me. Fear makes my body weak, makes me weep, but I sing our songs and clap our sticks all the same. When that purple dawn bleeds up from the horizon and the colours of the world emerge from the dark around us, we see her.

Oh! She is beautiful. This glorious giant of the deep blue, ageless as Time itself, bringer of blessed life to the bagarrook and munmundiik of my Biik. The magnificence of her gracious form, gentle in its power, peaceful in its dominance, inspiring of evangelical awe within even the staunchest of disbelievers. Within even the savages who rip her apart right now. Because in their shrieking and yelling is the shrill ring of terror. They know their pitiful smallness, that at any second, if she so chooses, one mighty thrash of her fluke and they would all be dead. Even while I try to diligently sing these songs of honour for our betayil, a compulsive urge wants to change the words, decimate the tune, scream out at the top of my lungs.

Kill them! Kill them all!

Yet I know this is not the way of Mother Whale and her children. And so, she is stabbed and hacked until her blood runs red into the sea. Harpoons shatter her blowhole, lances plunging into her lungs. Ropes slash and knot around her, cutting into her flesh, reining her flailing body to the side of the boat. She is still alive, still sentient and knowing, understanding it all, feeling it all, as they hack at her flippers and fluke, throwing them to the sharks swarming to feast on her butchered body. That giant soulful eye, lit with the presence of her ancient murrup, sees everything. The horror, the cruelty, the teeth of the darrak tearing at the dismembered pieces of her own body, the men's jeers ugly with orgiastic bloodlust.

Look to us, I howl in my mind. *We are here with you. We see you.*

And I throw all my hope and wishes to the stars in the sky, the Liwik so long quiet around us, Mother Whale resting in the safe arms of Warnmarring, that this betayil's giant eye sees us instead. How I hope it is us, singing to her soul from a windswept ocean cliff, that she sees in her dying moments, not the savagery raging around and through her.

Look to us.

How I hope, with every fibre of my broken-hearted being, the sacred betayil can see us now so that she knows she is not alone.

Later that afternoon, her desecrated remains are unleashed from the whaling boat and discarded into the sea. For most of the day, our two captors have watched the carving up of the betayil with a fervent glee. When her body is released, they race down to the water's edge to launch their boat. Scavengers, ever hungry for easy exploitation, they hook her remains to their vessel and tow her to the nearest shore on the mainland, directly across from our island prison, in full view of the ridges where we fish.

Years ago, I would stare longingly at that stretch of clean sand and imagine pressing my feet into its coolness, like I did on the beaches of my Biik. Imagining myself wandering the curve of the bay back and forth, scouring the tidelines for Warrayin's treasure. Some days, I would stare at those shores while my hands moved in autonomous motion, weaving what binuk we could from the island's wily bobad grass. Staring until my eyes stung from the glare of the reflective white sand. Then staring still more, until shapes would emerge along the gleaming coastlines, boys playing marngrook, girls collecting shells.

Clear as the shining day, I would see my mammam, Yearl Yearl, sprinting along its length with delighted abandon, remembering now to dodge the fragile nest of the burribarri. I would see my manggip, Boyerup, splashing and diving like a Koormamgarrook, searching for fruits of the sea, practising holding her breath in preparation for the time when she would descend into the giant kelp forests with her bagarrook kin. So long I would stare, and when I saw this vision strongly in my mind, I imagined myself waving to them from these not so distant rocks, pretending they were the boulders of Babayin Betayil near our women's sacred places. And I would fool myself that any minute now, Bobbinary would launch his gurrung into Warrayin and with a few powerful strokes of his strong arms, he would arrive to carry me back for a feast and ngargee around our blazing campfire.

Not anymore. Not for so many years now. Not since the whalers infested these waters with their murderous work. I turn to those shores now and see a bloody graveyard, strewn with the remains of all kinds of betayil. I have seen too much of their blood staining the white sand red, pooling into the clear, calm waters, tainting the vision forever. I had looked there as a soothing balm, for hope, for a harbour to hold my wishful dreaming, to play out in parallel the life I so desperately wanted to continue living. Now it holds the nightmare of the sacred whale, my family's totem, the revered being I am duty-bound to honour and care for, being mercilessly tortured and killed. One by one, they disappear, while I stand raging in my futile impotence with only song and daal kalk as my pitiful shields of protection.

Over the next few days, the ngamudji will pick apart the remains of the whale until only her bones are left. From her flayed body, they will sever her lips, her tongue, her cheeks, her eyes, those parts of her that would sing to her kin, rub up against her child, see the world with wise understanding. And they will boil down these parts of her majestic body into a few barrels of oil. Pleased with themselves, they will return with a handful of white man's treasure rattling in their pockets, fine threads caressing their backs, a swagger as if they were someone of importance or value. But Meendutgarrook and I know the truth. We see them for what they really are. The betayil see them for what they really are.

Warragul.

Night falls and he latches onto my arm to pull me into his wilam. Still etched on his skin, the stench of his vile exploits fume in the air, always there, no matter how soft his clothes are now or how bright the buttons on his coat shine. Before he pushes me onto the bed, he takes a piece of cloth from his pocket and rests it on his timbered trunk. Carefully, deliberately, he pulls it back to reveal his souvenir.

One enormous, gleaming, lonely tooth.

Hers.

BUNNULL LAANG
Mountain of Stone

Around and around the island, Meendutgarook and I walk. Back and forth along the flattened headlands, up and down the slopes of slippery granite. Blasted by the salt-laden crash of wind and water on the southwestern cliffs, sheltered in the resilient groves of moonah and peppermint to the north and east. We know the finest place where the kelp forests flourish, how deep we should dive for our fruits of the sea and exactly when Darrak the shark will be patrolling too close.

Tucked away under the base of a windswept scrub or hopping through the undergrowth of a fledgling tea tree, we know which bird, which lizard, which tiny kuyim will be making their homes in their favoured location. Down at the ocean's edge, whether it swells in a placid lull or foams with a chopping rage, we know which wirrap will be biting, at each outcrop of rock, at any given switch of the seasons. Every foot of this hulking beast is known to us now. We can walk it in the dark. We know the song of its every rumble, crack, whistle and grumbling sigh.

Our wilams are long embedded, earth and tree rising around them, hunkering them into the land, holding them close whether through driving rain or baking sun. Clusters of ngamudji vegetables sprout in forgiving soil, sculpted stones lay waiting to grind roots and seeds, cleaned and covered wells hold the rain to water us all.

There is certainty in this prison estate, a monotonous thread of easy knowledge. Unchanging, as the cycles of time endlessly repeat, like a trapping vortex that swirls around only us. We remain tethered here in an isolated stasis, but we know just beyond our bouldered edges, the world spins in dizzying transformation.

Outside, nothing remains the same. More and more of the foreigners' ships glide along the coastline, claiming everything they see as if it has always been their own. Less and less life thrives in Warrayin. No splashing of inquisitive seals, no aerial acrobatics from dolphins, no waving flukes from journeying mother whales. The children of Sea Country do not play anymore, they are dead bodies piled on a ngamudji's ship. When we stand on the peak of our rocky Biik, we can see Country on the mainland lose its very self, dunes and hilltops flattened, rivers and streams denuded, giant trees toppled after centuries, taking whole communities of creatures crashing to oblivion with them. Silence has descended, the shocked hush of irreparable decimation. A silence I first felt as a young bagarrook laying in the dunes of Warnmarring, ears pricked and listening for sounds of the koormam on Korriyong. Hearing nothing, but feeling the thickness of that quiet roll over the bay like a deafening boom. A vile sickness, spreading its infection across mountains, valleys, bays and the ocean, season after relentless season.

Viral, pervasive, fatal silence.

No Country now for those bagarrook and bubup on that Biik, I murmur.

Around the campfire, nothing to do but watch the flames lick the cooling air, I tell Meendutgarrook the story of my grandmother, for possibly the hundredth time. How it was late at night and I, as a bubup of eight, should have been fast asleep, but the Elders were talking knowledge and I was eager to learn. How my Gugungiyup held something soft and white in her wizened hands. Something I had never seen before, not made from any substance I knew, no skin, fur, reed or feather, to exist on our Biik.

I know now it was a white man's shirt, I say, the story spoken in the same way each rendition.

Yet, Meendutgarrook is patient and attentive, as always, a thirst to learn like I had. Still have, but the yearning is pushed down so deep, buried under so much numbness, I sometimes forget the yulendji I will never know, the thought of which is almost more than I can bear.

And my granny whispered to the murndigarrook around her, to the fire, to the air, to Warrayin rolling beyond the sand dunes. To the Liwik in the days when they were listening. The ngamudji are here. And if they don't leave, I fear it's the end of our world.

Tonight though, something is different. That yearning has risen from its buried depths and thrums like an aching wound in my chest. Remembering myself as that child, so curious, happy and innocent, remembering the shores of Euroyuroke, our country of burribarri, remembering my own children.

My first ones, birthed on my sacred Biik, Boyerup and Yearl Yearl, their scars still raised on my chest, would be grown now. They would bear their own ceremonial scars, and I, their babayin, the one who should have lit their path of yulendji, have missed it all. *Do they remember me?*

In a grove of turrung, barely a short walk from our wilam, white bones of little ones were buried in the ground too soon, claimed now by the spreading moonah, the roots, like mothers' arms, forever holding them. My beautiful Bobbinary, his father's mammam, wrapped in an eternal embrace with his bubup liwurruk Isabella. *Do their spirits walk beside me?*

And I think of Martha, just six years old when she became the only one left after the sickness swept the others away. Always pressed against my side, there, watching with nine-year-old eyes, when her sister Nancy was born under the same moonah. Pulled from my side at twelve, barely a munmundiik, no ceremony allowed, no yulendji bestowed, taken by her ngamudji father to the new places imposed on that desecrated Biik across Warrayin. And then again with Nancy, even younger, a child of ten, ripped from my arms and whisked away on the sealer's cursed gurrung.

How I wept and wailed, how I struck at my breast and clawed at his face. How the blows glanced off me and I barely felt their force, so agonising was my mother's pain at losing my babes once again. And how I could do nothing. No word, no action, no song, no ceremony, would change this relentless fate, would bring any of my bubup back. *Do they yearn for me, like I for them, all these years later?*

On the other side of the fire, Meendutgarrook's hands rest on her rounded belly. It has been so long since her body bloomed with child. I think of the path her fate has trod. How, after the sickness took her first- and second-born, the grief closed her body shut. Even when the seed of a bubup started to grow, it was only for a short time. Before her belly had even started to bloom, they too were swept away in an outpouring of blood and tears. And yet here she now sits, swollen with a baby nearly full-grown, ready to reveal themselves to the world.

Another bubup for me too. Tucked away in the safest corner of our women's wilam, wrapped in the finest of our skins and blankets, my youngest manggip, Emma, sleeps. She is my world, my djurt, the constant light I cling to. Brave one, curious and clever, she could run before she cared to walk, all of seven years but intuits the world like a murndigarrook. Her labour was the last great push my body had to offer, before she closed herself to the toil of building beings, birthing them into a turbulent world, and suffering them being ripped away. Sometimes I wonder if it was our sleeping Liwik sending Emma to me as the balm that might heal my burning edges, the year before they took Nancy from me. Only so many times can a babayin's heart be shredded. Only so many times can it bear to be repaired again with rebirth.

Whatever the reason, if there is one at all, for the bright spark of djurt, the old soul of my youngest manggip Emma, I muse pensively, *I am grateful.*

Silence sits heavy around us tonight. Perhaps it is the stillness of this subdued booroonth, eerie in its sense of waiting readiness.

Not a flutter of breeze in the trees, no crashing boom from a wind-swept swell, just stillness.

Looking up to a cloudless Sky Country, Meendutgarrook points to the shimmering, shy cluster of Seven Sisters, suspended in their perpetual journey for the briefest of moments, directly above us.

Tell me about Munmundiik.

So many times she has asked for their story, eager and hungry to have the mysteries of our Old Ones unwrapped. So many times I tell her the yulendji I know, golden threads of Lore that weave the patchwork of a beautiful tapestry, never finished.

But tonight, as my mouth opens to speak, it's not words which come, but a great rush of that yearning I try so hard to subdue with the numbing monotony of our island existence. On this tranquil, harmless night, it erupts so forcefully within me, I am powerless to stop its weeping, the agony of years spent wishing for another lifetime.

A lifetime where I am the teacher, the knowledge keeper, the story holder, as my birthright had destined me to be. Walking the trail of our bagarrook songlines along the undulating dunes of Mindayi, bathing in our holy waters, bleeding in ancient ceremony, our Munmundiik keeping watch out to sea, bearing witness to my earning of ageless wisdom. So many layers of yulendji I should have learned, knowledge nurtured and passed along to grow the next generation in the ways of our Old Ones. That unbroken line of women I am born from, so endless it stretches into the Time when memory first began.

Flooding from me is the anguish of countless years of aching, the constant remembering and desperate forgetting of images, memories, treasures and life stolen. The precious light in my children's eyes, the flick of emu feather skirts, whale songs resounding across the bay, marriages promised, ngargee planned, the thudding of feet in dance, drums and clapsticks beating in harmony, hands held around the firelight of a women's kuunh, flashes of my husband's searing gaze, wavering voices of the murndigarrook surging in ancient songs. And again, my Liwik's yulendji, the pathway of its learning once stretching before me on an ageless songline, waiting to fill my murrup with joy and passion and purpose. Gone, nearly forgotten. Now but a phantom echo whistling on a lonely mornmoot.

I cover my face with trembling hands, hoping my liwurruk has not seen my tears.

Tell me about Munmundiik, she says again.

A pressure hammers in my brain. *What of value do I have to tell?* After so many years, what now can I teach my insatiable Meendutgarrook, whose starving eyes and questions scratch at my mind in hopeful desperation? What now can I teach my sleeping bubup wrapped in her kuyim blanket, who should be lying in the luscious fur of the wallert wallert, surrounded by whole communities of kin on the glorious estate of the Burinyong-Balak? Not here. A rock in the middle of a raging sea. In the sadistic playing fields of another kind altogether, with no knowledge, no rules, no morals, only savage whim and ruthless gratification.

What of value do I have to tell? For so many years now, the fragments of my song and story, knowledge and teachings, visions of ngargee and yingali, have swum in endless loops around my head, searching for a way out to those I was duty bound to teach. I have yearned for those joyous nights under a starry blanket of booroonth, so much like tonight, of dancing, choruses of songs, feasts of our Biik's generous offerings. And my people, so many people I love, gathered around glowing firelight, cleansed in the smoke of our sacred branches, sharing story, after song, after song, after story.

We should be with our people, is all I can whisper to my kin, my voice cracking under the weight of the endless, crushing loss.

Meendutgarrook rushes to my side, loving arms wrapping around me. *I know.*

And she is sobbing as well. Clinging to each other like a mini cluster of Two Sisters in our desolate orbit, we, once more, try to shed the perpetual cloak of our shared grief. Munmundiik in Sky Country passes over us and Meeniyan slips away to rest below the distant horizon. At last, our tears subside with the darkness.

Is it enough? I ask in an uncertain whisper.

Her eyes shine with a profound understanding. Is it enough that I share all the stories I know over and over, sing our songs with only two strong voices, stomp our feet against stony ground in our favourite dances of betayil and barrunan, so far from the bays of our Biik.

It is enough, she whispers back.

We are still awake as Nyawiinth's first light filters through the wilam. In a glowing halo of pink and gold, Meendutgarrook stands to greet the rising sun. Arms outstretched, she is like Wootokorrook, the morning star, gracing the world below with her blazing beauty.

Then suddenly she falls. And cries out in pain.

The baby is coming.

Two excruciating days and nights and finally the baby arrives, exhausted, barely moving. Meendutgarrook holds him to her breast, suckling him with the wisps of energy she has left, even as blood still seeps from her shattered body. More days pass by in a feverish nightmare as I try to keep babayin and bubup alive.

Finally, the miraculous powers of woman prevail. Stronger and stronger, the couple fortify in unison, Meendutgarrook's body begins to heal and the tiny boy she names Barrunan thrives under her devoted care.

When at last it seems the dangers have passed, the sealers return, and we are bound once more into their enslavement as if nothing at all had happened. No acknowledgement of the miracle that had been achieved, no understanding of the extraordinary rescue of a mother and child from the precipice of death. Only deliberate indifference, beyond naming the bubup John. And, in spite of her body being bruised and battered from the rigours of a dangerous birth, Meendutgarrook is called upon to cook, clean, mend and wash, and satisfy her captor's desire.

Even as she begins to bleed again.

Weeks later, standing shoulder to shoulder on the headland, Emma clutching my hand, the babe swaddled tight to Meendutgarrook's chest, we watch the sealers lurch their boat out into Warrayin again. Only when the vessel rounds the cliffs and disappears from sight does relief begin to soften our limbs. Then, Emma turns to us, hands planted on her hips, and sighs in exasperation.

I just wish they wouldn't keep coming back!

A burst of laughter bubbles from within both Meendutgarrook and me, and it is like the sun erupting from behind a bank of heavy cloud. We are flooded in my little girl's innocent light, a truth spoken with a child's earnest forthrightness.

I see Meendutgarrook's laughing face, the flash of her wide, toothy grin, a flare of youthful radiance. I see the sleeping newborn swaddled to her breast, and beyond, my Emma skipping back towards our wilam.

Love softens my rigid limbs.

Even if it is just the four of us, I think to myself, *we are a family.* Together, we are enough.

DJINDIBIK
All Gone

Our catch is plentiful today. Emma and I clean and scale the wirrap, ready for roasting on a fire. My manggip is a brave one, adventurous, saltwater blood pumping through her veins. Always bursting with an eagerness to launch herself into Warrayin and play at seals and mermaids, practising her best diving and breath holding, even in the chilliest of waters. Soon, she will be ready to venture to a sea kelp patch and learn the ways of the Koormamgarrook, merging with the swaying stems, slowing her heartbeat, discovering the secrets, the wonders, the dangers, of the underwater world. Even here, so far from the Biik that is etched in her blood, my daughter swims like the Boonwurrung bubup she is.

Back at our women's wilam, we slow roast the skewered fish over low burning flames. From one of the sealer's camps in a distant bend of the moonah grove, we hear the sounds of Meendutgarrook, busy with some strange labour. Emma sings out to her that the wirrap are ready and my liwurruk takes her place by the kuunh, baby Barrunan nestled at her breast. Tiny wrists now filling out with the chubbiness of a thriving bubup, he will soon be ready to hold his own head up then discover the excitement of self-propelled motion on tender hands and knees.

For the rest of the afternoon, Meendutgarrook is away from the wilam while Emma and I fortify baskets made of sturdy turrung kalk and ngamudji rope to catch the crabs and crayfish around the rocks off the north eastern ledges. When she returns, I anxiously watch my kin's fixed purposefulness, barely glancing at me, her whole focus on the mysterious task that has occupied her over the last few days in the sealer's wilam. An unsettling fear swells in the pit of my stomach, something unknown sits in the slope of her shoulders, the crease of her brow, the grim set of her unsmiling face.

Just before Nyawiinth slides down to meet the blue line on the western horizon, Meendutgarrook comes to us, Barrunan swaddled to her chest, struggling to carry an enormous kuyim rug, the blanket of her captor. So big, it is the size of two grown men and impossible to carry by one bagarrook alone, so she has come to ask, hesitantly, if I can help.

Of course, liwurruk, I say, the uneasiness rising to constrict my chest. I tell Emma to tend to the fire then Meendutgarrook and I carry the rug across the island. A long, plodding walk over stony rises and falls, and we arrive at an isolated pocket of peppermint trees. Enough of a grove to shelter from mornmoot and the storm clouds she brings, but lonely nonetheless, no dense canopy of cradling moonah to evoke the feeling of being held within a turrung mother's arms.

It is when she takes me under the bending arch of the thickest part of the grove that I see why we are here. A rush of recognition and suddenly, all of my joints dissolve to water. I fall to my knees, drowned, upon the ground.

No.

For up in the connecting branches of the tallest turrung, Meendutgarrook has constructed a platform. Just like our Elders do in the sacred trees of our Homelands, when a beloved's breath had left their body. A bed raised high so Biik can reclaim the flesh of its child, leaving only the kalk for the mourners to gather and carry and grieve. To farewell, finally, in sacred ceremony, sent to their whale for the journey across Warrayin to Karralk.

No, my liwurruk, no. This cannot be.

Eyes dark with an unbearable sadness, Meendutgarook lifts her skirt to show me the cloth tied between her thighs and around her waist, stained red with a slow seep of blood.

No, is all I can whisper as the world comes crashing down around us.

One last night, we sit around our women's kuunh. Children asleep in our laps, the crackling fire warm and peaceful, tears unabating, dabbed with cloths against our desolate cheeks.

Tell me again what the murndigarrook said, she asks solemnly. *About me and Barrunan.*

Still I see that little girl shining in her beautiful face, collecting shells in the tidelines with her younger cousins. Still that child, nearly woman, who wove delicate baskets on the beach in our women's circle, stealing glances at her promised as he left to go hunting kuyim and barrimil with the other men, waiting patiently for her Elders to decide when they could be married. Still she is there, that munmundiik of fourteen, frozen in a sweet point in time. Even now, as her body grows ever weaker, draining of blood, draining of life, draining of the will to keep fighting.

They said when the weather turned cooler, when the hunting grounds were green, when they could bring all of the clans together at Kullurk for a giant feast, that would be the time for your wedding ngargee.

How many moons would that have been?

Probably two more.

Only two more?

I think so.

So close. So close to being married to my Barrunan.

Yes, so close.

She smiles that stunning, broad, cheeky smile, Meendutgarrook's smile, so loved by everyone, and says, full of mischief, *But I was with him in my dreams.*

One last night, and we remind each other of every exquisite contour of our Country, a ceremony of sacred remembrance.

We remember the wide, gentle, enclosing bay, gifted by Mother Whale, and the hours of swimming and diving in her saltwater, collecting shells, finding treasures, the giant tooth of Wiyagabul Darrak once. Of lying in the gleaming white sand, sunning ourselves after a long swim, watching the burribarri mothers shepherd their fledglings across the dunes on their stick legs. We remember the fecund wetlands, linking arms with each other in an undulating valley of water, lined with giant trees and teeming with every kind of bird you could think of.

This was our home, the estate of our youth, clan of the Yalukit-Wilam, and all ours to play in over countless, endless days.

And we remember the adventures into the other places of our Biik, the enormous weaving river of the Birrarung, shrouded in mist and wonder. The lush slopes of towering mountains, adorned with trees that could touch Sky Country itself. Into the estates of our promised ones and the sister bay where Babayin Betayil rests beside her calf. More streams of the sweetest water coursing down the prominence of Wonga, sustaining so much life, almost impossible to believe after so long on our prison island. And we remember our women's cliffs, stunning in their shades of reds, oranges, purples and pinks, faces of the Old Ones protruding out, Munmundiik, Karkarrook, Wootokorrook, luminous and alive, weathered by sea spray and mornmoot, sacred places of the Bagarrook Warrayin since the props first held up the Sky.

As the last night transitions to a new morning, Meendutgarrook makes me promise to honour her in the old way.

Even here, she says, her voice fading, but adamant. *Even here, I believe Mother Whale will come for me. She will. So I need you to prepare me, with ngargee, with yingali. Promise me.*

An eon stretches between us as my mind tumbles over all the knowledge I do not know. All the times I had to wait on the shores, gather our food, prepare the women's circle, our ngargee gurrubayin, while the murndigarrook fulfilled sacred business according to the yulendji their initiations had unlocked. That day on the beach with Bindergarrook carrying the sacred remains of her baby in a tightly woven binuk, watching the women walk her around the rock of Babayin Betayil, how I wanted to follow, to learn. But that ritual was not my right to see, that yulendji not mine to know.

Promise me, she repeats, her tone high-pitched now, aching with sadness, with fear, with determination.

Gripping her cold fingers with all the comforting strength I can gather, I look deep into her searching eyes and make the vow. *I will.*

Those words are the reassurance she needs. Relief radiates through her expression and body. She knows now she can let go. That I will catch her in her fall. That her murrup will be held in the joy, the light, the love of her people's ngargee.

Later that day, we make the slow walk to the place Meendutgarrook has chosen, a solemn procession, Emma clutching her hand while I carry her bubup, wrapped in a snug kuyim bundle, on my back.

Holding her face with my trembling hands I tell her, *I love you.*

I cannot sleep that night. Every thought is of my Meendutgarrook. My liwurruk, my sister, my countrywoman, my life companion. The one who has walked with me, held me, uplifted me, comforted me. The one who has saved me from drowning in the endless maelstrom of our vicious life. The one who knew me, the one who loved me.

At first light, I go to her place of rest. Her eyelids are closed. Her body is cold. Meendutgarrook is gone.

My days now are caring for two bubup, all by ourselves, on a granite island thrust up from the sea. My nights are staring into the fire while the bubup are fast asleep. And waiting. Waiting for enough days to cycle past. For Meeniyan the Moon to grow full, then hollow out, then grow full again. For then it will be time.

Dark clouds cluster on the horizon, readying for the storm they will bring to our island tonight. In one of my bilang, I carry a blade and the fresh leaves of the moonah. The other is Meendutgarrook's sacred dillybag. Leaving Emma to care for Barrunan, I walk the sombre path to her resting place under the sweep of the tallest peppermint tree.

As much as I try to be wise and calm like the murndigarrook I remember, as much as I know what I will see when I arrive at Meendutgarrook's resting place and as much as I know the power of Biik's purifying force, when my eyes first alight upon my liwurruk's sacred remains, an uncontrollable wail forces its way into the ether, echoing around the branches of the watching turrung. Yingali for saying goodbye has started.

Standing on the edge of the island's towering southern cliffs, storm clouds rumbling in the distance, the swelling of Warrayin building in the waves below, I sing with all my might to our Mother Whale, Babayin Betayil. Calling, shouting, wailing, for her to come and take this deserving bagarrook across the stormy sea to Nyawiinth as he lays his head along the blue line of the horizon. To help her find the pathway of Karralk and ascend the brilliant golden rays of the setting sun to Pindayi.

Without the red ochre of our women's cliffs speaking our symbols of joy and family, the very essence of our sacred business, I reach for the blade in my bilang. On my upper arm, in the place that signifies enduring love for my liwurruk, I make the cut and let the kulmul bleed freely onto my hands. Placing them over Meendutgarrook's woven binuk, I try the only way I can think of to steep her sacred remains in the lifeblood of her ngargee, to try and envelop her for the last time in the beauty of her culture and Country. To send her on her hallowed journey painted with the very blood of my being so she knows just how much I love her. Just how much I will miss her.

Surging waves begin to crash against the cliff as mornmoot flies in a squall around the headland. For one last time I sing out to Babayin Betayil. I tell her my liwurruk's name.

Meendutgarrook.

And when I lower her kalk to the ledge below, I let every atom of my loss and grief, despair and desolation pour from me, sobbing and screaming, into the ocean below.

Cradling my bubup tight that night, I feel every crash and boom of Warrayin's mighty force rumbling through the bedrock, and I know her cleansing swell has reached Meendutgarrook's sacred bilang. On the howling wind, I think I hear the cries of my Liwik calling in yingali for her murrup to find its way. And just as my exhausted body drifts into tumultuous slumber, I smile, because I know I hear, calling to me across the wind, the beautiful, sonorous song of our Mother Whale carrying my Meendutgarrook to Karralk.

BINDJIRRU
YALLAMBI
Two Together

Another boat lurches in the rising swell, laden with a meagre pile of my and my children's belongings. Manned by a small pack of ngamudji, dressed well in finer cloth but the treacherous glint of an old sealer still lurking in their eyes. My children, Emma and John, who is now a wily four-year-old, are already on deck, eyes wide in excitement, in trepidation, the lure of an unknown adventure sending a bewildering thrill through their little bodies.

I try to get to them as quickly as I can but I am rigid on the rocky ledge, unable to prise my feet from the only Biik I have known for so many seasons now. This giant, rugged beast, ancient and immovable, relentlessly buffeted by a wild Warrayin, a beacon of bleak isolation. And yet, I know every inch of its stony back, every heaving sigh and rumble, every tiny offering to be found, season after season, to miraculously keep us alive. A harsh teacher, hated and loved in equal measure. It holds my bubups' bones in its austere arms, the echoes of their play, their laughter, the light they brought to a soul floundering in imposed exile. And among the steadfast embrace of our moonah grove, every slope and bush, boulder and turrung, of this lonely, mighty Biik, the shadowed memories of Meendutgarrook walk.

Now I am to leave it.

Once more, the sealer's boat launches into the ocean and once more, that sudden seed of naive hope bursts open for a glorious moment, imagining a world where we might be voyaging home. And once more, as we head towards the direction of the setting sun, even further away from my Homelands, I feel the rising of my aching murrup, those last threads of it still tethered to my beautiful Biik, brittle and thin, on the verge of breaking forever.

Irrevocably altered, the Country on the mainland is not the one I remember looming into view all those years ago. Then, mighty trees ascended into the clouds on distant bunnull, sweeping dunes clothed in blankets of green, dense and thriving, only broken up by a sparse dotting of foreign wilams.

Now, the newcomers cover the valleys like a poisonous weed, no turrung left, no blooming warrak bursting with brilliant red and orange blossoms to soak in a sweet drink. All flat Biik now, penned animals, birdless skies. Stolen, stripped bare and bent to the will of the ngamudji.

Soon we reach an even smaller island of granite than the one we left. Panic shoots through my chest, clutching at my constricted throat.

Not here. Not this place of nothing. No graceful moonah here, no peppermints sweeping their leaves across the stony ground, giving shelter to tiny kuyim. Just looming peaks of bouldered slopes, brushed clean by an insistent mornmoot and the battering ocean, always seething, even on a still day. Only the wiry stamina of grass, scrub and saltbush can endure here, clinging to life with grim determination. On its peak, a tower rises, a fiery light emanating from its apex, built by the ngamudji to warn their passing ships of this wrathful Warrayin's hidden perils.

The boat draws ever closer. As the sky swirls black above us with a gathering storm, a mirror to the despair darkening my heart, a voice wails in my pounding head.

No!

In one swift manoeuvre, the boat docks.

That night, with a tempest seething inside and out, I stand on the very edge of the granite cliffs and scream, *Why?*

Arms outstretched, body shuddering, Warrayin rises into the ether around me, salt spray levitating like the mists of Birrarung, infusing into my bones, freezing me to the core. It's like I am in the fever of a nightmare. I wonder if I really stand on Biik or if I am, in fact, drowning in a raging Sea Country swelling to swallow the entire land. And then I see, with blinding clarity, that the bald beast of stone under my feet is the body of a colossal betayil. Petrified, calcified, frozen in Time, the whale stands stiff in rigor mortis, a sentinel warning of the graveyard ahead, a memorial to all those murdered and stolen and lost at the end of the world.

I scream again into the deafening abyss. *Why?*

I wait for a response from my Liwik, for the awakening of the whale underneath me, for the answer to this question that has burned inside me since that boat first broke my entire world. Mornmoot howls, Warrayin roars, but no answer comes.

Instead, a small hand takes hold of mine, pulling me from the edge of the cliff, back onto safer ground. My manggip, Emma, soaked and shivering, face questioning.

Please, Mama, come inside?

Suddenly, I see all of them again, in her beautiful, soulful eyes. My mother, my husband, Meendutgarrook, my kin, every single one of the bubup born from my body, every single one of the women born before me, standing in that endless line through Time. I see them all, looking back at me with love. A girl of eleven, with the murrup of an Old One. Showing me a lighted path out of the dark. I squeeze my bubup's brave hand and I let her take me back inside.

Every day is the same on this next island prison, numbing, unchanging, season upon windswept season. Only the spine of this island is flat ground, the rest of the body slides, at various degrees of treacherous declining, into the churning sea. Not a place for the scramble of young, reckless legs, so Meendutgarrook's Barrunan, stays enclosed in the sealer's fenced wilam, rocky sand pits for his playground. Through the ages of four to five, my cousin's Barrunan finds his delight in the smallest of things. Knowing every insect, every loose stone, every returning bird in the confines of his patch of

Biik. From six, the sealer takes him under his arm, pushing endless words into his head, teaching him their scribbly shapes on his crisp paper. He is more like a John now. But I still make sure to point out his true namesake whenever the creatures dive in the agitated Warrayin wrapping around the island, whispering in his ear, *They are barrunan like you are Barrunan.*

He whispers back, *Dolphin.*

Keeping an unending kuunh lit in his tower, the ngamudji remains on the island all the time. Like dutiful slaves, Emma and I are bound to cook and clean and wait on his command. Some days, when the form of his stooping shoulders, the glare of his pasty skin, the habitual spitting of his phlegm onto the ground, become overwhelming in their constancy, I feel my repressed rage rising. Those days, when he stands on the edge of a sloping rock wall smoking from his clay pipe, I see myself rushing like an enraged koonwarra at a wretched bunyip, thrusting him over the edge, making sure he plummets to a crashing death, even if it means I plunge into oblivion too.

Braced, ready to launch, a tugging turns my head. And Emma is there, arms laden with binuk and linganlingan, eager for our daily pilgrimage to Warrayin. Trudging away from the sealer's stone and mortared wilam, our footsteps pad lighter along this island beast's backbone. Slowly exhaling, letting go, until we arrive at the sanctuary of our fishing rock.

Here, feet bathing in a sheltered bay, saltwater medicine cleansing our murrup, the echoes of Meendutgarrook's voice swirling around in the ether, I tell my daughter, this blossoming munmundiik, everything I know. All the yulendji I was gifted before I was taken. All of the wisdom, ceremony, Law and Lore of her Biik and her people. I tell her of our Protectors of Sea, Sky and Land, Babayin Betayil the Mother Whale, Bunjil the wedge-tailed eagle and Waa the raven. Glorious kwiyup-kwiyup she has never seen, Koonwarra the swan, Ngayook the white cockatoo, Tulum the duck, the sweet stick legs of the Burribarri hooded plover. Incredible creatures of the land no mind could ever imagine, Kuyim the kangaroo, Barrimil the emu, Wallert Wallert the possum, Kurrburra the koala, Kowan the echidna. And so many more.

Every day is the same, except with my Emma in our Warrayin haven. For a child born and raised on barren rocks surrounded by restless seas, there is so much she has never seen. But here, in our suspended reality by a secluded, complicit slice of women's Sea Country, I make sure it all comes alive in her eager imagination, dancing in the gleam of her fervent eyes. I tell her everything I know about our Homelands towards Galinbarriam, across the distant, blue expanse where Nyawiinth rises from his nighttime sleep. Our clan's stunning stories of Meeniyan the moon, the Seven Sisters in Sky Country, Tooraddin the fearsome Bunyip, the Murrumbungiatta who, with Barrawarn the magpie, raised a sacred liyan to hold up the blanket of Sky Country, opening the whole world to light and space and Time. And in any patch of sand I can find, I draw the shape of our Biik, a kangaroo bent around two bounteous sister bays. Our land of plenty, bulaadu mountains and valleys, mighty rivers of mist, verdant wetlands, trees standing ten times taller than the lighted tower on our desolate island prison. Eyes wide with wonder, I can see that she conjures up every fastidious detail of our Country in her mind until it lives and breathes in her being like it does in mine.

And as my manggip grows from a budding munmundiik into a fledgling Bagarrook Warrayin, as her body embarks on the first tentative movement towards womanhood, I tell her about the sacred rituals of our women's business. Of ancient songlines arcing across endless stretches of beach, walked and sung by an uncountable number of women who course in her blood. About revered faces in rugged cliffs, immense Keeping Places enfolded in undulating dunes, colossal trees holding holy caves of birthing at their base. Our family's peninsula of sand at Yellodungo, the place of our custodial totem, knee deep in the waters of Warnmarring, where it is possible to be just one step away from an enormous betayil and her inquisitive bubup, where you can look into the depths of a mighty whale's eyes and see the universe unfold.

One day I will take you there.

I whisper the promise in Emma's ear and feel her spirit soar. Between us, a tiny flame sparks, the warmth of which I have not felt for so very long. Just a glimmer, tender and shy, of a feeling long buried in my blunted body.

Hope.

And in that wondrous moment, I am certain of our return.

WIRRIGIRRI
Messenger

Black and white lines imprinted on paper show a woman and man standing rigidly beside one another. Trembling, my finger traces the contours of the bagarrook's face.

Even in this strange impression, flat shapes on fragile material, I know her cheeks, her chin, her nose, her eyes. This is Martha. Even after thirty years have formed her into her own, grown woman, I can still see the soul of my newborn bubup staring back at me.

Standing by the door, the delivering captain waits for the sealer to write a return letter. As the paper passes between the men, the wirrigirri suddenly convulses with a wheezing cough.

Panic shoots up my spine and I pull Emma behind me, the echoes of my lost bubup clamouring a warning call in my mind. I gesture to Barrunan, but the sealer already has him by the arm, pulling him in step between himself and the captain as they saunter down the steep track to the moored vessel below.

She's having another baby.

Distracted, a fearful pulse still pounding in my neck, I turn to see Emma running a curious gaze over the paper accompanying the photo.

Surprised, I ask, *You know what that says?*

Not really, she responds with a pragmatic shake of her head. *Only a few words. Like baby.*

Pointing to the scribbles on the page, Emma shows me the ones she knows. Loops and lines running in neat rows. Not like

235

the markings I remember. Emblazoned in ochre tones of pink, yellow and orange, contrasted against the black of our oiled skins ready for ngargee, telling the stories of belonging and responsibility, totems and family. Bunjil's wings, Koonwarra's tracks, the fluke of Babayin Betayil. Painted so long ago on my skin, present in my mind like it was yesterday.

One day soon, I assure my manggip, *I will write our clan's language on your body for ceremony. You will know the wurrung of your People better than the ngamudji's tongue, I promise.*

Three days later, the youngest one succumbs first. Vulnerable body burning hot, Barrunan convulses with every consumptive cough. Overwhelming him with terrifying speed, I watch helplessly as his eyes, usually shining with the glimmer of Meendutgarrook's light, sink into the sockets of his bones. Wan and hollow, his delicate face haunts me with images of my bubup all those years ago, the infant Isabella still at my breast, cheeky mischief-makers John and Robert, all taken in one ferocious swoop. And my mammam Bobbinary, conceived on his Country, ripped away still in my womb, the perfect replication of his warrior father, but never a match for the ngamudji's virulent disease. And now it is back again.

Battling through an aching, sleepless night, Barrunan's parched lips fret in a feverish mumble. Switching from burning to freezing, sweating forehead to icy hands, hour by weary hour sees his tiny body yield yet more to the onslaught of a fearsome foe.

By first light, he has lost the war.

Wrapped in the patchwork kuyim rug fashioned for him by his babayin's fingers, the sealer lowers him into a freshly dug, shallow grave. Watching the shovelled dirt slowly disappear the kuyim cloth, and the tender yanyean inside it, another fissure splits through my fractured heart. Yet another bubup's bones laid for eternity on a rocky island so far from the Biik of their birthright.

Two days later the sealer is unable to get up from his bed, shivering and sweating, under attack from the same invisible assailant.

Anxiously I watch for signs that Emma might succumb too but we both seem to have a merciful veil of protection for now. With the sealer unable to light the fire of his tower that night, the island sits in darkness, a gloomy booroonth heavy with clouds, shielding any light from Meeniyan or her twinkling djurt. As the soundscape of the night shudders with the ngamudji's worsening cough and Warrayin's booming waves, I lie awake listening for, hoping for, the sound of a white-masted ship, lost and adrift without the island's beacon of light, crashing against her fearsome granite cliffs.

I am still awake when Nyawiinth emerges in Galinbarriam, a bleed of purple transmuting into shafts of gold and pink, bursting through blooms of billowing clouds. No ship has been wrecked on the rocky boulders below our wilam. Instead, from the extended arms of the mainland peninsula that enfolds their bay, a boat makes haste in our direction.

KUUNH YINGURR
Bright Fire

Gripping Emma's hand in mine, the comfort of her shoulder leaning into my body, we huddle on a timbered bench, watching the sealer labour for every gasping breath.

Seated in a ngamudji's enormous shelter for the sick, built with the stone ripped from Biik underfoot, I can see outside the sweeping shifts in the landscape of this invaded saltwater Country. Giant turrung felled and carved into pieces to form endless rows of square wilams. Soil pressed hard into wide tracks, devoid of reed or grass or saltbush. No sheltering branches for kwiyup-kwiyup here, no materials for nests, no trees with ancient hollows, no branches for the wallert wallert's drey. Without birdsong, without the call of animal kin, the land here is quiet. Once more, that familiar, thick silence which resounds with the decimation of life.

Except, of course, for the ngamudji. Everywhere in this hospital wilam, their stares bore into me. From the patients, pale like moor-roobull in their creaking beds, to the man with the bearing of importance, tapping bodies and declaring prognoses, to the women busy following his every order, buzzing like bees around a cherished blossom. I see them steal their glances at my manggip and me, our dark skin gleaming against their whitewashed walls, wondering, appraising, judging.

Some stare at me with a primal fear, as if I am a wild creature stalking them, lying in wait for my chance to rip them apart, and maybe I am. Some glance at me with a shadow of shame clouding

238

their earnest expressions for they know what their kind have done. They have watched, mute, from the sidelines, no courage to combat the cruelty, no will to make amends. Why would they when they are so richly rewarded by the murderous thievery of others like them? One woman surveys me with a miserable pity, and I want to shake her and school her uncomprehending ignorance with all that I know and all that I am.

I meet her doleful eyes with an unashamed stare. *I am Nannertgarrook.*

The woman turns away.

Beside me, Emma balances the photo of her older liwurruk on her knee, searching every person moving through the hospital, glancing back to the picture for comparison. Much as she has heard many stories of her sisters, told over long days and nights by me and her Aunty Meendutgarrook, she was only a bubup swaddled in kuyim cloth when Nancy was ripped away. Even greater the time span between the youngest and eldest daughters, nearly twenty years, Martha a fully grown bagarrook when Emma was beginning to suckle at the breast.

Suddenly, she launches from her seat beside me into the open arms of a beautiful bagarrook, standing fixed in the doorway, brown skin gleaming in the late afternoon light. Locked in a steadfast embrace, these two sisters, one a girl of thirteen, the other a woman of thirty-two, would seem to be no more than strangers, except for the inexplicable knowing of kin that surges through their shared blood.

A sudden sob escapes me as I watch my daughters hold each other, both born from my body, but in epochs far apart. In faint whispers, I hear them talking with each other, quickly, excitedly, in the sealer's tongue, words I know tumbling together, alongside unfamiliar ones I struggle to understand. When they finally part, I see for the first time, the full swell of my older manggip's pregnant belly. My Martha, firstborn to my captor, now a grown bagarrook leading a life I can barely comprehend. So many ceremonies missed, so much life lived separate, but a babayin can always see the bubup she cradled in her arms. Those days when I was the centre of her world, round eyes gazing up to me, for my knowledge, my strength, my love.

Stretching my arms out towards her, I lightly touch my Martha's full, glowing cheeks, wondrous, joyous, at seeing my manggip again. An awkward shyness clouds her eyes and I widen my smile to show her just how much I have missed her, just how tightly I have held her in my heart all these years.

Looking to her swollen belly, I marvel at the miracle of our sacred women's business. These ceremonies I have missed too, the carrying of my child through a bagarrook's greatest challenge, the fear, the pain, the awe, the untold jubilation of giving birth. And it is my ritual too, as I hold my daughter in her profound initiation, I become the grandmother, her gugungiyup, elevating into a higher realm of knowledge, the yulendji of the murndigarrook. So much denied when my daughters were taken from me. But my Martha stands here now and we can finally move forward together.

Bending before her, I place my hands on the swell of her blooming baby. Closing my eyes, I draw from the deep recesses of my memory to find the thread of an ancient song. Softly, I sing a murndigarrook's chant of love for this new murrup venturing into the world.

Under my touch, I feel Martha's body pull away. When I open my eyes, I see the flush of embarrassment firing across her cheeks as she glances furtively to the ngamudji watching us. For the first time, I notice a white woman hovering behind my daughter, a benevolent smile fixed in place as she watches our tremulous reunion.

Lifting my hands from her belly, Martha pats my shoulder and moves away to the side of her father's bed. Still smiling, the white woman follows her, barely turning her head as she passes by me. Immobilised by a sickening wave of sadness, I stand, locked in place, paralysed by an acute understanding.

My bubup is ashamed of me.

I watch as Martha sits down by the wheezing sealer and takes his hand in hers. Waves of turbulent sorrow crest before me, my knees begin to buckle under the drowning weight. Before I can crash to the floor, Emma takes my arm and guides me back to our wooden bench. Each step matches the pounding in my head.

My bubup is ashamed of me.

Night falls, and Emma and I still sit at the old sealer's bedside, watching his struggle for each phlegm-filled wheeze. In and out, a puff of air whistles, and each time I wish it was his last. But he labours on.

As he lies there fighting an attacker who is finally bigger than him, I think of the countless days he has taken from me. Slow-motion eons of hours, eating away at my youth, my learning, my yulendji. I think of all the spitting words, the merciless beatings, the searing violations, the times he turned his wrath on not just me and my liwurruk, but his own children. Not a man, but a warrugul, dragging us all down the descent of Muyiipnallook.

And then, in one implosive, resplendent moment, it is over. The breath stops. The sallow face shrivels. The murrup falls into the hell of his own making.

My enslaver is dead.

And I am free.

Time suspends. Serenely still, the room around me is quiet. My daughter is curled up on a chair, head resting against a wall, asleep. Meeniyan the moon gleams, soft and knowing, through the window.

Silence. As every fundamental element of my universe is shattered and reshaped. I am free.

I can go home.

And then, the waves crash over me. Sobs command my whole body, all-consuming, sinking into every fibre in my being. An epic upwelling of my long-held, pent-up eons of rage and grief, loss and heartache, pouring out soundlessly on the thieved floor of that ngamudji hospital. Then slowly, slowly, as the saltwater finds its level, the gentle rising and releasing swell of profound relief. And a bone-deep joy, kindling my soul into a lighted kuunh yingurr.

I can go home.

BARRINGDJIGURRI MARRAMBAYIK
On My Knees

Playing with my grandchildren as if they are her own, the smiling white woman from the hospital talks to Martha's husband about finding passage on a ship for Emma and me. Plotting the various possibilities in words I try hard to understand, the ngamudji sometimes look my way with an encouraging nod, other times they murmur in downcast tones as if they are planning a voyage to the end of a collapsing world.

Around me, sand-coloured walls are stacked high with stone pulled from the depths of this Biik, marking the parameters of this wilam where Martha and her ngamudji husband live with the family of the white woman. So much adornment hangs on the walls that I blink wearily with the overwhelm. Strange too is the resonance of so many people in one space after years of unbroken isolation, the unbridled squeals of fighting bubup, the animated conversation of finding a sailing ship and occasionally, the murmurs of my two daughters preparing dinner in the ngamudji's kitchen.

Closing my wirring to the noise around me, I keep my focus on Martha. With Emma's help, my manggip prepares bright coloured vegetables and cuts of red meat to place in the pot over the hearth's kuunh. Heavy with a ready child, her lumbering body is weary and slow moving. Every now and then, Martha steadies herself against the wall, rubbing her head. I notice her flushed face, her swollen hands, and a nervous fluttering stirs in my stomach. Whenever

I stand to help, my daughter admonishes me, telling me to sit, telling me not to worry.

An uneasy pulse thuds through my body, so I look out of the wilam's windows with restless eyes, searching the surrounding Biik for something, a familiar turrung, a totemic animal, a reassuring sign. Or, I hope, a woman's plant storied in my yulendji that might help my daughter. But all I see is a grassy slope, flanked by the straight lines of trees of an unknown timber, devoid of leaves, strangely unclothed in the cool air, alive but wearing a mask of death. No kurrburra munching on fragrant branches, no wallert wallert nesting in hollows with their young. Just more straight lines with verdant shrubs dotted with bursts of colour, pretty but foreign. Whether they hold value for medicine, or kwiyup-kwiyup, or the flutter of balam-balam, I do not know. But they are not plants for women's business.

That night, Martha shows Emma and me a place for sleeping, two beds fashioned from the ngamudji's soft cloth. Before she leaves, I tentatively grasp her fingers and stroke them, hoping she does not recoil from my touch. Without the others watching, she smiles at me gently.

I ask, *You well?*

I'll feel better when the baby is out.

I will help?

No, no, I'm being well cared for. I have everything I need. You just get some rest.

I want to let her know that I can see the strain in her face, that her back is bent under the growing weight, that her swollen hands and feet are thickening. I want to let her know I have knowledge which might help, that I still remember some of the things my murndigarrook taught me. I want to let her know I am her babayin and I love her, so much, even though I was not allowed to be a part of her new world. And I want her to know, so desperately, I did not want her to be taken from me, and that I have thought about her every day since. But I cannot find the words she will understand.

As she turns to leave, I clutch at her hands again, unwilling to let her go.

You, your sister, me. We go together to Biik.

For the briefest moment, I see the flicker of a curious light in her dark eyes, so much like mine. One quick, searching flame which burns out in seconds.

Martha shakes her head with a laugh. *My husband.*

I know. I say nothing more because I do know, all too well, the power they can hold. Cruel, like the false one, enslaving me on islands further and further from my home. Or magnificent, like the one I have yearned for ever since. The one I will see soon.

As she leaves, I ask, once more. *Can I help?*

No. There's nothing you can do.

I love you. A whisper, as my daughter closes the door.

Echoing around me is the mellow, somnambulant beat of Warnmarring's lapping waves. I am nestled next to my Bobbinary, fast asleep, his velvet skin melding into mine as we hold each other close under the blanket of booroonth. Across my shoulders, a delicate hand opens like a night flower blooming for Meeniyan the Moon. My Boyerup, in a drift of peaceful dreaming. Beside her, as always, Yearl Yearl lays with his limbs flung wide, hair tousled in a curly mess. *My family*, I think dreamily. *Soon, soon.*

Pushing through the haze of sleep, an insistent mopoke calls. My eyelids flick open. I know what that call means. And I am up, rushing to Martha's room, even before her scream shatters the still night.

Lying in a pool of her birthing water, Martha's face is distorted in pain. Around her, with cloths and tarnook of steaming water, her husband and the white woman hover anxiously. At her side, I grab my manggip'o arm and try to lift her from the bed. To encourage her to move and sway, squat and stretch, in the way our women have done for millennia. I want to take her out from the confines of the ngamudji's wilam and into the sheltering arms of an enfolding turrung, bathing in the warmth and light of the ceremonial fire, belly rubbed in the red and orange ochres of life and joy, air cleansed and cleared with the purifying smoke of the moonah and eucalypt. But every time I try to bring her into a space of ceremony, the ngamudji pull me away and school me as if I am a child.

No. Over and over again. *No.*

And each time I want to grab their shoulders and shake them. Tell them that I am Nannertgarrook, a babayin who has birthed nine children, who has sung the songs of women's ngargee at hundreds of other births. Who has been taught by the wisest of murndigarrook the ways to keep a struggling mother relaxed and open in her time of great initiation, the way to coax a hesitant bubup out from the safety of their mother's womb. But I cannot teach this sense into them. So, instead, they keep pulling me away and telling me, *No.* Even as my daughter begins to bleed.

When a sombre band of important ngamudji arrive, led by two men in fine clothes with bags of white man tools, I stand firm.

Yandjali! No men here. I shake my head and command in my mother tongue. *Yandjali! This is sacred women's business, you men have no place here. Around our bodies, around our womanhood. Be off with you.*

Face brightening red, the oldest man turns to Martha's husband and barks his order. *Get her out of here.*

Firm hands grip my arms and lead me to the door. Twisting and shouting, I try one last time to make them understand.

Yandjali! This is not your business! You can never understand our womanhood. You will never bleed. You will never grow a bubup in your own body. You will never know the pain and joy and sacredness of our woman's initiation, birthing them into the world. Go away, you ignorant fools. Yandjali!

The last thing I see, before they close the door on me, is my manggip, lying supine in pain, bleeding and wailing, her terrified eyes staring at mine.

All I can do is grasp Emma's hand and lead her outside, taking embers from the low-burning fire in the hearth as we go. Together, we light the fire of women's ngargee and encourage the smoke using whatever green leaves this strange, subjugated Biik offers. I sing loud and strong, calling to our Liwik, to Babayin Betayil the Mother Whale, Bunjil the eagle, Waa the raven, our Protectors of Sea, Sky and Land. In a wavering wail, I call upon Munmundiik and Meeniyan the moon, luminous above us in the exquisite expanse of a shimmering night sky. And I sing the songs of our Old Ones, the murndigarrook from Time Immemorial. Emma grows louder too, and together we weave our women's ngargee gurrubayin. We slap our bodies and stamp our feet, we sing until our voices strain with exhaustion, chanting, calling, pleading and wailing. Even when we hear our beloved Martha's cries of pain, we sing, as our murrup splinter and our hearts shatter into untold pieces.

And then, all is silent. The descent of an aching hush. I grip Emma's hand, waiting, willing, hoping for a bubup's cry. But it never comes.

Instead, a stabbing pain, like the plunging of a sealer's sharpened knife into my chest, brings me to my knees.

MURRMURRWIIN MORNMOOT
A Furious Wind

Echoes of my beautiful bubup's humming rise and fall in the ether around me. Through a haze of glimmering light, I see the stunning contours of my Emma's face slowly emerge.

Babayin? Her voice sounds thin and far away, taut with devastation.

Struggling to pull my mind through the daze of sleep, I blindly reach around, grasping the soft curves of her small fingers.

Babayin?

Her voice is sharper now as she calls again, and I feel my floating murrup, adrift on a lilting mornmoot, slam back into my body. At once, I feel that stabbing pain still piercing into my heart and my eyes shoot open, fully focused now. With stark clarity, I see the glaring whitewashed walls looming around me and I realise where I am.

No! No! No!

Even though only a hoarse whisper escapes my parched lips, I can see the essence of my desperate wail ricochet around the cold stone walls. *Not here*, I rail in my mind. *Not here in the death trap of the ngamudji, the place where their Moorroobull linger, where the sealer's murrup was snatched into Muyiipnallook.*

Emma stares down at me, her gaunt face pinched with grief, eyes red from tears. I try to sit up, but a weakness overcomes my body that I have never felt before, like its very lifeblood has drained away through the wound gushing in my fractured heart.

Please don't leave me, my bubup whispers.

I love to look at my beautiful girl. A glorious munmundiik on the very cusp of womanhood, about to step onto the ancient pathway of her Old One's songlines. Stroking the smooth contours of her blossoming face, I make her a promise.

When we return to our Biik, we will make your emu feather skirt. When the kulin bring back the barrimil from their hunt, they will save the best gangan for you. We will go to Monmar and we will sink our feet into the cool sand. After all those years on the rock. We will walk along the tideline and collect the finest shells for your bilang. And then, we will sit in our women's weaving circle, tell the stories of the moonah and the Munmundiik, and string those shells on the kuyim sinew to decorate the band of your skirt. Would you like that?

Staring at me with wide, solemn eyes, Emma nods.

I promise you, your dilburnayin will be the most beautiful.

The stabbing pain in my chest plunges deeper, and my hand flies from my bubup's face to claw at the layers of ngamudji cloth covering my heart. Panic burns in my body and I see it mirrored in Emma's stricken gaze.

Where is the ship to take us home? We need to go home.

My call reverberates down the hallway and I hear footsteps clatter along the wooden floors. A ngamudji woman arrives and bends over me, putting a sweet liquid to my thirsty lips. After I drink, I clutch her arm, speaking slowly so she will understand.

I am Nannertgarrook. My Biik is Burinyong-Balak. You say Westernport, Port Phillip. Me and my bubup, we need the boat to take us home.

A swirling fog starts to creep into my mind, but the building urgency to see my manggip and I onto our boat keeps my focus clear. Even as the pain drives further into my chest, I clutch the woman's arm tighter.

We need a boat.

Fear flares in her expression and I can tell she sees me as a warrugul, a savage who holds no yulendji. I want to tell her about the true savagery I have seen but she yanks her arm away and bustles quickly down the hallway and out of sight.

Turning back to Emma, I try to ease the panic I see rising in her dark, dreading eyes.

I will take you to meet your sister Boyerup, your brother Yearl Yearl, and together we will go to the home of the Koormamgarrook, the mighty boulder that rises from Warrayin like Mother Whale. We will watch Nyawiinth sink down to rest and you will see Karralk, when those golden rays of the setting sun stream up into Sky Country. Once again, my mind threatens to be pulled into a rising fog but I push it away and call out in rising desperation. *We need a boat!*

Tears spill down Emma's tender cheeks as she whispers to me a soothing hum. *Shhh, Babayin.*

I smile at her and feel an upwell of powerful love flood through me for this wonderful girl with the bright shining eyes, my very last born bubup.

I will tell you a secret. Our murrup walk up Karralk when we leave our bodies, when we take our journey to Pindayi. And can you guess who carries us there?

Our whales take us, Mama.

Clever one, my manggip, special one. A desperate urgency to keep her safe, to get her home, pounds through my agonised heart.

We need a boat! I am wailing now, over and over. *We need a boat!*

More footsteps rush down the hallway, a man leading the woman this time. A sharp prick pierces my skin and a jet of cold shoots up and down my arm. The fog I have been fighting spreads through my body thick and fast. But I can still hear the man ask for my name.

Eliza, the woman replies.

Fierce, righteous anger propels the words from my mouth. *Not Eliza. Not No-one.* My words are clear and strong. *I am Nannertgarrook.*

Gentle fingers stroke my cheek, and my Emma's luminous face comes into my clouded view, smiling at me through rivulets of salt-water tears, love radiating from every fibre of her being.

And in that moment, I have the blinding epiphany.

I am dying.

There is no time for me to get on that boat to make the journey home. No time to wrap my arms around my Boyerup and Yearl Yearl, kiss the lips of my Bobbinary again. No time for my flesh to be taken by Biik, for my kalk to be painted in ochre, for it to be sung in ceremony and placed for my whale to carry to Karralk.

Take us home. I plead to the doctor, to the nurse, to any ngamudji who is listening. *Please take me home to my family. I need my whale. I need to get to Karralk. I need to get my bubup to her Biik.*

Once more, the sweet sounds of Emma's humming envelop me in perfect, delicate tenderness. *We will get home, babayin. I will take you home.*

All I can see are her wide, dark, desperate eyes.

And my heart breaks for the last time.

I love you, bubup. I am so sorry you were born when the world had ended.

Epilogue

Do you hear that Wind?

That desolate murrup screaming across these shores, still trapped on a raging Mornmoot?

Yes, that Wind is Me. Forever howling my story into the abyss.

I am Nannertgarrook.

Can you hear me? Will you hear me?

Or will you be like the Others?

Turn your face away, turn your back to me.

Pretend you do not hear.

Pretend you do not see.

Pretend you did not know.

Or will you say, like the Others, it was all so long ago.

But I am still here. Still waiting for my whale.

My murrup still trapped.

On this relentless murrmurrwiin Mornmoot.

Blasting your newfound southern shores.

I am Nannertgarrook.

Forever chained. Forever stolen. Forever screaming my fury at the invaders who destroyed it all.

Glossary of Boonwurrung Words

babayin	mother
Babayin Betayil	Mother Whale
bagarrook	woman
balambalam	butterfly
baldu	to fall
bambun	aunty
barndana	message stick
barrawarn	magpie
barrimil	emu
barring	tracks, walking paths
barring djinang	footprints
barringdjigurri marrambayik	on my knees
barrunan	dolphin
bayadin	moonbird, muttonbird
berrenberren	flee
betayil	whale
Biik	Country
bilang	dillybag
bindjirru yallambi	two together
bfinuk	basket
birrimbayin	wife
bobad	reed (poa grass)
Boonwurrung Biik	Country of the Boonwurrung Nation
booroonth	darkness, night sky

255

bubup	child/baby
bulaadu	plenty
buldjinganu	devil
Bunjil	wedge-tailed eagle, moiety figure
bunnull laang	mountain of stone
Burinyong-Balak	Boonwurrung Clan Estate on the Mornington Peninsula
Burrabong	name of the freshwater creek running to Bushrangers Bay
burribarri	hooded plover
daal kalk	clap sticks (from the musk daisy)
dilburnayin	emu feather skirt
djambana	talking together
djindibik	all gone, empty
Djou-Djou	Mother Whale's calf
Djouap	French Island
djurt	star
Euroyoroke	St Kilda
Galinbarriam	East
gangan	feather
gugungiyup	grandmother
Gurriin	South (place from where storms come)
gurriin	storm
gurrubayin	initiation circle
gurrung	canoe
kalk	bone/sticks
kanaan	women's stick
Karralk	place of the rays of the setting sun over the ocean, pathway to Pindayi

Kobin Koolin	Embracement Ceremony
konye	look!
koonwarra	swan
koormam	seal
Koormamgarrook	Women of the Seal and Kelp
Korriyong	Phillip Island
kowan	echidna
kulin	man
Kulin	Confederacy of 5 Nations (contemporary term)
Kullurk	favoured, permanent home site of the Burinyong-Balak Clan Estate
kulmul	blood
kurrawan	reed (flag)
kurrburra	koala
kurrun	wattle
kuunh	fire
kuunh yingurr	bright fire
kuyim	kangaroo
kwiyup-kwiyup	birds
kye	hey!
lambamurr	apparition of one who's passed
liik	headband
Liwik	Old Ones/Ancestors
liwurruk	sister
liyan	forked prop
Lowandjirri	Boonwurrung Clan Estate near Wilsons Promontory
mammam	son
manggip	daughter
mardan mardan	crying crying

marmin	father
marn	ball
marngrook	football sport
marrambayik	I am
Meeniyan	the Moon
mindalk	wombat
Mindayi	serpent/whirlwind
monameit	wonderful, great
Monmar	Point Nepean
moonah	coastal moonah (melaleuca lanceolata)
moonip ba mannip	embers and ashes
moorroobull	ghost
mornmoot	wind
morr	currant
Mumilam	West
munmundiik	older girl
Munmundiik	Seven Sisters, the Pleiades
murndigarrook	female Elders
murnong	yam
murrmurrwiin	furious, angry
Murrumbungattia	old spirit beings from north countries – separation of Sky Country story
murrup	spirit/soul
muryok	cockleshell
Muyiipnallook	Hell (constantly falling through a narrow space and never stopping)
nangorrong	husband
Nerrm	Port Phillip Bay
ngamudji	white man
ngargee	ceremony
ngarrambil	white ochre
ngarweet	clan leader

ngayook	white cockatoo
nyaalinggu	return
Nyawiinth	the Sun
nyudha	no
Pareip	Spring (the season)
parnmin	rain
Perrin	Winter
Pindayi	place in Sky Country where departed souls journey to
poorneet	tadpole
tarnook	wooden bowl
thooamee	listen!
Tooraddin	bunyip, emu-like creature that lurks in wetlands
tulum	duck
turrung	tree
Waa	raven, moiety figure
wallert wallert	possum
Wamoom	Wilsons Promontory
Warnmarring	Westernport Bay
warragul	savage
warrak	banksia
warrana wurrba	song/lament of sorrow
Warrayin	Sea Country
werrun	dingo
wilam	home
wirrap	fish
wirrayit	far away, a distance
wirrigirri	messenger
wirring	ear

wirrirap	cleverman
Wiyagabul Darrak	Old Man Shark
womindjeka	coming together
Wonga	Arthurs Seat
wongurrunin	ignorant, stupidity
Woorroowee	place of sorrow ('sorry place')
Woorwoor	Sky Country, sky/heavens
Wootokorrook	the morning star
wundul	brother
wurrdin	abalone
wurrun	manna gum
yadabiling	beloved
Yalukit-Wilam	Boonwurrung Clan Estate from Werribee to Brighton
yanadhan	until we walk the path again
yandjali	go away, leave!
yanyean	older boy
yarradjinan nyilam	a bad dream, nightmare
yearl yearl	sea snail
yellinguth	yesterday, the past
Yellodungo	place of the yaludang (structural prop for wilams), Mother Whale ceremonial site
yingali	ceremonial song
yulendji	knowledge
yurok	eel
yuwarrabuk djidhu	run away

Sources

For a full reading list, please visit the page for
I Am Nannertgarrook *at simonandschuster.com.au*

Clark, Ian D., ed., *The Journals of George Augustus Robinson, Chief Protector, Port Phillip Aboriginal Protectorate*, six volumes, 1839–1852, 2014.

Drummond, Sarah, *Exiles and Island Wives: History, Fiction and Breaksea Islanders*, (PhD thesis), Murdoch University, 2015.

Fels, Marie Hansen, '*I Succeeded Once': The Aboriginal Protectorate on the Mornington Peninsula, 1839–1840*, ANU E Press and Aboriginal History Incorporated, 2011.

Jones, Pauline, ed., Historical Records of Victoria, Foundation Series, Volume One, *Beginnings of Permanent Government*, editor-in-chief Michael Cannon, Victorian Government Printing Office, 1981.

MacFarlane, Ian, assoc. ed., Historical Records of Victoria, Foundation Series, Volume 2A, *The Aborigines of Port Phillip 1835–1839*, editor-in-chief Michael Cannon, Victorian Government Printing Office, 1982.

——Historical Records of Victoria, Foundation Series, Volume 2B, *Aborigines and Protectors 1838–1839*, edited by Michael Cannon, Victorian Government Printing Office, 1983.

Plomley, N.J.B., ed., *Friendly Mission: The Tasmanian Journals and Papers of George Augustus Robinson, 1829–1834*, 2nd edition, Queen Victoria Museum and Art Gallery and Quintus Publishing, 2008.

Acknowledgements

To the Ancestors – everywhere I walk on this beautiful continent of ours, I feel the resonance of thousands of years of life and love, and the extraordinary depth of the symbiotic harmony between Country and the Old Ones. I acknowledge with pride, wonder and gratitude, the thousands of generations of Ancestors who have cared for and cherished this land since Time Immemorial.

To Nana Eliza Nowen/Gamble – Nannertgarrook – even in the face of the apocalypse, as all you knew, loved, hoped for and cherished was ripped away, you prevailed, continuing your legacy of yulendji, strength and courage through your daughters and descendants.

To Nana Emma, Aunty Martha, Nana Eileen, Aunty Joanie – this is the through-line, the golden thread, the extraordinary, staunch bagar-rook who kept Nannertgarrook's yulendji alive, through generation after generation of subjugation, fear, hostility and prejudice. Thank you for ensuring that ancient, delicate, flickering flame stayed alight, and for passing it from generation to generation, ready for the time of its rekindling into a blazing kuunh yingurr.

To Aunty Gail Kunwarra Dawson – for the long, encouraging yarns followed by a brisk 'Alright, get back to it.' For your steadfast support and belief, rich and profound cultural knowledge, and dedicated rigour in reawakening our sleeping language and women's business. You are a graceful teacher, like the swan, and I'm so thankful for your gentle leadership and generosity.

To my Bunurong/Boonwurrung aunties: Senior Elder Aunty Pat Keenan – for your precious, priceless biocultural knowledge, your many decades of dedicated research, and those old family stories of Granny Eliza, Nana Emma and the 'fighting Fitzies'; Aunty 'Wadjil' Terri – for your deep empathy and capacity to see and understand the breadth of the lives and souls that came before; Aunty Dyan Summers – for your staunch and inspiring commitment to our Country, cultural arts and women's business.

To Aunty Fay Stewart-Muir and Aunty Caroline Briggs – for so many years of passionate dedication to caring for our language, culture and community, forging pathways with your firesticks for others to follow.

To the extraordinary Anita Heiss – quite simply, this novel would not exist without your committed encouragement and unwavering faith in me to tell this story. I will be forever grateful, tidda, for the incredible opportunity you have given me, and your gracious dedication to profound truth-telling.

To Tara Wynne at Curtis Brown – thank you for bringing me into your fold and for your words of wisdom, encouragement and belief.

To Meredith Rose, Anna O'Grady and the wonderful team at Simon & Schuster – thank you for the warm welcome, steadfast support and commitment to truth-telling in story. Particular, heartfelt thanks to Allanah Hunt – for your deeply sensitive and compassionate editorial eye, and generous engagement with every layer of the story.

To my beautiful family: Mum, Jode, Bean, Teegs, Renato – thank you for being unwavering cheerleaders, for always having my back and for the constancy of your love and belief in me; Grandma Coz – for your ever-generous support and for always stepping up to help keep all the plates spinning; Samantha Bennett – for walking those songlines with me, sharing the joy of the salt spray and shells, holding hands through the ache of all that is lost, remembering, honouring, finally weaving the threads after waiting so long. I treasure you, cuz.

To Rove and Ruby – my very heartbeat, the light in my soul. I could never have stood in the maelstrom of this story without knowing you were always right there, my safe harbour. Forever thankful to be us three peas in our pod.

Frances Andrijich

Tasma Walton is a proud Boonwurrung woman from the Saltwater Country of Melbourne and surrounding coastlines. She is an award-winning actor and has appeared in numerous television productions, including *The Twelve, Mystery Road, Rake, Cleverman, Deadloch* and *The Secret Life of Us*; for her renowned role of Dash McKinley in *Blue Heelers* she received a Best New Talent Logie Award. Her films include *Mystery Road, Sweet As, How to Please a Woman, Kid Snow, Looking for Grace, Blessed* and *Fistful of Flies*, for the last of which she won the Sochi Film Festival Award for Best Actress. Tasma's first novel, *Heartless*, was nominated for an ABIA Award for General Fiction; and the first book in her children's series, Nerra: Deep Time Traveller, was longlisted for the DANZ Children's Book Award. She has worked in various writer's rooms and workshops in the development stage of many film, television and theatre productions. Tasma's most cherished role is playing mum to her eleven-year-old daughter, Ruby.